Kirk stepped forward, hand extended.

"Commander—" He stopped as he saw the pips on the visitor's uniform. "*Captain* Riker." Kirk shook Will Riker's hand. "Jean-Luc told me the good news." He smiled at Deanna Troi at Riker's side. "All of it. Congratulations to you both. On your marriage, and your new command."

But even then, Kirk felt a tightness in his chest, because the smiles and words of greeting Riker and his bride returned were forced and grim: the smiles of old friends with bad news. Deanna's dark Betazoid eyes fixed intently on Kirk, and in the intensity of her gaze, in the knowledge that it was onto his emotional mood she focused her empathic powers, Kirk suddenly knew the worst.

"Spock," he said quietly.

Riker nodded, and Kirk felt the gravity of Qo'noS shift beneath him, as if all the stars had been wrenched from the heavens.

As if something within him, too, had died.

OTHER BOOKS BY WILLIAM SHATNER

with Judith & Garfield Reeves-Stevens

Star Trek: Totality
Captain's Peril

Star Trek: The Mirror Universe Saga
Spectre
Dark Victory
Preserver

Star Trek: Odyssey
The Ashes of Eden
The Return
Avenger

with Chris Kreski
Get a Life!

with Chip Walter
Star Trek: I'm Working on That

STAR TREK®
CAPTAIN'S BLOOD

WILLIAM SHATNER

WITH JUDITH & GARFIELD REEVES-STEVENS

Based on *Star Trek*
and *Star Trek: The Next Generation*®
created by Gene Roddenberry

POCKET BOOKS
New York London Toronto Sydney

POCKET BOOKS, a division of Simon & Schuster, Inc.
1230 Avenue of the Americas, New York, NY 10020

This book is a work of fiction. Names, characters, places, and incidents are products of the authors' imaginations or are used fictitiously. Any resemblance to actual events or locales or persons, living or dead, is entirely coincidental.

Originally published in hardcover in 2003 by Pocket Books

 STAR TREK is a Registered Trademark of
Paramount Pictures.

This book is published by Pocket Books, a division of
Simon & Schuster, Inc., under exclusive license from
Paramount Pictures.

ISBN: 0-671-02130-3

First Pocket Books paperback edition January 2005

10 9 8 7 6 5 4 3 2 1

POCKET and colophon are registered trademarks of
Simon & Schuster, Inc.

Manufactured in the United States of America

For information regarding special discounts for bulk purchases,
please contact Simon & Schuster Special Sales at 1-800-456-6798
or business@simonandschuster.com.

The books in this series have been about love.
Love in all its brilliant, passionate, fiery colors.
And love in its agonizing aftermath,
filled with pain, disillusionment, and gray depression.
There is a balance, of course. Hard to find, but it's there.
I hoist my fluted glass to love, because only by love
do we shape the universe.

Once again, I acknowledge my co-writers,
whose talents and friendship I treasure;
Margaret Clark, for all her patience;
and Carmen LaVia, for all his skills.

. . . And bid the planets and the sun
Their own appointed orbits run;
O hear us when we seek thy grace
For those who soar through outer space.

—THE NAVY HYMN
J. E. VOLANTE, 1961

CAPTAIN'S BLOOD

Prologue
The *Galileo* Gambit

Spock remembered heat.

He remembered the shuttlecraft shuddering around him, the last frantic beats of a dying heart. His own heart, now, he knew.

Dying.

It was the way of things.

No matter that logic had so many times been circumvented. No matter that fate and luck and James T. Kirk had so many times intervened in the flow of cause and effect; inevitably everything must die.

Vulcans were no exception.

"Mister Ambassador?"

Spock opened his eyes. Meditation eluded him.

Even in the shadows of the ground transport's passenger compartment, lit only by the slow green flicker of passing streetglows, he saw the worry in Marinta's expression. Romulans were so free that way. In truth, there was much these lost children could teach their Vulcan forebears.

Spock focused his thoughts on chance—his one last chance to make that transfer possible.

Reunification.

It was all that mattered to him now.

"We're almost there," Marinta said.

Spock knew that wasn't what she meant.

"I am fine," he assured her.

Marinta smiled. "I don't believe you."

Spock raised an eyebrow at the young woman with whom he had worked for almost half a standard year, ever since the dark days of confusion following Shinzon's coup and the slaughter of almost every member of the Romulan Senate. He had no reason to question Marinta's loyalty to his cause of reuniting Vulcans and Romulans after more than two millennia of bitter estrangement. But the respect he had reluctantly come to accept as his natural due as a senior Vulcan ambassador was something she seldom demonstrated. Spock decided it was that refreshing freedom from formality he appreciated most about her.

After more than a century and a half of life lived within the protective cloak of total logic and emotional self-control, Spock craved freedom.

That craving drove him now. Just as he recognized that the war between his two halves—human and Vulcan—had once dominated him before he had achieved his own unique balance. But now that same struggle still continued, unresolved, between the Vulcans and the Romulans. Only the scale was different.

Spock's personal battle ended decades ago, when V'Ger had come to claim the Earth, though the scars of that victory would be with him forever.

Now he wanted—he *needed*—to bring the same peace of acceptance to his chosen people. That same freedom.

Before he died.

"You're doing the right thing." Marinta spoke quietly, as if she sensed his thoughts. Being Romulan, it was entirely possible that she did. Vulcan telepathic traits were encoded in Romulan and Reman DNA, and not always dormant.

"That is not in question."

"I sense your doubt."

"Not doubt," Spock answered. Then surprised even himself with his confession. "Remorse."

Through the dark windows of the transport, Spock watched as the ancient stone streets of Primedian scrolled by, rough-hewn, black as space, overlaid with centuries of urban soot. And in the shadowed intervals between pools of pale green light, reflected in those same dark windows he glimpsed the faces of the dead.

Lieutenant Latimer. Pierced by an alien spear.

Lieutenant Gaetano. Crushed by alien hands.

Both of them dead and buried on Taurus II.

Because of him.

"There is no need for remorse," Marinta said.

He looked back at her. "Still, it exists."

Marinta's dark eyes flashed. "Mister Ambassador, I submit that reaction is not logical."

But Spock caught the smile she tried to suppress and unexpectedly found himself doing the same. No one else he knew these days, at least not under the age of one hundred fifty, would dare take him on in logical debate. "That is not the issue. Remorse is an emotion. Logic plays no part."

"I thought you believed logic plays a part in . . . everything."

"The words 'logic' and 'believe' do not often belong in the same sentence."

"Then what you are about to do," she said slowly, "does it flow from logic, or belief?" Marinta, despite her brave challenge to him, sounded confused. Spock couldn't blame her. If he allowed his own constrained emotions to surface, he knew he would betray the same hesitation.

Spock kept his face neutral, his lined features more akin to carved stone than flesh. But with his stark words, his heart, his memories escaped all shielding.

"I once commanded a shuttlecraft crew. The *Columbus*. Our mission: to investigate a quasarlike object. We were forced down. There were seven of us when we crash-landed. Only five survived to return to the *Enterprise*."

Marinta was quick to form a conclusion. By telepathy or insight, it didn't matter. She was correct either way.

"That's why you feel remorse. For the loss of those two crew members."

"They were my responsibility. They were not the first to die under my command. Nor the last. But they are the two I remember most clearly."

"Because . . . ?"

Spock glanced out the windows again. The transport was slowing. Like a failing heartbeat.

"They died while I attempted to lead by logic. I, and the others, survived only when I set logic aside." Spock again surprised himself. Though Doctor McCoy had speculated on the motivation behind Spock's decision at the time of the incident, this was the first time Spock had confessed it aloud.

Uncharacteristically, Marinta offered no comment or judgment, as if waiting for him to continue. But Spock said nothing more.

The transport stopped and Spock felt it settle slowly as its wheels withdrew. In this most ancient of Romulan cities, where the planners of the central streets and plazas had been among the first outcast Vulcans to land on this world, old technologies were a tradition.

Spock pulled his ambassadorial robes close. They were lighter than those he usually wore, since he had forgone the traditional jewels and silver embroidery of his office. Spock had no desire to stand apart from his cousins. Much of Romulus was still impoverished in the aftermath of the Dominion War, harsh conditions made worse by Shinzon and the subsequent disruption of government services.

He rewarded Marinta's quiet patience.

"After repairs, the *Columbus* achieved a decaying orbit. We had, at best, almost an hour before we were forced down again. I chose to ignite all our fuel at once. Not for propulsion, but as a signal. One with little chance of being detected. A signal that meant the *Columbus* would burn up in minutes."

Spock again felt the heat of that terrible moment. The buffeting of the thickening atmosphere. The acrid bite of burning insulation as the temperature rose. The unspoken accusations of his crew. The approach of death.

"But obviously the signal was detected," Marinta said.

Spock drew a breath, dispelled the past. "The signal was detected." He sat forward in his seat as he waited for the armored compartment door to be opened by the bodyguards outside. "And now I am preparing to commit the same act of desperation. To ignite all the fuel, as it were." He held Marinta's gaze. "It is not logical. But I *believe* it is my last best hope."

"*Our* best hope." Marinta's bright smile was undisguised.

Spock nodded. "For both our people. One people."

The door puffed out, then hummed as it slid open.

Primedian's night air was cold, unusual for the season. The musty, layered scent of age enveloped Spock, and for a stifling moment he felt as ancient as the city's weathered blocks and roadways.

Two private bodyguards—Romulan, in drab and featureless civilian garb—stood outside, their stern features harshly shadowed emerald by a single, overhead streetglow that shone straight down. Each guard had a microcommunicator in one pointed ear. Narrow disruptor tubes in magnetic holsters were strapped to their forearms, their outlines almost concealed by the fabric of their sleeves.

"It's time," Spock said, to himself as much as to anyone else.

But Marinta reached out and lightly placed her hand on a fold of his robes, taking care not to touch his arm. "Mister Ambassador . . ."

Spock looked at her, waited.

"The shuttlecraft. I've read so many accounts of your life. It wasn't the *Columbus*. It was the *Galileo*."

In defiance of his self-mastery, Spock felt his stomach tighten. She was right. *How could I have forgotten? Have I grown so old?*

"Of course," he said calmly, fiercely walling off anything he thought, anything he felt. He had commanded the *Galileo*, not the *Columbus*. "I misspoke."

If Marinta sensed anything of his inward struggle, she did not share it with him.

She merely took her hand from his robes. "I'll . . . wait for you here?"

"That would be best."

Saying nothing else, Spock stepped from the transport, into the night, into what must happen next.

But his lapse of memory tore at him, spurring the unwanted memories of heat and smoke and . . .

He saw two figures in an alley. Dead eyes locked on his in bitter accusation.

Latimer and Gaetano, both in their antique uniforms. Sodden with fresh blood.

Spock's guards saw his reaction, spun together, disruptors already in their hands as they aimed across the street at . . .

The empty alley.

Like burrowing snakes, the disruptors slipped back up the guards' sleeves.

"Did you see something, Mister Ambassador?"

Spock answered by walking toward the private entrance to the towering coliseum, robes swirling around his boots.

The bodyguards hurried to match his pace.

No sign of what Spock felt or thought was visible in his demeanor.

But within, he was consumed by doubt and felt the first insinuating tendrils of what any human would recognize as panic.

His decision had been made. His path could not be altered any more than a decaying orbit could escape the siren call of gravity.

But he had commanded the *Galileo*, not the *Columbus*.

And just as he was haunted by the mistakes he had made in the past, he feared the mistakes that still remained before him, and already felt remorse for those who could be harmed because what he must do next might somehow be wrong.

Consumed by doubt, displaying confidence, Spock strode into the first coliseum built on Romulus, where three thousand Romulans were waiting to hear his message of peace and reconciliation.

But what Spock felt or how he looked didn't matter.

Because exactly fourteen minutes later, those three thousand Romulans saw Spock die.

1

The swinging *bat'leth* blazed in the sun of Qo'noS, as if the Klingon sun itself reached out a fiery arm to strike down James T. Kirk.

Huffing, puffing, drenched in sweat, Kirk instinctively calculated the blade's killing arc, then threw himself sideways beyond the reach of his opponent.

He pulled in his free arm to hit the unforgiving surface of the combat pit with his shoulder. With his other arm outstretched, holding his own *bat'leth* as a counterbalance, he sought to stabilize his center of gravity.

For one sweet moment, airborne and in swift action, Kirk knew his form was perfect, his tactic sound.

Then his shoulder struck rock-hard clay and it was as if he'd landed on an agonizer set to level eleven.

Breathless as brilliant fireworks of pain receded from his wide-open eyes, Kirk watched the shadow of his opponent rise over him, to block the searing sun and the yellow Klingon sky. He saw his opponent's blade lift straight up, preparing to deliver the *k'rel tagh*—the ritual stroke of major severance.

Flat on his back in the combat pit, Kirk knew he was

seconds away from decapitation. And that's where he saw his chance.

His opponent had underestimated him.

A more experienced *bat'Wahl*—*bat'leth* warrior— would have responded to Kirk's position by performing a series of *k'rel meen* lunges, first double-slicing across his chest to disable the pectoral muscles he could use to raise his own *bat'leth* in defense. That preliminary attack would be followed by one, possibly two, *a'k'rel tagh* attacks—minor severances—to detach one, possibly both of Kirk's arms. Only then would a true *bat'Wahl* deliver the *k'rel tagh*, when his opponent was deserving of a warrior's death and no longer capable of counterattack.

A perfect counterattack is what Kirk had before him now. One swing of the tip of his blade in a disemboweling *meen p'Ral* stroke left to right across the fighter's stomach and the bout would be over.

But even as Kirk instinctively calculated the proper trajectory for his swing, he also saw the exhaustion in his opponent's eyes.

There was a better way for this fight to end.

Kirk threw his arms up and shrieked in fear!

His opponent's blade swept through the humid air and struck Kirk's unprotected neck, and—

—sliced through cleanly, the holographic projection of the deadly tip flickering only once as the circuits in the practice weapon registered the kill.

"Ya got me," Kirk moaned.

His opponent giggled.

Kirk pushed himself to a sitting position, grimacing as he pulled his opponent close to his chest, ignoring the pulsing pain of his sprained shoulder in the joy of hugging the most precious being in the galaxy.

Joseph Samuel T'Kol T'Lan Kirk, child of James and Teilani.

Their child had been born of love just five years ago. Their child had been born a monster.

Kirk, the father, was human; all too human, he sometimes feared.

Teilani, the mother, was *Chalchaj 'qmey*; in the standard Klingon language: a Child of Heaven. Among the second generation of a colony of genetically engineered Klingon/Romulan hybrids created to survive in a galaxy devastated by an anticipated all-out war with the Federation. But, in the dark times of the hybrids' creation, in an era when the Klingons and the Romulans were uneasy allies, feared the Federation, and believed war was inevitable, genetic engineering had its limitations.

So Teilani and the others had been further enhanced, with human organs harvested from prisoners of the Empires. The secret, when revealed, forever changed Teilani. Innocents had died so she could live.

Kirk had tried to assuage her guilt. He had told her—and he still believed—no person is responsible for the world in which she was born, only for the world she leaves when she dies. The past must be accepted so we can concentrate on changing the only thing we can—the future.

Kirk knew his words and his love had never removed all the darkness from Teilani's soul, but he had brought her moments of light and of love, as she had brought the same to him. And now he followed his own counsel, and accepted the past he had shared with her, even as he accepted the tragedy of her death on Halkan.

But part of Teilani remained, in his memories, in his heart, and in the child they had created together.

A child like no other, whose genetic heritage continued to defy McCoy's attempts to sequence and understand it. A child whose constantly shifting appearance and unpredictable growth spurts continued to make him—or her—unique among the biological histories of every known world in the four quadrants.

But the science of Joseph's existence, the complexities of his DNA, his ultimate fate or form as an adult . . . none of those mysteries mattered to Kirk. Just as he had seen beyond Teilani's virogen scars, without question or struggle he could see into the heart and soul of their child.

Kirk gave love. Kirk gave acceptance. Kirk felt both given to him in return. And Kirk was grateful that he had finally lived long enough to understand that, in the end, nothing else mattered.

Kirk leapt to his feet in the combat pit and rubbed his hand on Joseph's smooth-skinned skull, as if tousling nonexistent hair, making his son squirm away, laughing.

"Son" was how Kirk thought of Joseph these days. Though, he conceded to himself with undiminished wonder, "daughter" was just as appropriate, which was why Kirk had bestowed upon his child two feminine names from Teilani's side—*T'Kol T'Lan*. Someday, when whatever maturation process was locked within Joseph's genes expressed itself, Kirk hoped that his and Teilani's child would choose the name and identity that pleased him, or her. If, indeed, a final gender was something that eventually would develop.

But for now his child was simply Joseph. Tall and

precocious for a five-year-old, his stature and intellect closer to that of a human child of nine or ten, his once rosy skin now a soft gray-brown striped by the single band of dark, almost Trill-like spots that swept up his spine and over the top of his scalp, fading away just above the diminutive Klingon ridges of his forehead and the already elegant tips of his Romulan ears.

McCoy termed the child's build as scrawny, and his quickly growing gangly limbs revealed a few odd planes and lines to show that his musculature wasn't exactly human, nor precisely Klingon, nor Romulan, nor Vulcan. Strictly speaking, those four species were the sum total that had contributed to Joseph's genetic makeup. But where McCoy could be certain that Kirk's DNA was one hundred percent human, among the genes that had been artificially blended to create Teilani, the best genetic engineers at Starfleet Medical couldn't be certain that there were not some whispers of other species hidden within the billions of base pairs of the child's commingled amino acids.

"Time for lunch," Kirk said. "Then lessons."

Joseph held up a hand, three perfect fingers and one perfect thumb. "Two more rounds," he pleaded.

Kirk smiled ruefully. The past few months, almost every conversation with his son had become a negotiation. The request for two more rounds was obviously meant to provoke a counter of one more round. Which was probably all that Joseph wanted, anyway.

But Kirk knew all about that kind of negotiating tactic. He had been taught by experts, and so, it seemed, had Joseph. "You've been spending too much time with your uncle Scotty," Kirk said.

"Daa-ad."

Kirk tried not to laugh. Joseph was looking deeply

offended that his father would even think such a thing. "Hit the sonics. Then lunch."

"And then two more rounds?" Joseph persisted.

Kirk smiled at his son, losing his battle but not the war. "Lessons, mister. Scoot!"

This time Joseph acquiesced gracefully—*This time,* Kirk thought—tossed Kirk his holographic *bat'leth* projector, then ran like an ungainly stork to the wooden ladder at the far side of the elliptical pit.

Kirk marveled that a child so uncoordinated in running could thrust and parry with his *bat'leth* so deftly. And his piano playing was already at the level of a skilled adult, though his math—usually a related skill—was lagging behind the average for even a five-year-old human. Joseph still didn't have the faintest grasp of calculus, and without that rudimentary background, warp mechanics would be forever beyond him.

Kirk frowned even as he reached that dismal conclusion. His child was only five, and already he was placing the ultimate burden of expectation on him—a Starfleet career.

"I say this with respect," Worf suddenly growled from behind Kirk, "but you should be ashamed of yourself."

Kirk started. He had been so engrossed in watching Joseph clamber up the two-meter ladder to leave the pit that he hadn't heard Worf approach.

"I beg your pardon?"

Worf, more imposing than ever in his combat-training garb of suèded burgundy leather, scowled as only a Klingon could. Despite his best effort to show deference to his guest, the disdain in his voice was impossible to disguise. "You *let* the child beat you."

Kirk bristled. He, Joseph, and McCoy had been guests of the House of Martok for two weeks, and only now were the subtleties of Klingon etiquette coming into focus. Joseph was even developing a taste for *gagh*, though whether that was because the living worms actually tasted good to his Klingon taste buds, or because he was playing to his father's unexpected squeamishness, Kirk could not be sure.

But even given the blunt directness of Klingon hospitality, Worf's rude accusation surprised Kirk.

"Of course I let Joseph beat me," Kirk said, trolling for more details.

But Worf only shook his heavy head, as if rendered speechless by disgust.

Kirk tried again. "I take it you don't approve."

"It is dishonest," Worf thundered. "Such behavior gives the child a false sense of security. It teaches him that adults cannot be trusted. When the time comes to face true combat, he will fail."

Kirk sighed, wiped the sweat from his forehead, and looked past Worf to find McCoy leaning on the wooden railing that surrounded the ceremonial pit. But his old friend paid no attention to Kirk and Worf. He was fiddling with a medical tricorder, no doubt reviewing his latest scans of Joseph. Since McCoy's full retirement from Starfleet Medical, the study of Kirk's child seemed to have become his new mission in life.

Still, another human ally was what Kirk needed now, to sort this out with Worf. He was here to help his child explore his Klingon heritage, but his own lessons in understanding Joseph were a challenge to him as well. Kirk started for the ladder closest to McCoy, reasonably certain that Worf would follow. And he did.

"He's five years old, Worf. He won't be facing true combat for—"

Worf cut off his explanations. "If you are serious about teaching your son his Klingon heritage, he should have already been blooded."

Kirk paused with one hand on the ladder. There were some parts of parenting he had no doubts about. "I've also got his human, Romulan, and Vulcan heritage to work in there. He's *not* going to be blooded. Not at age five."

Worf growled again. Louder this time.

But Kirk merely handed him the holographic *bat'leth* projectors. Each unit was the size of a traditional *bat'leth*'s haft, with its three handgrip openings and leather wrappings. The actual twin batwing blades and spikes on each side were missing, to be created instead by small holoemitters and low-power forcefield generators. The projectors were a clever invention, enabling combatants to feel when an illusory blade had made contact, yet preventing the weapon from inflicting harm. Needless to say, the projectors were not a Klingon invention and Worf did not approve of them, either. But since even the wooden *bat'leth*s used by Klingon children could cause nasty cuts and bruises, Kirk had opted for safety over cultural purity.

Kirk stepped off the top of the ladder and walked along the railing toward McCoy. At ground level, all around him, the Martok estate was an explosion of dark purple summer-growth vegetation in more subtly differentiated hues than Kirk could identify. Wild *targ* roamed the forests to the east, in the midst of which stood the ancient ancestral castle of the House of Martok. It had a solid, imposing appearance, almost pyramidal, reminding Kirk strongly of the Great Hall housing the Klingon High Council. Why it was considered an ancestral castle, Kirk wasn't certain. Less than a century ago, the House of Martok had wrested the castle from the House of Krant, which had wrested it in turn from the House of Fralk, which had rebuilt it after slaughtering the entire House of Tralkar, which originally had defeated the House of Fralk during an imperial interregnum four hundred years earlier, following the defeat of . . . The rest of the endless history was a blur to Kirk, who had tried to follow Worf's recitation on the occasion of the first dinner held for Joseph. From that evening, he had retained little more than the impression that Klingon real-estate transactions were extremely complicated, and often bloody.

"So what's today's diagnosis?" Kirk asked McCoy.

The doctor, simply clad in civilian trousers and a loose black shirt that looked suspiciously Vulcan in design, kept making adjustments to his medical tricorder and didn't bother to look up. "For Joseph, or for you?"

Kirk leaned against the rough-hewn wooden railing that surrounded the combat pit. He heard the ladder creak as Worf climbed up. The sound made him rub his strained shoulder. "I already know what my diagnosis is. What about my son?"

McCoy slipped a thumb-sized, cylindrical plaser from a small pouch on his belt. For all that his snow white hair and narrow build made him look frail, his movements were sure, his hands steady. At one hundred fifty years of age, McCoy was reaching the upper limits of recorded human life spans, aided by internal skeletal actuators, synthetic organs, and his latest implant—an experimental, artificial mitochondrial biogenerator based on one of the remarkable subsystems built into the late Lieutenant Commander Data. In truth, Kirk thought a trifle grudgingly, his old friend looked better than he had in years, and his voice displayed no loss of gruff authority as he ordered Kirk to turn around.

"Joseph's diagnosis is as close to textbook Romulan perfect as the tricorder can scan. For all that running around you were doing down there, his heart rate barely rose, but his blood-flow pattern went through a massive reconfiguration."

Kirk flinched as he felt the plaser's medical force-fields go to work on his shoulder, tightening stretched ligaments and loosening tight muscles. "Explain," he said. A few years ago, he might have worried at the words "massive reconfiguration" being applied to Joseph, but he was used to it now.

"Blood flow to his muscles increased by twenty-three percent, shifting from less critical areas: intestines, both livers, and the secondary heart. How's that?"

Kirk stretched his arm over his head, turned back and forth. The pain in his shoulder was gone. He grinned. "Good as new. Thanks, Bones."

McCoy made a sound halfway between a snort and a laugh. "You, my friend, are held together by spit and baling wire."

Kirk stiffened. "What kind of bedside manner is that?" He was still in command of his faculties—or at least most of them, he told himself. The last thing he needed was someone else to remind him of his own mortality.

"I save that for patients who at least make an attempt to follow my medical advice."

Kirk turned back to McCoy. "I make an *attempt*."

McCoy rolled his eyes skeptically.

Kirk felt he might as well be having another conversation with his five-year-old. "You were saying about Joseph . . ." he prompted.

McCoy slapped his tricorder to his belt and the device hung there by molecular adhesion. "Jim, to be blunt, to be medical, your boy . . . that is, your child . . . is a hybrid. Genetically, hybrids can often tend to be stronger than their individual parents, their genetic makeup more robust. I can't say for certain there aren't more unusual growth spurts in his future, but my instincts tell me that Joseph's physical development isn't anything you or I should be worried about anymore."

Kirk read between the lines, realized what McCoy wasn't saying. "Then what should we be worried about?"

McCoy nodded to Worf as the Klingon joined them. "That other half of him," the doctor said. "His mind, his spirit, what makes him human."

"Or Klingon," Worf said.

"Or Romulan or Vulcan," Kirk added. "I know all this, Bones."

Then McCoy surprised him by saying, "No, Jim, you don't know."

Kirk tapped his fingers on the wooden railing. If there was anything he disliked more than an argument, it was an argument he had had before.

"Bones, that's the point of this exercise," he said. "I can teach Joseph everything I know about his human heritage. But he's more than that." Kirk turned to Worf. "That's why I'm relying on my friends to help him learn about *everything* he is. Where he came from. All the possibilities for what he might become."

"Then you must stop letting him win," Worf said.

"More important than that," McCoy added, "you have to give Joseph some structure in his life."

Worf nodded approvingly. "Discipline. That is the warrior's way."

Kirk rubbed at his face, knowing he shouldn't get caught up in this discussion, but unable to remain silent. "He *has* structure."

McCoy shook his head. "Because you make him take sonic showers and study the junior Academy-entrance curriculum? That's not enough, Jim. Joseph needs a home base. He needs a stable community. A chance to make friends."

"He has friends," Kirk argued, defensive. "You, and Worf, and Spock, and Scotty and—"

"His own age," McCoy said. "Worf's right. Joseph shouldn't be sparring with his father in a Klingon combat pit and winning just because he's your son—or daughter. He should be wrestling with other children, climbing trees, getting dirt under his fingernails, scabs on his knees . . . being a child, and not . . . not a recruit in his father's personal Starfleet Academy."

Kirk felt anger grow in him as he listened to McCoy's diatribe, and he could see that his friend saw that anger in his eyes.

"You asked for a diagnosis—there it is."

A part of Kirk wanted to instantly discount everything McCoy had just said. But because it *was* McCoy who had said it, Kirk knew he couldn't. Instead, he fought his resentment, tried to make McCoy truly understand.

"Bones . . . I don't want to limit him."

"Children need limits." McCoy looked at Worf. "You're a father. It's the same for Klingons, isn't it?"

Kirk felt the heat of Worf's glare. "Yes. Limits provide security. Security provides confidence. Confidence provides courage. And courage is the key to surmounting all limits."

Kirk looked up at Worf, unintimidated by his size or attitude. "I thought you didn't get along with your son."

Worf's eyes narrowed, his nostrils flared, a predator about to attack. "We had . . . differences. Had I known then what I know now, perhaps those differences would not have been as . . . extreme."

"Well, Joseph and I don't have differences." Kirk had the sudden feeling that if he were not an invited guest of the House of Martok, Worf would have already landed the first punch in a fight for honor.

"Fathers and sons always have differences," McCoy said flatly.

"Other fathers. Other sons." As far as Kirk was concerned, the unwanted and unwarranted discussion was over. "I'm going to have a shower. See you both at lunch."

Worf grunted. McCoy frowned. And then all three men turned as one, Starfleet training to the fore, as they heard the first subtle tone of what could only be the carrier wave of an incoming transport.

The color signature of the familiar shimmer three meters away told Kirk it was a Starfleet beam, though the materialization—two figures, Kirk counted—was faster than he was used to seeing, as if Starfleet had achieved yet another incremental breakthrough in the technology.

Then, even before the effect had dissipated, Kirk recognized the new arrivals, and his first thought was that Worf might soon be in a better mood because of them.

Kirk stepped forward, hand extended. "Commander—" He stopped as he saw the pips on the visitor's uniform. "*Captain* Riker." Kirk shook Will Riker's hand. "Jean-Luc told me the good news." He smiled at

Deanna Troi at Riker's side. "All of it. Congratulations to you both. On your marriage, and your new command."

But even then, Kirk felt a tightness in his chest, because the smiles and words of greeting Riker and his bride returned were forced and grim: the smiles of old friends with bad news.

Kirk glanced at Worf and McCoy, saw they sensed the somber mood of the visit as well.

"Is Captain Picard well?" Worf asked.

Jean-Luc's well-being was the first thought that had come to Kirk, too.

"The captain is fine," Riker said. But Deanna's dark Betazoid eyes fixed intently on Kirk, and in the intensity of her gaze, in the knowledge that it was onto his emotional mood she focused her empathic powers, Kirk tensed, suspecting that Jean-Luc was not the reason for this unexpected visit.

Kirk suddenly knew the worst.

"Spock," he said quietly.

Riker nodded, and Kirk felt the gravity of Qo'noS shift beneath him, as if all the stars had been wrenched from the heavens.

As if something within him, too, had died.

2

It had been more than a year since Kirk had been on a Starfleet vessel, but he scarcely registered the difference between the artificial gravity of Riker's *Titan* and the natural heavy pull of Qo'noS. The starship's cool air tinged with the faint crisp scent of warm isolinear circuitry, the almost soothing hum of atmospheric circulators and scrubbers, the rushing pulse of water and coolant through hidden conduits; all the sensations of the mighty ship washed around Kirk without his notice.

He stood alone, his mind and being still in turmoil. How many times had he thought he had lost Spock? How many times had he thought the adventure of his own life was over? And always there had been a way back, the unseen chance, a . . . possibility.

Until now.

He stared at the image frozen on the main viewscreen in the *Titan's* darkened ready room. The coliseum on Romulus. The first to be built there uncounted centuries ago.

The flash from the explosion glowed through the rows of arched windows. That flash was the last thing Spock had experienced—seen, felt, known.

It had been a chemical explosive, or so the local Compliance Division had determined. Simple, primitive, deadly. No telltale radiation or antimatter signature to set off the security alarms. Triggered by a mechanical timekeeping device—again, no anomalous energy readings to raise suspicion.

The device had been placed under the elegantly carved stone podium from which Spock had addressed his audience. There were visual sensor logs of his speech—his impassioned plea—which had been transmitted live for other interested parties on Romulus, and recorded for eventual transmission over subspace information channels to Vulcan.

"*It is not a question of logic,*" Spock had said in the final moments of his life. "*It is not a question of emotion. It is a question that can be answered only by the blending of the two. Emotion and logic. Romulan and Vulcan. Two halves of a single entity that has too long been sundered.*"

Then Spock had paused to look around at his audience. He had taken a sip of water from a slender cup. And then the nature of what he said subtly changed, became more personal, and Kirk couldn't help but wonder if in some way Spock had known the next words he spoke would be his last.

"*There is rest enough for the individual being, too much and too soon, and we call it death. But for our people, Romulan and Reman and Vulcan, and all who will stand with us, there can be no rest and no ending.*

"*Only together can we then go on, frontier after frontier. First the stars, and then all the laws of mind and matter that restrain us.*

"And when, together, we have achieved understanding of all of deep space and all the mysteries of time, still we will be beginning.

"Together.

"Unified.

"Or—"

There the record ended.

The penultimate, still image of this recording haunted Kirk: Spock, holding one outstretched hand to his audience, reaching out to all the worlds of the Star Empire and Vulcan's myriad independent colonies, as the first yellow-orange glow of the bomb's detonation shone up from beneath him.

Reaching out from the grave, Kirk thought sadly, painfully.

The final image showed only the light that had consumed his friend.

After that, there was nothing; the visual sensors had been rendered inoperative.

Kirk slowly grew aware of Riker watching him, as were Troi and Worf. But McCoy still stared at the dark viewscreen, as if his thoughts were the mirror of Kirk's. Kirk had no reason to think that they weren't.

Kirk, Spock, and McCoy. The three of them had experienced so much together, to have lost one was to have lost a limb, a heart, a soul.

It came to Kirk that the others were waiting for him to say something.

He cleared his throat, so dry, so unwilling to make a sound. What words could there be to express such a loss?

Move on, Kirk told himself.

He closed his eyes, saw himself in the center chair of the *Enterprise.* His *Enterprise.* A crewman had been lost, but the mission must continue. The mission must *always* continue.

"Do they . . . do they know who's responsible?"

"Three groups have claimed responsibility," Riker said quietly.

"So far," Troi added.

Kirk looked at her, didn't understand. "A conspiracy?"

"Confusion," Riker said. "The political situation on Romulus is . . . chaotic, to say the least. Interim senators have been appointed to replace those assassinated in the coup, but they have no real authority until the new praetor has been confirmed—and months of internal bickering have to be resolved before that happens. According to our best intelligence, the real power, for the moment, seems to rest with the Imperial Fleet. They've at least taken responsibility for maintaining order on Romulan colony worlds, restoring trade routes, keeping the empire together."

"The Imperial Fleet," Worf huffed in derision. "They were *responsible* for Shinzon's coup."

Riker sighed, as if he and Worf had had this conversation before. Kirk recognized the feeling. "Yes, Worf. *Some* elements within the Fleet chose not to act against Shinzon."

"They did more than not act against him," Worf countered. "I have reviewed the diplomatic reports. Fleet leadership actively gave their support to Shinzon, in return for his offer to destroy the Earth."

Kirk knew that post-coup conditions on Romulus were still uncertain. He also knew that the political situation that had allowed Shinzon, a Reman slave—a *human* slave, at that—to rise to an unprecedented level of power might never be truly comprehended by a non-

Romulan. But he didn't care about any of it, unless it might have something to do with Spock's death.

Troi's distinctive, calming voice spoke next. "Worf, I've read the reports, too, and that's not what Starfleet Intelligence has concluded. A majority of Romulan military commanders *did* agree to not interfere in Shinzon's claim to be the new praetor. In return, they accepted Shinzon's promise that he would ensure the Federation would no longer be a threat to Romulan interests."

Kirk noted that while Worf seemed perfectly ready to argue with Riker, he immediately fell silent when Troi addressed him.

The Betazoid capitalized on that silence. "Most of those commanders were led to believe that promise meant Shinzon would take a more aggressive stance in the empire's relations with us. That he would unilaterally renounce the Cheron Accords, rearm the Neutral Zone outposts, and open talks with the Klingon Empire to reestablish their old strategic alliance. Instead, Shinzon set out to obliterate all life on Earth with an outlawed thalaron weapon. Apparently, he referred to that act as 'decapitating the serpent.'"

Troi stopped speaking, as if sensing that Worf was ready to respond. He was.

"We both were there," the Klingon softly said, as if floodgates were straining to contain a building torrent of rage. Kirk was impressed by Worf's restraint, decided he must have an interesting history with the counselor.

"And we both know," Troi said coolly, "that without the last-minute assistance of the Romulan fleet, the *Enterprise* might not have been successful in stopping Shinzon from reaching Earth."

She paused again to let Worf speak, but Riker took the initiative.

"Worf, this is not the time or place to debate Romulan politics. We know that the majority of Romulan commanders who supported Shinzon, or who at least agreed to not act against him, were appalled at Shinzon's plan to destroy the Earth. They know what kind of war that would have unleashed with the Federation. They know how their own empire would have been regarded by the nonaligned systems." He fixed his gaze intently on Worf. "And do you honestly believe the Klingon Empire would hold to its own promise not to develop thalaron weapons if they knew the Romulans already had them and had demonstrated they were willing to use them in an unprovoked first strike?

"Memory Alpha has *already* published a preliminary analysis of probable developments in the event Shinzon had not been stopped. They estimate that the Alpha and Beta Quadrants would have been consumed by total thalaron war within three years. Consider that. With entire planetary populations subject to extinction from a single thalaron strike by an undetectable cloaked warship, within a decade the infrastructure of interstellar commerce built up over centuries would be obliterated. A galactic dark age would follow, during which not one surviving world in the Federation, the Romulan and Klingon Empires, and the local nonaligned systems would have the slightest chance of mounting a credible defense against the Borg."

Riker was finished, but Troi was not. "Romulan military leaders have no love for the Federation," she said, "but they aren't insane."

Kirk was disturbed. Why was Riker—with Troi's help—going to such great lengths to explain himself to

Worf? After all, both men were in Starfleet, and Riker outranked Worf. Even the fact that Riker, a superior officer, was allowing debate in his ready room suggested some still-to-be-revealed agenda for this meeting. An unwelcome suspicion quickened Kirk's pulse.

"Captain Riker," Kirk said, "is there any reason to believe the Romulan military is involved in Spock's murder?"

Kirk's last two words were almost lost to the sudden dry constriction of his throat. His mind knew what must be done, the attitude that must be maintained. But his flesh betrayed him.

"Call me Will," Riker said. "And no, no reason at all. In fact, the military establishment has changed its unofficial stance on the topic of reunification of Romulus and Vulcan. They know how close Shinzon came to successfully attacking Earth. And I assure you, they are very aware that if the situation had been reversed, and a rogue Federation ship had come that close to destroying Romulus, the Star Empire would *have* to respond with an all-out counterattack. No matter the consequences."

Troi offered a small shrug. "You see, Captain Kirk, just as we don't fully comprehend the Romulan political system, they truly don't understand why the Federation didn't declare war on them in the aftermath of Shinzon's attack—that lack of response is unthinkable to them. Right now many Romulan leaders still believe that *our* ongoing negotiations with them are simply a stalling tactic while we develop our own thalaron weapons."

"The end result," Riker added, picking up on Troi's point as if he and she were two halves of a joined mind, "is that the Romulan military is eager to establish peaceful relations with all the members of the Federation. Our diplomats don't really believe the military would welcome unification, but neither will the military oppose initial discussions. Not as long as it means increased contact and openness with Vulcan."

Troi completed their explanation. "That's why Ambassador Spock was able to take such a high-profile presence on Romulus, to actually announce where he would be speaking so that ordinary citizens could join the debate on unification."

Kirk nodded. "In chaos, he saw opportunity. So like him."

"Unification was his dream," the counselor said softly.

Then McCoy spoke his first words since the sensor log had been played, almost as if he were speaking to himself. "He must have seen it coming. He *must* have."

Kirk looked sharply at his friend. "Bones . . . ?"

"Did you hear what he said, Jim? Those last words of his. It was as if Spock *knew* he was going to die."

Kirk sighed, not surprised that McCoy felt as he did. But he didn't see why the doctor was so upset by the idea that Spock sensed his own mortality. "We're all going to die, Bones."

"Speak for yourself," McCoy said. "Spock *knew* those were going to be his last words. He was putting himself up as a target."

"For what possible reason?"

McCoy waved a thin arm toward the viewscreen. "For *this*. His chance to deliver a powerful speech that all of a sudden becomes his legacy. Do you think anyone would be paying half as much attention to this speech of his if it hadn't been his last? Typical . . ." McCoy shook his head.

Kirk now understood what had provoked the doctor. Everyone grieved in his or her own way. McCoy's way was to deny what had happened, transferring his anger and his sorrow from Spock's killers to Spock himself. Also typical.

"Doctor McCoy," Troi said gently, "in the few times I've spoken with him, Ambassador Spock never appeared to be the type of person who would willingly seek out death just to prove a point."

McCoy gave the counselor a twisted smile. "Well, then, my dear, you don't know Spock." He rocked back in his chair. "Who saw him last?"

"There were three thousand Romulans in the audience," Riker began.

"No, no," McCoy interrupted. "Not who *saw* him—who was *with* him? *Before* he went on stage."

Kirk instantly saw what McCoy was suggesting, was surprised he hadn't thought of it himself.

"Spock's *katra*," Kirk said.

"He's done it again, Jim."

Kirk saw that Riker and Deanna appeared confused. He tried to explain. "There is an aspect of a Vulcan's personality, what they call their *katra*, that, under certain conditions, can survive physical death."

Troi nodded. "I've heard the stories."

"It's not just a story, Counselor," Kirk said.

"Damn right it isn't," McCoy muttered.

"The point Bones is trying to make," Kirk said, "is that if Spock thought or suspected that he might be in danger, he . . . would first have taken steps to see that his *katra* was preserved."

Troi and Riker exchanged a glance. "A mind-meld?" the Betazoid asked.

"A specific type of meld," Kirk said. "Possibly with

whomever it was who was with him before he took the stage."

Riker put his hands palm down on the smooth wooden conference table. "Captain Kirk—"

"Call me Jim," Kirk said.

"Jim," Riker continued. "Do you agree with Doctor McCoy? That Spock might have known what was about to happen to him?"

"If Spock had suspected he might be facing an assassination attempt, then he certainly wouldn't have accepted it," Kirk said forcefully. "He's not afraid . . . wasn't afraid . . . of dangerous situations, but he'd never go willingly to his death." He glanced over at McCoy. "Not like this, Bones."

Riker half-smiled, though Kirk could see the sadness that lingered there, as if the new starship captain was too familiar with the loss of a friend. "I see you two don't agree."

"It's not a disagreement," McCoy snapped. "Jim's wrong, I'm right. That's a different matter."

Kirk knew better than to take the bait, and remained silent.

"Then how would you like to resolve it?" Riker suddenly asked.

"Resolve what?" Kirk answered.

"The truth," Troi said.

"About what happened to Spock," Riker added.

McCoy glared at Kirk. "And how do y'all suggest we do that?"

"By going to Romulus," Riker said, "and investigating Spock's death firsthand."

McCoy straightened up in his chair, surprised. Kirk leaned back, thoughtful. So there *had* been an unspoken condition underlying everything Riker and Troi had said. Riker had intended to make this offer from the beginning.

And, Kirk sensed, there was something else being hidden, as well.

"What about the Romulan authorities?" he asked. "Aren't they investigating?"

"The Compliance Division is," Troi said. "They're the equivalent of the local civilian police. They're treating Spock's death as a criminal matter."

"But from everything you've said, Counselor, Spock's . . . murder . . . wasn't a criminal act. It was political."

Troi gave Riker an intense look. "Given the current situation on Romulus, the civilian authorities don't have the power—or the will—to act against the political authorities."

McCoy slapped his hand on the table. "You just told us there was no political authority on Romulus."

"Other than the Fleet," Kirk added.

"No one," Riker said, "is saying this is going to be easy. It is quite possible that Spock was killed by a disaffected faction of anarchists who have never acted before, and who will never act again. People impossible to trace and impossible to bring to justice."

"It's equally possible," Kirk pointed out, "Spock was assassinated on the orders of the Fleet leadership—people paying lip service to talk of unification, who have no intention of allowing it to proceed."

Riker nodded. "And if that's true," he said, "then Spock's assassination *could* be the proverbial tip of the iceberg, proof of a powerful group submerged within the chaos of Romulan authority. A group determined to defeat any efforts toward a new era of peace between the empire and the Federation."

Almost without conscious thought, Kirk felt an odd relief, almost a dislocation of his emotions, realizing he was no longer focused on his loss in the past, but on the mission that lay in the future.

"Will," he said, "do you have any reason for thinking such a cabal exists?"

Riker tapped the controls of a small padd on the table before him. The viewscreen on the far wall changed its display to show what was obviously a Romulan warship, but one that literally bristled with armaments. A scale at the side of the image gave an indication of the warship's size—at minimum twice the length of Picard's *Enterprise*.

"What is that monstrosity?" McCoy asked.

"The *Scimitar*," Worf said.

"Shinzon's ship," Riker elaborated. "With a fully functional thalaron weapon capable of obliterating the biomass of an entire planet with a single discharge."

Kirk understood. "Yet it was a slave's ship."

"Exactly," Riker said.

With that, Kirk knew what the Federation feared, and why Riker had come to him.

A ship like the *Scimitar* did not arise from empty space. It was undeniably the result of a massive Romulan program of research and development. Even Starfleet's mind-boggling Martian shipyards would be hard-pressed to construct such a vessel in under two years. And add to that a thalaron weapon capable of planetary destruction . . . Kirk's mind raced through the implications. How many intermediate models had been built and tested? All of this designed, prototyped, tested, refined, and brought online without Starfleet detecting any hint of it.

And then, in the end, the *Scimitar* had been placed in

the hands of a slave who single-handedly eliminated the existing government of Romulus.

"You think there are more of those," Kirk said.

"No question," Troi said.

"The Romulans admit as much, to a point," Riker added. "They're saying this class of vessel was intended for use in the Dominion War, but that the war ended before the spaceframes were complete. Same story for the thalaron weapons—developed to be used against the Dominion homeworlds in the Gamma Quadrant, but never brought forward to operational status."

"Can they account for the unfinished ships and weapons?" Kirk asked.

Riker shook his head. "Supposedly destroyed by Shinzon once he took control of the *Scimitar*, so that no one could oppose him."

McCoy gestured to the screen, unconvinced. "How does a slave gain control of *that?*"

Worf's gruff voice caught everyone's attention. "There is only one way," he said bluntly. "Someone who was not a slave gave it to him."

Kirk suddenly felt indescribably tired. A voice within him cried out, *I left this behind! My duty is to my son! This belongs in the care of a new generation!*

Except . . . Spock was dead.

So how could he say that this was not his fight?

"A puppetmaster," Kirk said, wondering if the exhaustion he felt was apparent.

"That's one theory," Riker agreed. "Someone, or some group within the Romulan power structure, perhaps even a reconstituted Tal Shiar, was responsible for elevating Shinzon to a position of relative power. Responsible for—"

"Killing Spock," Kirk said.

"Starfleet can't investigate on Romulus," Troi continued, and to Kirk it seemed her words were well rehearsed. "Federation diplomats are limited in how far they can push for results."

"But a civilian," Riker continued, then looked over at McCoy, "*two* civilians, with close ties to the victim, if *you* investigate, then that's something the Romulan authorities will understand, and the Federation's friends among them can help."

McCoy's laugh was forced and angry. "So now we have our strings pulled by the Federation puppetmaster to go looking for the Romulan puppetmaster."

"The alternative is to do nothing," Riker said, "and hope that what we fear most is wrong."

"Which is," Kirk said, "unacceptable."

Worf nodded.

Riker appeared to think the meeting had run its course. "Will you do it, Jim? Will you go to Romulus, investigate Spock's murder to see if it might be connected to an even greater threat to the Federation than Shinzon posed?"

Everyone at the table, including Kirk, knew it was impossible for him to refuse. "Yes," he agreed.

"That's it?" McCoy suddenly said. "You're not even going to ask any questions?"

Kirk didn't understand the reason for the doctor's outburst, and neither, it seemed, did anyone else.

"Bones, there'll be time for questions later."

"What about the most important one?" McCoy asked. He looked triumphantly around the table. "Given all the machinations and string-pulling going on around here, can anyone prove that Spock really *is* dead?"

Riker had no answer for that, and for a moment, Kirk felt a completely irrational moment of hope.

It didn't last.

There were three thousand witnesses to the truth, and multiple unaltered recordings.

Spock was dead.

All that mattered now was the mission.

3

SOLTOTH CAVERNS, ROMULUS, STARDATE 57473.1

He was tired, he was sore, he fought to keep despair from overwhelming him, but he was not dead.

Even now, one standard week after his outrageous gambit, Spock still tasted the primitive explosive's sulfuric sting in the back of his throat. His ears still rang with the echo of the blast. His muscles ached from the force of the concussion that had slammed first against his body armor, and then against him.

The fall back from the podium had seemed to take forever, and, indeed, T'Vrel confirmed that he had momentarily lost consciousness. But whether that was a result of the explosion or of the shock of instantly being contained within an incompressible level-four forcefield, she could not say.

No matter the cause, the terse Vulcan healer maintained that Spock's unconsciousness had actually been a benefit. Enough people had seen him thrown back from the podium to rule out such tricks as transporter substitution. Before dozens of close-up witnesses, he had crumpled to the stage floor in a limp confusion of sprawling limbs, the chemical he had sipped from his water cup providing a convincing froth of what appeared to be green blood at his lips.

The Vulcan defenders onstage, different from the unwitting Romulan bodyguards who had escorted Spock to the coliseum, had successfully kept witnesses back while they frantically called for healers, so that when the carefully timed fire spread across the stage floor and the blast-fractured structure began to collapse, there was no question but that it was Spock who had been caught by the explosion, it was Spock who had been abandoned onstage, and it was Spock whose body was mangled beyond recognition by fire and crushing debris.

That part of the plan, at least, had unfolded satisfactorily.

Less satisfactory to Spock was the lack of explanation for the illogical aftermath of his plan. That was the conundrum that troubled him as he walked slowly along the high-ceilinged cavern tunnel for his daily meeting with T'Vrel. The tunnel's walls were rough volcanic rock, carved by particle beams centuries ago, cold and dark now, lit only by occasional facets of emerald light. And though Spock knew that the nature of this rock explained the past and foretold the inevitable future of the twin worlds of Romulus and Remus, he did not yet see how his own fate was also contained within it, like a hidden vein of dilithium, waiting for its discovery to unleash a revolution that would change the face of the galaxy.

As a planetary system, Romulus and Remus shared similarities of their birth with Earth and its moon. Once, geologists believed, the twin planets were a single body, which, for convenience, they called Romii.

Then, five-point-three billion years in the past, another planetary body, at least sixty percent the size of Romii, and in a retrograde orbit, collided with the giant protoworld.

In a matter of hours, the stupendous impact had stripped the crust from Romii, and in less than two hundred years, it was estimated, that ejecta had coalesced into a single body that would eventually cool to become the planet now known as Romulus, still spinning quickly with the force of that ancient, cataclysmic collision, eventually becoming an abode of life.

The other half of Romii, composed primarily of its heavy core elements, had been superheated by the impact and the concurrent energy release of its axial revolution being stopped dead. After two million years of erratic oscillations before stable orbital resonance was achieved, the result was the planet Remus—perhaps the richest world in the Alpha and Beta Quadrants in terms of exotic mineral wealth, yet rendered virtually uninhabitable because it was gravitationally locked to its sun so that one day equaled one year, keeping the same face in constant sunlight, and the opposite side in perpetual night.

The planet's unusually heavy gravity for its size, one-point-five standard G for a world barely the size of Mars, plus its complex chemistry produced an atmosphere of sorts. And billions of years later, when the Vulcan diaspora limped into the Romii system in their ragtag fleet of sublight ships, they found two life-bearing worlds: Romulus, with its complex ecosystem and oxygen atmosphere, a reasonable length of night and day, and virtually no mineral wealth with which to build a civilization; and Remus, inhospitable, devoid of life except in the unique zone of habitability existing in the perpetual twilight of its unmoving terminator, but with the mineral treasures to build not just a world's civilization, but an empire's.

Thus it was in the petri dish of the Romii system that the maverick offshoot of the Vulcan race split again, becoming the ruling elite of Romulus, and the subjugated slaves of Remus. Yet both branches of the original colonists maintained that savage edge that was their heritage from their pre-logic Vulcan ancestors. In the Romulans, that savagery became the fount of cold and cruel calculation, making them masters of intrigue and manipulation. In the Remans, it became the fount of physical strength and a penchant for direct action.

But those colonists who first chose the rewards they believed awaited them in the mines of Remus, and who were later joined by native generations of Romulans exiled for their crimes, then their sins, and, eventually, for their political beliefs, had to devote the majority of their existence to mere survival. The Romulans, in the comparative paradise of the world they had chosen, had time to look beyond themselves and build their empire. The military might that forged that assemblage of worlds became an equally effective tool for ensuring that the Remans fulfilled their half of the social contract—supplying the material wealth that enabled the Romulan expansion, while being given none of it for their own use and betterment.

Two thousand years after the first landing on Romulus, no one could say exactly when it was the Remans had become a slave race, and no Romulan historian would dare to investigate. It was simply the way things had always been and always would be.

The Remans, however, in their stories and traditions, in their secret schools in which the Old Ways were passed down through the generations by spoken word alone, still remembered a time when things were different, and thus could imagine a future time when things would be different again.

A ruling race that believed in the permanence of their society.

A slave race that knew that all things must change.

In the histories of a thousand different worlds, that same situation had led to only one result—

Revolution.

And all because two worlds had collided five billion years ago.

Those shock waves still resonated through history.

But Spock had yet to feel them.

T'Vrel was waiting for Spock in the starkly lit and austerely furnished canteen, as she always did this time of day.

The courtesy was something else Spock had noticed with his advancing years and rank. He no longer had to wait for anyone. Somehow, he became the more important participant in any meeting, and so he invariably became the last to arrive, even when he arrived early.

"Ambassador," the healer said, politely acknowledging his presence. They were the only two occupants in a canteen built to seat one hundred Romulan troops, and as usual, T'Vrel spoke in one of Vulcan's more esoteric scholar's dialects.

In keeping with T'Vrel's preference for efficient conversation, Spock acknowledged her presence in turn with a simple nod. Considering her background, he knew it was the correct response.

T'Vrel was a Surakian. Of all the different offshoots

of Vulcan empiricism, among which no truly major differences existed, the Surakians were those who attained the *Kolinahr* through the ongoing pursuit of the strictest interpretation of Surak's teachings. As was typical of her particular school of logic, T'Vrel's head was shaved, the clearest expression of the Surakian disdain for ornamentation of any kind. Her clothing consisted of a plain dark brown robe, with a simple, floor-length lighter brown vest of Guylinian cotton, from the province of Surak's birth.

Also, as would the others of her school, T'Vrel had renounced personal possessions, and in the normal course of events, she would have been expected to live a fully communal existence, dedicated to the advancement of knowledge above all else.

Many of Vulcan's greatest scientists and philosophers had been Surakian, or had been shaped by their schools. But, intriguingly, for all that they sought out new information and experience, not one Surakian had ever followed Spock's path and sought a career in Starfleet. Their focus was strictly on Vulcan. Everything else was extraneous.

Except, of course, the Romulans.

In the view of the Surakians, the Romulans were an affront to the Vulcan psyche. Until the renegades had been returned to the fold, the grave insult their ancestors had paid to Surak would continue to be an unhealed wound.

Before Spock could take his place on the green metal bench across the table from T'Vrel, the healer had scanned him with her medical tricorder and gave her verdict. "You are well enough."

Spock wondered what it was about physicians, how they all managed to sound like McCoy to him. Or was it just that he missed the human doctor's company, and sought to find it elsewhere?

"News?" Spock asked. He glanced at the tray she had set out for him. Old Romulan military rations. The Soltoth Command Post dated back from a time before the Earth/Romulan wars, when the Star Empire had taken on the Hiram Assembly. The war had gone badly at first, and had reached the outskirts of the Romii system. This complex of volcanic caverns deep within Romulus, attainable only by transporter, had been intended as an impregnable bunker from which the Imperial Fleet could prosecute the defense of the homeworld.

The bunker had not been necessary. The worlds of the assembly were now Romulan colonies. The Hiramnae themselves an extinct species. It was the Romulan way.

"No change," T'Vrel answered. "Claims of responsibility from three organizations. The Compliance Division will release the coliseum to its owners in two days to allow repairs to commence."

"No word from Vulcan?"

"Regret at the loss of a senior diplomat on leave, who was acting on his own without official sanction."

Spock kneaded a food pack to activate its heating chemicals. He had expected more from the Vulcan diplomatic community, and T'Vrel seemed to sense it.

"You are surprised by their response?" she asked.

"Disappointed," Spock answered.

"Surely, that is an emotional response."

"It is not every day one dies. I had expected a more . . . pronounced reaction."

"Define 'a more pronounced reaction.' "

"A public call for an investigation into the circumstances of my death. An official effort to begin one."

"The Vulcan embassy has expressed full confidence in local compliance officials."

"Then they are lying."

That his inflammatory accusation drew no outward response from T'Vrel was not remarkable to Spock. Surakians had the same perfect control of their autonomic systems as the greatest *Kolinahr* masters.

"They are being diplomatic. It is their function."

Spock placed the heated foodpack on the tray before him, squeezed the activation corners, and the soft-sided pouch hardened to become a low, rectangular bowl as the top surface split open. He sniffed the aroma of centuries-old *plomeek* soup.

"Agreeable?" T'Vrel asked.

Spock paused, surprised. For a Surakian, to inquire about a purely subjective experience was illogic of the most extreme. Food was fuel. Palatability was not an issue. She had even had to switch from the scholar's tongue to a more common Vulcan dialect to ask the question.

So Spock ignored it, refusing to be pandered to. He peeled the serving utensil from the foodpack, tapped it on the table once to harden it, then used it to stir the ancient soup.

"Given the inexplicably low-key response to my assassination," he said, "logic suggests that I have miscalculated the effect I wished to create."

"Now you are being diplomatic," T'Vrel said, still in the common dialect. "The miscalculation is shared. You did not act in this alone."

Spock appreciated T'Vrel's willingness to share the responsibility. But though he had had considerable help in putting his plan into motion, the final decision had been his. None of that was worth stating to a Surakian, though. To repeat information already known was illogical.

"Have you any insight into conditions which we did not allow for?" Spock asked.

"One."

That admission did surprise Spock. "Indeed."

She returned to the scholar's dialect she preferred. "The existence of an unidentified party already engaged in covert efforts to change the existing political structure on Romulus."

Spock took a mouthful of the *plomeek* soup, and was momentarily surprised by how flavorful it was. The Romulan military had long ago learned what Surak had so eloquently stated, that a military force proceeds by the nutritional well-being of its members.

"The existing political structure on Romulus was chaotic before my assassination," Spock said. "To all appearances, it remains chaotic." The political fallout from Shinzon's coup was what had prompted him to take the extreme step of manufacturing a legend by becoming a martyr to the cause of unification. By itself, the deceit behind such a concept would be disagreeable to a Vulcan, even illegal if attempted on a world within the Vulcan sphere of influence. But Romulan society was much more apt to take action based on emotional reactions. Thus, as he had done once before, in command of a doomed shuttlecraft long ago in the past, Spock had seen the logic of emotion, and had acted on it.

But T'Vrel had even more surprises for him.

"Upon consideration," she said, "the existing political structure on Romulus *appears* to be chaotic."

Spock put down his utensil, his appetite gone. Had he risked everything based on false assumptions? "Explain," he said. The Vulcan healer had switched back to a common dialect, subtly implying that he was at fault for not being able to reach the same conclusion she had.

"The aftermath of Shinzon's coup brought uncertainty to Romulus. Many groups vying for power, each looking for advantage over the other. None willing to speak out against or for unification with Vulcan. None wishing to cause friction with Vulcan 'influences' in particular, or Federation 'initiatives' in general.

"You, Spock, chose to exploit those chaotic conditions, by presenting yourself as a martyr, an emotional rally point for the many groups to coalesce around—a logical decision supported by the elders of my *s'url*." The healer used the Vulcan word for a Surakian school of logic.

"Yet now it appears my logic was uncertain," Spock said.

T'Vrel nodded once in acknowledgment. "Our plan to have the new government of Romulus endorse unification depended on the fact that our manipulation would bring stability and order.

"What it appears we did not consider was that another group saw the same chaos we saw, and decided to exploit it as we planned to exploit it, to further their own cause."

"What cause?" Spock asked.

"Unknown," T'Vrel answered. "All that we can infer is that the failure of our plan was caused by our attempt to bring order to a situation that was already ordered."

"In other words," Spock said, "our logic was sound, but our analysis of initial conditions was flawed."

"Yes."

Spock steepled his hands, pleased that an explanation was in hand, frustrated that a new plan would have to be developed.

"Have you given consideration to what new steps we might make to further our cause?" he asked.

"Yes. But the situation is more complex than it first appears."

Spock refrained from interrupting, knowing further explanation would follow, and it did.

"There is only one reason why news of your assassination was not followed by the predicted outpouring of Romulan sentiment for unification: The other group that we failed to identify is actively *against* unification."

"If that is true, then it would appear I died for nothing."

"Regrettable."

Spock decided he had been deferential long enough. "Not regrettable. Unacceptable."

The Vulcan healer did not respond to Spock's challenge directly. Instead, she asked, "What new action do you propose to take?"

Spock was puzzled by the question. Because it had only one answer. "Identify the other group intent on manipulating Romulan politics."

"That could be dangerous," T'Vrel said evenly.

For just a moment, Spock wondered if this was how McCoy felt in their ongoing debates. "Explain," he said again.

"We have just now, seven standard days after your staged assassination, deduced the existence of the other group that has thwarted our plans from the beginning."

Spock understood at once. "Then it is likely that they already know of our existence."

T'Vrel nodded. "And since their goals are antithetical to our own, logic dictates they will attempt to stop our efforts."

Spock drew on his own *Kolinahr* training as the full meaning of T'Vrel's conclusion became apparent to him. In the normal course of events, there would be many ways to stop a rival political organization. But in this case, given his own apparent death, the next, most obvious way the other group would move to stop him would be to ensure his actual death—a crime for which there could be no punishment.

"How much time do you estimate we have before the unknowns move against us?"

T'Vrel didn't answer.

She didn't have to.

The caverns of Soltoth echoed with a sudden explosion.

The emerald facets failed as their broadcast power source was interrupted, bringing on impenetrable darkness.

Time had run out.

4

RISA, STARDATE 57473.1

What the hell? Picard thought. *It's not as if she can fire me.* So he gave his honest opinion. "With all due consideration, Admiral, I decline your invitation."

But the response Kathryn Janeway gave was not any of the ones Picard had expected. No expression of disappointment or determination, just a flash of a smile through the mesh of her face screen.

Rather than argue or accept his last statement, the admiral simply slashed her *épée* to the side in salute, said, "On guard," and took up the classic position.

It's going to be like that? Picard thought. *So be it, then.*

Returning her salute and her smile, he matched her pose, right arm extended with his *épée* raised to parry her expected thrust. And in that same moment, all the details of their surroundings left him.

The rush and crash of surf on the beachside of their arena faded from his awareness, taking with it the cacophony of the Risan parrots' odes to dawn.

The early heat of morning vanished, as did the cool shade of the jungleside's lush foliage, which artfully shielded their exertions from the sprawling resort complex.

Picard even erased the idea that he, merely a Starfleet captain, was about to attempt to inflict grievous bodily harm—or, at least, a simulated version of it—on a Starfleet admiral.

All that mattered was that two fencers faced each other on a long and narrow *piste*, and that in five points, there would only be one.

Picard's honor demanded only one outcome, all considerations of rank and career advancement be damned.

"I thought Spock was a friend of yours," Janeway said, serious, as if intending to continue their conversation instead of commencing their match. But then, as if her words had been a deliberate attempt to distract, she sprang forward with a lunge to her opponent's chest, forcing Picard to retreat as he parried in the *tierce* position.

"I know the ambassador," Picard responded, countering with an expert *riposte* that defeated Janeway's *quinte* parry and found her left shoulder. Unfortunately, the instant the hit registered on the scorecard projected on his helmet screen, a matching tone and sharp pressure registered her hit on his own left shoulder.

The match had begun. Picard kept mental score: *Tied one all.*

"Or should I say, I knew him," he added as he and the admiral returned to the *en garde* lines glowing on the two-meter-wide and fourteen-meter-long mat that was their battlefield. "And I mourn his death." He took up the first position, his *épée* held in presentation. "*En garde.*"

"Don't you want to see his murderers brought to justice?"

The tips of their weapons circled each other as each sought an opening.

In *épée* competition—a favored form of fencing at Starfleet Academy—the formal attack/counterattack order of combat by foil was dispensed with. Both fencers could go on the offensive and score at any time. Thus initiative was rewarded.

"To obtain justice on Romulus under current conditions—" Picard moved forward with a firm *patinado*, let Janeway parry, then thrust again, and again, to complete the phrase of action with a lunge, scoring a decisive hit in her solar plexus. He caught his breath, stepped back. "—would require a better man than I."

Two-one for the captain.

Janeway smiled sweetly as they returned to their starting positions. "Is *that* how you regard Jim Kirk? A better man? I always thought there was a bit of a competition between the two of you."

Picard declined to take the proffered bait. "Since you said this will be a civilian operation, it makes sense for Jim to go to Romulus. He's retired, and he and Spock were like brothers. So—"

"On guard!" Janeway said, and again sprang forward in a lunge that became a surprisingly powerful parry to Picard's offensive *coupé*.

Her *épée* scraped his from *foible* to *forte*, at last reaching the bell-shaped *coquille* that protected his hand, at which she added an expert twist that forced Picard's weapon from his glove.

She smiled again and went to retrieve it. There was no honor in scoring a point against a defenseless opponent.

Picard raised his mask to let the dawn breeze dry his sweat-covered face.

It was early, and given that Risa was known for its nightlife, the resort's fresh-air gym was almost deserted. The few beings who either had risen early, had not yet slept, or came from worlds with a completely different circadian rhythm were paying more attention to a *banth* match now under way in the low-gravity boxing ring closer to the beach.

Picard had long been an admirer of *banth*, but given that it required four hands to keep the spinning pins in motion, no human need apply. That restriction apparently didn't deter two Vulcans near a group of boisterous Bolians from following the contest, raptly. A lone human in a glaringly bright shirt with oversize tropical flowers printed in harsh, clashing colors seemed equally engaged, though he stood apart from the others. The pale legs revealed by the man's baggy shorts suggested he had not been on Risa long. His floppy sunhat was that of a typical tourist from Sector Zero-Zero-One.

Janeway returned Picard's weapon to him and again they took up their positions.

And again the admiral led her charge with verbal needling.

"Even with you aboard, Jim would still do the legwork. On guard."

This time, Picard was ready for Janeway's sudden lunge.

So of course the admiral feinted and drew him into a *septime* parry, driving his weapon down so she could tap his facemask with the button of her weapon, unopposed.

Picard frowned, annoyed both by the unexpected

shock of the impact and the buzz from his helmet speaker. Not to mention the fact that the bout was now tied: two–two.

"Are you all right?" Janeway asked.

Picard tugged on the padded bib of his fencing helmet to settle it securely around his neck and upper chest. "Fine," he said.

Janeway did not dispute his assessment. Her interest was elsewhere. "I do feel I'm owed an explanation for your refusal."

Picard paused for a moment, stood at ease with his weapon to the side. "Admiral, have I misunderstood your request?" In Starfleet, tradition held that an admiral's request was an order by any other name.

But Janeway understood that tradition as well as he did. "My invitation wasn't an order, Jean-Luc. Merely . . . a suggestion."

"To be blunt, then," Picard said, "I am within my rights to decline."

Janeway shifted into the ready position. "Explain your decision, then I'll give you mine."

Picard raised his own *épée*.

"I am a starship captain. Should I and my crew suddenly appear on Romulus—"

"*With* Kirk," Janeway interrupted.

"With any civilian," Picard agreed, "then clearly the Romulans would have no reason to believe we were there for civilian reasons. *En garde.*"

Other than a slight circling movement of his *épée*, Picard held position.

Janeway merely circled her own *épée* in response, as if refusing to be drawn into an attack.

"Correction, Jean-Luc. For the moment, you're a starship captain without a starship."

"The *Enterprise* refit is proceeding on schedule," Picard said. He feinted but the admiral did not react. "She'll be ready for her shakedown cruise in less than a month."

He feinted again, and this time Janeway responded with a lunge, forcing him back, though she didn't press her advantage with pursuit.

Picard wondered if they had both decided on the same strategy. If so, each of them was waiting for the other to make a mistake.

Janeway confirmed his suspicions as she stepped back to her *en garde* line, clearly trying to entice him to follow with a thrust, as if they were dancing, not fencing.

"If we're going to get into what the Romulans might believe," she said with a playful edge, "then believe *me*. No Romulan will understand that Starfleet is leaving you in command of the *Enterprise*, let alone any other ship."

Picard's annoyance was flowering into something greater. He gave a halfhearted lunge, which the admiral efficiently parried, but didn't counter. "I beg your pardon," he said.

Janeway's irritating grin flashed through her mesh again. "The *Stargazer*. The *Enterprise*-D. Two ships lost."

Picard felt a flash of temper but controlled it. He still didn't know if Janeway was truly trying to further their debate or merely provoke him into making an error. They were fencing on several levels, it seemed.

"Is there a point, Admiral?"

Janeway began a mechanical sequence of lunge, thrust, lunge, which Picard parried with equal efficiency and lack of style. This round would belong to whichever fencer had the best supply of patience.

"An important point, Captain," Janeway said. "Since no Romulan commander would ever be given a second command after the loss of a ship—even if the loss were not her fault—no Romulan *would* be curious about your presence as a civilian. In fact, most Romulans would be puzzled by the fact that Starfleet hadn't executed you for carelessness."

Picard suddenly slashed at Janeway's *épée* as if they were fencing with sabres. "There is no question of command error in the loss of my ships," he said through clenched teeth.

Janeway backed off, parrying his unorthodox attack. "Of course not. But Starfleet isn't the Imperial Fleet. I'm only saying how the Romulans would see your position, not how Starfleet does."

Janeway abruptly executed a *passata sotto*, dropping to the mat with one hand to support her, and lunging with such unexpected speed that Picard heard the helmet-buzz of her hit being recorded on his leg before he was even aware that her blade was a threat.

Three—two now, in the admiral's favor.

"Then answer me this," Picard grumbled as he tugged down on his thickly padded white plastron jacket. "What would the Romulan reaction be to a contingent of Federation civilians, all *supposedly* ex-Starfleet, showing up to investigate a political crime on Romulus—as if local Romulan authorities were incapable or untrustworthy of doing the same?"

"Well," Janeway said, maddeningly unperturbed, "according to the best cultural attachés at headquarters, the Romulans would think it was business as usual. Think about it, Jean-Luc. If the situation were reversed, they wouldn't trust our local authorities. So to them, it would seem completely reasonable for us not to trust theirs."

I'm doomed, Picard thought in resignation. *"En garde,"* he said grimly. But a sudden loud cheer from the *banth* ring, and an instant's hesitation in the circular motion of Janeway's *épée*, changed everything. Instinct took over and Picard lunged forward, thrust and parried, and thrust again.

Janeway retreated, forced back to the last two meters of the *piste*, triggering the warning tone. And even as that alarm rang forth, Picard slashed twice, back and forth, then lunged to strike her heart.

The score was now three–three.

"I understand they fence on Romulus," Janeway said breathlessly as they resumed position in the center of the *piste*.

Picard was reenergized. He had his focus back. "No doubt with sharpened broadswords and a lack of armor," he said.

Janeway's eyes met his directly through the mesh of their masks. "That would be the Klingons. Romulans, it seems, have adopted the human sport, with only a few rule changes." She presented her blade. "On guard."

Picard was ready.

"And those changes would be?"

"Minor," she said as she thrust and he parried. "Sabres in one hand, short daggers in the other."

"With or without armor?" Picard grinned, relishing the intensity. This round, there was no question of either of them waiting for a mistake—each was going for a full-out offense. The bout would soon be over.

"With, of course!" Janeway completed a powerful parry that almost forced Picard off the *piste*, making him swing his arms to the side to keep his balance, and leaving him so wide open to Janeway's inevitable thrust that she merely tapped his chest to score.

Four–three. Picard berated himself for overconfidence. The admiral was one touch away from victory.

"You see, to a Romulan," Janeway said, "it is much more desirable to let the opponent bear the humiliation of defeat without a scar to point to. That way there is no excuse for defeat—no claims of pain or injury preventing one from doing one's best. Victory is achieved solely through skill."

Picard stiffened, sensing insult. "Is that what your intentions are here, Admiral? Inflicting the humiliation of defeat, not the injury?"

Janeway shook her head behind her mask. "Jean-Luc, I'm shocked . . . shocked that you would think such a thing. On guard, by the way."

Picard began to lower his *épée* as if this time he intended to set aside the bout for further conversation. "With respect, Admiral, I believe I'm owed the truth," he said.

Janeway straightened, began to lower her *épée* as well.

Then Picard lunged so forcefully that even after he had scored his hit, he overran the admiral, *corps à corps,* and had to grab her arm to keep from knocking her full over.

"Romulan tactics, Jean-Luc. Well done." Picard heard the admiral's chuckle. Amusement, not annoyance. But then, she had been enjoying the upper hand.

The bout was tied four–four.

All that remained was *la belle touché.* Whoever scored "the beautiful touch" would be the victor.

As he and Janeway took their positions for the final time, there was another loud cheer from the low-gravity ring and a round of enthusiastic Bolian warbling. The *banth* match, it seemed, had concluded.

Janeway and Picard both glanced over at the dispersing audience, both checking that they were far enough away to be spared collision.

"*En garde*," Picard said.

Picard parried Janeway's expected lunge, then thrust with all the energy remaining to him, as in a seamless phrase of movement, Janeway moved from the *septime* to the *octave* parry, then countered with a forceful thrust, missing Picard by less than a centimeter.

Then Picard and Janeway backed off, each catching breath after giving their all. But their confrontation still lacked that final touch.

"You'd be back from Romulus in a month," Janeway gasped. "In time for that shakedown cruise."

"I understand Starfleet's concern in this matter," Picard said gruffly, searching for the right words to end their debate, if not their match. "I understand the Federation's concern. And any insight or experience I can share with anyone outside the Star Empire, I stand ready to do so in any way I can, at any time. But in light of my involvement in ending Shinzon's coup, in light of my previous run-ins with Romulan politics, *also* involving Ambassador Spock, I assure you, Admiral Janeway, I am not the man for the job. Not on Romulus itself."

"Funny," Janeway huffed as she somehow found the resources to renew her assault, "those are all the reasons why Starfleet thinks you're perfect for it."

That's it! Picard felt vindicated. It was just as he had suspected from the beginning. Janeway's "invitation" to go to Romulus to help Jim Kirk investigate Spock's assassination wasn't just a favor to the Federation's diplomatic corps, it was a plan hatched at Starfleet Command.

He abruptly departed from form and slashed the admiral's *épée* to the side, leaving her in no position to execute a *riposte* as he scraped his blade around hers, then brought it back for the final lunge.

That's when Janeway shouted *"Jean-Luc!"* and charged off the mat and past Picard to strike at—

A Vulcan!

Picard had only an instant to register that the Vulcan was attacking him from behind with an upraised dagger before Janeway's hand dug into his padded shoulder and pulled him down and to the side.

Instinctively, Picard rolled to use the momentum to right himself, and by the time he regained his feet, he knew that his attacker had been one of the two Vulcans watching the *banth* bout so intently.

Two of them, Picard thought. He threw off his fencing helmet, certain that the Vulcan who had assaulted him would do so only if he thought his companion was targeting the admiral.

But the admiral was having no difficulty with Picard's attacker, her blazing swordplay successfully preventing his deadly dagger from reaching her. Her skill told Picard all too clearly that Janeway had been toying with him on the *piste*—she obviously could have bested him five–nothing at any time of her choosing.

Even so, he sprang forward to help her, glancing as he did to the side, to see the second Vulcan five meters away, flat on his back and unmoving, a trickle of green blood running from his swollen split lip. Beside the Vulcan, a pale-legged human in the loud tropical flower shirt and floppy sunhat, now turning from the fallen body, to run toward the admiral.

Before Picard had covered half the distance to Janeway, the human was already behind her attacker. With a perfectly precise movement reminiscent of Data, the man grabbed the Vulcan's forearm and locked it in place as firmly as if he had the strength of five Vulcans. He then dropped his other hand to the Vulcan's shoulder and inflicted a nerve pinch.

An instant later, though, the Vulcan wrenched his forearm free, twisted from the pinch, and spun in a deadly arc to drive the dagger directly into the human's flower-shirted chest.

Before Picard's horror-struck eyes, the man stood motionless with an almost comical expression of puzzlement, then glanced down with mild curiosity as the Vulcan savagely twisted the dagger deeper into his chest. For a moment, the man frowned, then looked up at the by now equally puzzled Vulcan and employed a deft right hook to send him crashing to the ground.

Picard stared as the human took the dagger smoothly from his chest and examined its bloodless surface. And only then did he recognize the man's uncanny resemblance to Doctor Lewis Zimmerman and realized what had happened, and who had saved him.

"Your holographic doctor," Picard said to Janeway.

The Doctor looked up with a sudden expression of indignation. "I beg your pardon. I am not a possession."

Picard smiled, approached the celebrated medical hero of the *Voyager*'s Delta Expedition. "Of course not, and I meant no disrespect. It's just that . . . well, I have encountered other emergency medical holograms, but you, sir, stand apart from them all." Picard saw the Doctor's expression soften, decided he was on the right track, continued to lay on the compliments as he held out his hand. "It is a true pleasure to meet you, and to thank you for saving my life." He looked at Janeway, who regarded him with a look that suggested he might be going too far with his praise. "Our lives," he concluded, and left it at that.

"A pleasure to meet you as well," the Doctor said as he shook Picard's hand. "I'm sure."

Picard was startled at the incredible sensation of contact with the holographic being. The flesh had just the right amount of give, the inner structure of the bones was solid, and there was even heat and a suggestion of sweat. Absolutely astounding.

"I'd been watching these two," the Doctor went on. He removed a Starfleet medical tricorder from under his nonregulation shirt, pointed it at the unconscious Vulcan at his feet, frowned again. "Most curious. Despite his current condition, his life-sign readings are no different from when I scanned him ringside."

Picard wasn't certain he understood the Doctor's point, but then the hologram knelt beside the fallen Vulcan. First, he ripped away the unconscious being's tunic to reveal the armor on his shoulder that had protected him from the nerve pinch; then he found a small device hidden under his belt, and held it up for Picard's inspection.

"Very clever," the Doctor said. "Life-sign transmitter." He pressed a control tab on the device, checked his tricorder again. "And very interesting." He looked at Janeway and his smug attitude became serious. "This fellow's Romulan."

Janeway turned to Picard, and lightly tapped the button of her *épée* to his shoulder. "*Touché*," she said, and Picard detected no sense that she was in any way enjoying what had just happened. "Looks like Starfleet's not the only one who thinks you're the right man for the job."

Picard, at last, had run out of arguments to the contrary.

He *was* doomed, after all.

5

SOLTOTH CAVERNS, ROMULUS, STARDATE 57473.1

Even as the echoes of the distant explosion faded, even as the afterimage of the canteen's extinguished lights remained burned into his eyes, Spock was up and moving with T'Vrel for the emergency equipment lockers on the far wall.

Neither Vulcan inadvertently collided with a bench or table. Their exact memory of the room's layout, augmented by their sensitive hearing, made moving through the familiar area, even in total darkness, as unremarkable as if it had been well lit.

Spock heard running feet in the rock corridors outside the canteen, then the ionic hiss of an energy weapon he did not recognize. The sounds of one set of running footsteps ceased immediately, without the punctuation of a falling body.

To Spock, the logic of that was simple. The attackers' weapons were set to full disintegration.

Spock heard T'Vrel open the locker, heard her hands move confidently, selecting the items they needed.

"Here," she said, and that one whispered word was enough for Spock to pinpoint her, sweep his hand to meet hers, and take the first item that she offered him.

A thermal imager—Romulan fleet surplus.

He pulled the asymmetrical flat shield over his eyes, pressed the control switch at his temple and felt the restraint straps tighten in place. A moment later, a holographic image sprang to life before him, showing T'Vrel, the open locker, and the canteen in a blotchy smear of false colors, assembled from the emission of infrared radiation.

"Working," Spock said quietly. That one word was enough to tell T'Vrel that he could see what she was doing, and that no more words were necessary.

But Spock knew that betraying their location by sound was the least of their worries. The invaders would also be wearing similar imaging devices to move through the darkened caverns.

Spock heard running footsteps again, this time much closer to the canteen. Two sets.

Both he and T'Vrel paused in their collection of equipment, but just for a moment. The footsteps were recognizable, not only from the familiar sound of Vulcan boot heels on the ribbed metal floor, but from the distinctive pace. Soral and T'Rem were approaching on the run, two of the team of sixteen Vulcans who were currently quartered in these facilities.

By the time the sounds of the young Vulcans indicated passage through the canteen doors, Spock and T'Vrel were equipped and ready for whatever had to be done.

In the false color generated by Spock's thermal imager, the two Vulcans in the doorway appeared brighter than T'Vrel. The outline of their lean bodies glowed through the simple robes they wore. Both were overheated from running. *Certainly not from fear*, Spock thought. The two young Vulcans were Surakians, students of T'Vrel's own *s'url*.

To both Spock and T'Vrel, Soral made a series of broad, though precise, gestures—combat sign language designed to be intelligible even in the low-resolution reconstructions provided by the thermal imagers.

His information was succinct: Invaders had beamed in at three different locations, three individuals to each team. Thus far, at least four Vulcans had been killed, and the facility's own transporter room was under enemy control.

Spock's first conclusion was that the invaders were Cardassian. The concept of a triumvirate was the centerpiece of their dominant culture. However, the Cardassian Union had been brought to the brink of destruction by the Dominion War, and Spock could not see any logical motive for its leaders to expend resources on an operation to manipulate Romulan politics.

But T'Vrel had already jumped beyond Spock's line of reasoning.

"Cardassian *mercenaries*," she said in a low voice, beside Spock.

Spock did not contest her conclusion. There were certainly enough dishonored Cardassian soldiers in the quadrant unable to return home. Their connections to the Obsidian Order would only guarantee a war crimes tribunal which, by Cardassian tradition, would try them only after they had been found guilty. Such soldiers would be eager for employment by whoever could pay the price, and would have no motivation to question their assignments.

Spock considered the small cylindrical device that T'Vrel now held up. It was a Romulan sunpod flare, designed to explode in two distinct phases. The first phase would generate an encrypted electromagnetic pulse that would selectively switch off—for one-half second—the thermal imagers the Vulcans wore. Less than a millisecond later, the second phase of the explosion would produce a broad spectrum of infrared radiation and visible light powerful enough to overwhelm the circuits of the invaders' thermal imagers.

In the seconds it would take for the enemy imagers to reconfigure themselves, he and T'Vrel and the two younger Vulcans would have a decided advantage. Yet given that Soral and T'Rem were Surakians, schooled in the most ancient Vulcan combat arts, whoever dared enter this room was most unlikely to last more than a heartbeat, even without the deployment of counter-measures.

The only variable that Spock could not adequately incorporate into a logical prediction of the outcome of this attack was the invaders' use of disintegration weapons. But from the increasing sound of the approaching footfalls, an empirical answer would soon be furnished.

Soral and T'Rem exchanged another set of rapid hand signals with T'Vrel. Then T'Rem leapt lightly onto a bench, from there onto a table, and finally sprang to a position above the entrance door, clinging to the wall like an enormous insect.

Though the details were too fine for Spock to see in his imager, he recalled a wiring conduit that ran along the wall above the doorway. It apparently was all the support T'Rem needed to hold herself in position. Her display of agility and strength was impressive.

Now Soral made a twisting movement and Spock saw the smeared orange outline of the student's long cotton vest flutter to the floor to the side of the door, still incandescent with his residual body heat. The young Vulcan then slipped behind a food dispenser, flattening his body against the carved rock wall so he would be unseen when the invaders entered.

It appeared Soral had determined that the rapidity of the invaders' advance through the corridors indicated they were not using sensing devices to map an area before entering. What they lost in precision, they gained in speed. The tactic also meant they gave no energy signals to their enemies that could be used to locate them. *Cardassian tactics once again,* Spock concluded.

T'Vrel gestured to him, and Spock took his place beside the open equipment locker, a countermeasures case slung over his shoulder, and in his right hand a Romulan disruptor. The weapon had no stun setting, so Spock had switched it from lethal neural disruption to molecular decohesion. If he had to, he would take another's life to preserve his own. But, he calculated, blasting loose rock from the room's low ceiling might be enough to repel the invaders without causing unnecessary fatalities.

Then he waited.

He heard more boots running and the hiss of two more weapon discharges, one of them followed by a crashing of rock and metal.

Spock noted the direction of the noise and judged that one of the facility's geothermal power converters had been destroyed. The invaders clearly wished to prevent any circuit reconfiguration that would divert life-support power to the lighting grid. That also suggested the invaders were counting on the darkness continuing.

The thought reassured Spock. It meant the sunpod flare would likely be an effective, nonlethal weapon.

The enemy entering the canteen would be temporarily blinded, and in those few seconds they could be captured. Alive. Learning the invaders' identity would certainly reveal their motives, and that knowledge in turn would open other logical pathways to victory through negotiation, escape, or combat.

The sounds of footsteps slowed as the unseen enemy approached the canteen door from the corridor.

Spock's sensitive hearing caught the faint metallic *snick* of the sunpod flare being armed by T'Vrel.

Then three large humanoid forms of false yellow rushed into the doorway, halted, and swept the room with an ungainly and unidentifiable rifle-like weapon.

Spock had just enough time to note that the invaders did not have the distinctive, cobra-neck silhouette of Cardassians before his imager switched off. A moment later, he felt the heat of the sunpod's release of blinding light.

Spock bolted for the doorway, fully expecting Soral and T'Rem to have subdued the blinded invaders in the few seconds it would take him to get there. But when his imager switched back on again, less than three steps later, he saw a different outcome.

Soral was trading a flurry of deadly hand strikes with one of the invaders, weaving and ducking to avoid being shot by the attacker's rifle.

Spock quickly reached a new conclusion: The fact that the enemy was engaged in hand-to-hand combat instead of using disintegrators strongly implied they intended to *capture* whoever was in this room.

Then T'Rem dropped from the wall above the other two invaders, striking one with her fists and the other with her feet. As both were thrown off balance, stumbling forward, the young Vulcan tucked into a roll as she reached the floor, and leapt in an instant to her feet.

One of the invaders whirled about, awkwardly brandishing his rifle as a staff. But T'Rem simply flipped over it and struck him once again with her feet. The force of her blow sent him flying backward into a bench.

T'Vrel was at the invader's side at once. Spock didn't have to see what happened next. The touch of two of the Vulcan healer's fingers in the appropriate *katra* point, and the invader would be paralyzed.

Soral and the third invader battled on in silence. Both combatants' movements were so fast they strobed across Spock's computer-generated vision.

Ignoring his disruptor, Spock held his hand ready to strike, using his other senses to answer the last question he had about Soral's attacker: Which species of humanoid was attacking them?

He smelled the sharp hot scent of the emitter node on the invader's recently used energy weapon. Then sweat, not as pungent as a Klingon's, not as sour as a human's, insufficient in character to identify the species.

He listened to the sounds of the attacker's uniform, creaking as if made from actual animal hide and not military fabric engineered for silence. He heard the attacker's steady breathing, controlled and focused, through his nostrils, not his open mouth, despite his strenuous exertions.

Spock processed all these impressions in less than a second, but none led him to a logical identification of Soral's attacker.

But just as he had been a teacher of James T. Kirk, so Spock had been a student of the human captain. Logic was not the only way to approach a challenge.

Spock watched for his opening, acted, thrust his hand forward to grab at the shoulder of Soral's attacker, trusting his instinct and training. The Vulcan nerve pinch would require no more than half a second.

And yet, in that half second, incredibly, Soral's attacker sensed Spock's presence as well as his attack.

Almost simultaneously, the invader blocked another strike by Soral, then ducked and twisted and spun to face Spock.

Spock responded without conscious thought, whipping his free arm out to block the barrel of the attacker's rifle as it swung for his head, to make it fly from his attacker's grasp. At the same time, Spock changed his target from the attacker's shoulder to his face, determined to rip off the attacker's imager, reducing him to blindness.

But the attacker did not block Spock's hand as it closed like a vise—on a cold metal mask without image inputs or eye slits of any kind.

At the bottommost range of Spock's own imager, the attacker's leg and boot rose up and struck backward into Soral's chest.

Spock heard bones crack. Saw Soral drop to the canteen floor.

In the same instant, the attacker's hands were around Spock's throat. Spock's head was slammed forward.

Spock reached up, grasping, his hands slipping to one side of the metal mask. His fingers raked across bare flesh, and into the soft ridged muscles of a batlike ear.

And at his contact with that ear, even as taloned hands squeezed his throat and shut his senses down, Spock had his answer.

The attackers had no need of imagers, nor could they be blinded by light through the metal masks that shielded their eyes, because they perceived their surroundings by sound.

The advantage of night had always been theirs because all in their world were born in darkness.

The identity of the other group who wished to interfere in the fragile politics of Romulus was no longer unknown to Spock.

His attackers were the other lost children of Vulcan. Remans.

6

S.S. CALYPSO, STARDATE 57480.3

There was no center chair.

Kirk paused on the scuffed metal deckplates outside the single turbolift, and looked at what passed for the bridge of the commercial astrogation vessel, *Calypso*, in more detail.

In particular, he stared at the center of the bridge, at the deck, trying to see any marks in the traction carpet that might indicate the captain's chair had been temporarily removed for repair.

But he couldn't easily find the center of the bridge.

It wasn't even circular.

It was boxlike, rectangular, more like an inflated interior of an old-style shuttlecraft.

On the main level, four steps down from the elevated deck on which the turbolift opened, along each side of the bridge were three duty stations, each with two chairs, and two sets of displays and control boards cantilevered out from the bulkheads. But instead of the displays being aligned flat to the bulkheads, so that command staff in the center of the bridge could see each duty station at a glance, all controls faced ahead, like desks in a classroom.

And what they faced wasn't a large, central viewscreen—there were three of them, side by side on the sharply inward-angled forward wall. The rightmost screen displayed an engineering schematic of the *Calypso*—little more than a blunt-nosed, cylindrical main module about the same size as a single nacelle from an old *Ambassador*-class ship, with a slight, tapered bulge at the rear of the ventral hull, and two swept-back, outboard warp nacelles, also cylindrical, suggesting technology that was decades removed from state-of-the-art.

A dozen other smaller displays angled down from the ceiling of the bridge, and a handful more were arranged in what seemed to be a random fashion on the port and starboard bulkheads. Brightly colored conduits threaded among stark switching boxes made the rest of the exposed bulkheads resemble the outside of a Borg cube. Behind Kirk, also on the upper level, was a small room with a deck-to-overhead transparent wall. Inside the room was a wide black desk, apparently bolted to the deck, covered with scattered padds, and ringed by more displays on the bulkheads and overhead, all angled so they could be seen only by whoever sat behind the station.

And the air had a damp and musty smell, as if the ship recently had been used to transport livestock and the ventilation system had yet to be purged.

Kirk wondered what Spock would say when he told him about this sad excuse for a starship.

And then he remembered.

The shock of loss was just as strong as it had been the first time he knew Spock was dead. Just as strong as it had been every other time these past ten days when he had realized he would never again be able to share anything with his friend.

"Not quite Starfleet specs, is it, Captain?" Admiral Janeway smiled warmly at Kirk as she approached him from the lower level.

Kirk almost gasped. He had been so discomfited by his thoughts of Spock, so bothered by the bridge's layout and condition that he hadn't even noticed Janeway's presence among the other technicians on the bridge. The fact that she wore a drab civilian outfit of tan jacket and gray trousers didn't help. All the technicians were civilian, as well: three humans, two Bynars, and a Tellarite with a bad cough. They all seemed to be working on the same disassembled control console, arguing over which circuits to tear out next and throw onto the deck with the others.

Kirk tried to ignore the unprofessional chaos, held out his hand to shake Janeway's as she came up the steps. "Admiral." He looked around again. There were scrapes on every pale green wall, gouges and nicks on every piece of equipment. He could picture the way Spock's eyebrow would rise at the sight of such disrepair. "She *is* spaceworthy, is she?"

Janeway's smile grew wider, as if she had no sense of what Kirk was feeling, what he was hiding. "Mister Scott and Commander La Forge are in the engine room, determining that even now. But I don't think they'll find anything surprising." She gestured to the room behind the transparent wall. "Care to join me in your office?"

"Office?" Kirk repeated.

Janeway waved her hand past a sensor patch and a section of the wall slid to the side. "After you," she said.

Kirk took a breath, stepped into the room, and knew he would be damned before he would ever call it his office.

"When Captain Riker told me Starfleet would be providing a ship . . ." Kirk began.

"You expected a Starfleet vessel," Janeway concluded for him. She still hadn't lost that all-knowing smile, and she waved her hand again to close the sliding door.

"I expected a *ship*." Kirk was determined to make Janeway understand this wasn't a training run he had agreed to. A man was dead. A great man. And his unknown killers lived. "One worthy of the mission."

With those words, Janeway finally seemed to sense what lay behind the steel in Kirk's tone. Her smile faded. "I understand. And your expectations have been met. This *is* a Starfleet vessel."

Kirk frowned. "Admiral, the noncertified shuttlecraft that first-year engineering students take apart and reassemble at the Academy are in better shape than this . . . barge."

"Which is what makes it perfect for espionage missions."

That stopped Kirk. "Espionage?"

Janeway paused, as if mentally testing different replies before committing to speak one aloud. At last, she chose her approach.

"Captain, I will not presume to say I can understand what you feel at the loss of your friend. But I do hope you understand that more than a friend was lost. Ambassador Spock was a powerful force for peace, whose influence extended far beyond the Federation's boundaries. As an arm of the Federation, Starfleet has been given the mission to determine if the people who killed

Spock did so as a strike specifically against the reunification of Romulans and Vulcans, or if there was a larger purpose, one directed against the Federation itself."

Kirk had been out of Starfleet too long. He was tired of admirals and their long-winded justifications for everything they did. He missed Komack and Morrow and Bennett, the bold leaders of his day, who simply took action when it was required, and left the explanations to the junior staff responsible for filing reports. He started to interrupt, but Janeway wouldn't let him.

"I know that's not what you care about right now," she said. "I don't blame you. You've done more for the Federation than we could ever ask of anyone. You deserve your own life. You deserve time with your child."

"What I deserve," Kirk said without waiting for Janeway to give him an opening, "is you getting to the point."

A flicker of a smile played over Janeway's lips, as if she appreciated Kirk's blunt approach. "All right. In the matter of Spock's murder, Starfleet has a mission, and *you* have a mission. Those missions overlap." She gestured to include the battered bridge before them. "So Starfleet is making one of its most valuable Q-ships available to you, so you can—"

"Throw myself on the barbed wire in advance of the main force," Kirk said coldly. He had known what was expected of him since the unusual briefing with Riker, Troi, and Worf on the *Titan*. He understood exactly what Janeway meant.

But she didn't understand him. "Barbed wire? Something to do with . . . horses?"

"Combat," Kirk said. "Centuries ago, barbed wire was strung across battlefields and beaches to slow invading forces. The first soldiers to reach the barbed-wire fences would throw themselves down on it, so those behind could run over them without slowing."

This time, Janeway didn't fight her smile. "Don't worry, Captain. Starfleet will give you time to get out of the way."

Kirk stared out at the bridge, and from this vantage point he immediately saw the purpose of its design: The flow of information went in only one direction—*to* the commander. From this room, looking through the transparent wall, the captain of the *Calypso* could see every display screen his crew worked at, even though each of those crew members could see only his or her own. Data therefore filtered up to this . . . office, and whatever information flowed out was limited to what the captain chose to share.

But on a Starfleet vessel, the mission came before the man, and all information was freely available to everyone cleared for bridge duty. That was the only way something as complex as a starship could be managed—with complete trust in all personnel. No secrets. No doubts. No delays.

Three conditions which Janeway now refused to meet.

"You look like there's something else you need to say," Janeway prompted.

Kirk wondered what the point would be. But he tried anyway.

"Captain Riker made my position clear. I'm to be the point man. I lead the investigation. I distract and annoy the Romulan authorities. But in the end, I'm not to think it's anything but a Starfleet operation."

Janeway gave Kirk a measuring look. "Captain Riker may have said more than he was authorized to say."

Kirk was equally tired of the formality of Starfleet's chain of command. He was sick to death of protocol. "Riker didn't *say* anything he wasn't supposed to. I said: He made my position clear."

Janeway raised her eyebrows, silently asking for clarification.

Kirk gave it to her. "Trust me, Admiral, I was in Starfleet before you were . . ." Kirk couldn't bring himself to finish that particular thought. In truth, he had been in Starfleet before virtually anyone else in Starfleet today had been born. And he was tired of being reminded of that too. "I know how Starfleet operates," he continued instead. "I know what you can say, what you can't, and I don't care anymore. I'll carry out my mission, and Picard, I'm sure, will be your eyes and ears to be certain Starfleet's interests are protected."

Kirk was surprised by the sudden icy glare that came to Janeway. She leaned back on the desktop, kept her eyes locked on Kirk as if he were a cadet and she his Academy instructor. "I'll only say this once. You're going to Romulus as part of a team. A Starfleet team. You and Jean-Luc. Doctor McCoy, Mister Scott, Commander La Forge, and Doctor Crusher."

"And Joseph." Kirk matched Janeway icy glare for icy glare.

Janeway nodded, conceding the point. "And your child."

"Who is no more part of Starfleet than I am."

But Janeway shook her head, patted the desk. "As I said, this is a Starfleet vessel. It goes where obvious Starfleet vessels can't go. Half the time, its supposed owners rent it out for legitimate private cruises. Geological mapping of non–M-class planets. University research expeditions. The other half of the time, Starfleet officers, in civilian clothes, with carefully constructed false identities, sit behind this desk and carry out missions Starfleet can't be seen to be involved in.

"The only difference between *those* missions and this one is that we don't have to create a false identity for you. You have a reason for going to Romulus. That's all anyone needs to know." She stood up again, spoke the next words almost as if they were a threat. "Even you, *Captain.*"

"That's 'mister.' I'm retired."

"I mean it as a form of respect."

To Kirk, it felt as if the temperature in the "office" had dropped by fifty degrees. He couldn't be certain of the reason for Janeway's hostility toward him, but the very fact it existed was enough to kindle the same kind of obstinacy in himself.

"There's a better way to show respect," Kirk said.

Janeway waited for him to explain.

"Tell me the truth about this mission."

"I have."

"The whole truth."

Janeway tapped her finger against the desktop, then shrugged. "Even I don't know that."

Kirk was momentarily distracted by a flash of sparks that jumped up from the open console surrounded by technicians, down on the bridge proper. "So I have a mission. Picard has a mission. And then . . . there's a third mission?"

Janeway wasn't going to give up anything more. "Maybe even a fourth or a fifth," she said, almost as if she deliberately meant to taunt him. "This has all been arranged by Starfleet Intelligence. I've been told what I need to know. And now you've been told, too."

Kirk studied Janeway carefully. He didn't know her

well, but he had read of her astonishing voyage
through the Delta Quadrant. He had been impressed
that against impossible odds, she had brought her crew
and her ship back from certain death, like a modern-
day Shackleton. And he had met her Mirror Universe
duplicate, held her in his arms and fought at her side,
and from that experience knew firsthand the inner
strength and force of will that was common to both re-
flections of the woman.

But he hated the fact that she stood before him now
not as a legendary starship captain, but merely as a
Starfleet functionary. Somehow, he doubted that she
would be entirely comfortable with that role. He decided to find out.

"Admiral," Kirk asked her, "when did you stop
being a captain?"

He saw her eyes narrow, knew she understood the
criticism he intended. But to Kirk's disappointment,
she held herself in check, revealed nothing of what she
might really be feeling. "We're on the same side, Captain Kirk."

But Kirk shook his head. "No, we're not. Unless—
and until—you tell me what the real purpose of this
mission is, you're just noise in the signal."

Janeway forced a smile. "Then get used to the static."

Part of Kirk appreciated the fact that Janeway
wouldn't back down, that for all that she made a point
of showing him respect, she treated him as an equal. He
hoped she felt the same about the way he treated her.

But if there was anything more to be said between
them, that conversation would have to wait, because
suddenly the office door slid open again, and Joseph
skipped in, clutching his much-too-large duffel bag to
his chest.

"Hi Dad!" His voice was bright, full of energy, full of promise. Kirk, as always, was astounded at the effect his child had on him, as if some of that energy miraculously flowed into him, recharging, reinvigorating. Suddenly, Janeway and her Starfleet machinations weren't that annoying, or important.

"Hi Joseph." Kirk reached out to rub his hand over Joseph's ridged, bald scalp.

"Hello . . . Admiral," Joseph said to Janeway.

Kirk was surprised. He didn't think Joseph and Janeway had met. He glanced at the admiral, but she wasn't looking at Joseph in acknowledgment. Instead, she was looking at something past him.

Kirk followed her gaze, expecting to see something more going on on the bridge. Instead, he saw the sensor patch that controlled the sliding door.

"Joseph," Kirk asked, "have you met Admiral Janeway?"

"No, sir."

Kirk hadn't expected that answer. "Then how did you know who she is?"

"Uncle Scotty said she was here."

Janeway held out her hand to shake Joseph's. "I'm very pleased to meet you, Joseph."

The child squirmed with his duffel until Kirk lifted it from him. Joseph eagerly started to reach out his hand to take Janeway's, then stopped, looked at his palm, then quickly wiped it against his red coveralls.

"Sorry. I was in the mess." Apparently convinced his hand was clean, Joseph earnestly shook Janeway's hand. Kirk hid his smile as Janeway surreptitiously wiped her own hand against her slacks.

"So what do you think about this ship?" Janeway asked.

Joseph looked up at Kirk. "Permission to speak freely?"

Kirk saw Janeway smile at that phrase, but Kirk was pleased that Joseph remembered proper etiquette for talking with adults.

"Permission granted," Kirk said.

"Well, it's sort of messy," Joseph said. "But Uncle Scotty says the engines are outstanding! Under the dirt. He doesn't like the dirt. But Geordi says they can't clean it off." Joseph screwed up his face. "How come?"

Janeway looked at Kirk, passing the question on to him.

Kirk was already uncomfortable with having Joseph on this mission, even though no one expected danger. The worst that could happen was that the Romulans would prevent the *Calypso* from entering their system. But Kirk had always insisted on complete honesty from his son, and the only way he could expect Joseph to keep that commitment to his father was to be completely honest in return.

"Remember how we've talked about operational security?" Kirk asked. He ignored Janeway's flicker of puzzlement.

"Top secret. Need to know," Joseph said gravely.

"Very good," Kirk confirmed. "The answer to your question is top secret, so you can never tell anyone else about it. Understood?"

"Is the admiral cleared?" Joseph asked.

Janeway put her hand over her mouth and coughed. But Kirk had had a great deal more experience in not laughing at Joseph's unexpectedly adult pronouncements, and kept a serious expression. "She's in charge."

"Understood," Joseph said.

Kirk looked to Janeway. "Admiral . . . if you'd care to, uh, brief Joseph."

Janeway shrugged, clearly amused. "Very well, Captain." She took on an extremely serious demeanor as well, and turned to Joseph. "The *Calypso* is what we call a Q-ship. It's a Starfleet vessel, but it's in disguise. From the outside, it looks like a slow-moving civilian ship. But on the inside, it has Starfleet's best engines and shields."

Joseph's eyes widened. "Oh, oh! So if . . . if Orion pirates board the vessel, and they go into the engine room, they'll see all the dirt and think the engines are junk!"

"Exactly," Janeway said. "But for the disguise to work, you can't ever tell anyone about it."

"Yes, sir!"

Janeway gave Kirk an inquiring look. "And what year of the Academy is Joseph in now?"

Joseph laughed. "I'm not in the Academy!"

Janeway played along. "You're certain? You're behaving exactly like a proper cadet. I'm very impressed."

Joseph looked at Kirk, and Kirk could see his son, only five, going on ten most days, going on seventeen from time to time, had no idea what to say. Kirk helped him out. "Admiral Janeway has just paid you a compliment."

Joseph remembered his etiquette again. He actually stood at attention. "Thank you, Admiral."

"You're very welcome." Janeway turned her attention back to Kirk. "I think we're finished here, Captain Kirk. Jean-Luc will be able to fill you in on any details we've missed."

"Uncle Jean-Luc?" Joseph asked excitedly. "Is he here?" And then Joseph tensed as he realized his mistake, and added, "I apologize for interrupting."

"Not necessary," Janeway said gracefully. "And, uh . . . Uncle Jean-Luc should be arriving within the hour." She nodded at Kirk. "And I should be getting back to the *Titan*."

Janeway started for the closed door.

"Will you be staying on the *Titan?*" Kirk asked.

Janeway paused by the transparent door. "No. Between you, Jean-Luc, and Captain Riker, we're in good hands." She tapped the door. It didn't move. Then she waved her hand over the sensor patch, and the door opened. She looked back at Kirk. "You should have your engineers check the lock on this door. It's supposed to be keyed to command staff only." She smiled professionally at Kirk, then looked at Joseph. "A pleasure to meet you, Cadet."

Joseph jumped to attention again. "A pleasure to meet you, Admiral."

Then Janeway left and the door closed behind her.

As she stepped into the turbolift a few steps away, Kirk waved his hand over the sensor patch, and the door opened again, then closed at his second wave. "There's nothing wrong with this." He looked at Joseph. "Is there?"

"No, sir. But Admiral Janeway said your engineers should check it."

Kirk bent down to scoop up Joseph, and even as he straightened up he realized his days of lifting his son were coming to an end. He was getting too big. "Well, if an admiral tells us to check something, then we should, right?"

"Right!"

Kirk sighed. "I'm going to have to start strapping antigravs onto you." He gently slipped Joseph back to the deck. "I'll get your duffel."

Kirk picked up the cloth bag from the desktop, frowned at the weight of it. "Are you smuggling latinum in this?"

Joseph giggled at the door. "Daa-ad."

Kirk started forward, stopped as he saw that the door was open again. "Can you open that door?"

Joseph nodded.

"I guess that's what the admiral meant," Kirk said. He stepped out of the command room with his son. *Never the office*, he thought. "Let's go check our quarters."

"Okay," Joseph agreed.

"Maybe we can short-sheet Uncle Jean-Luc's bunk."

The transparent door slid closed behind them as they stepped up to the closed turbolift door.

"Okay," Joseph agreed again.

The turbolift door puffed open and they stepped inside.

"Deck four," Kirk said.

"What's 'short-sheet' mean?" Joseph asked.

Kirk grinned at his son. "We're going to learn a lot on this trip."

Joseph grinned back.

But as the turbolift door closed, Kirk looked again at the command-room door, wondering why Janeway had called his attention to it, and what other secrets she was hiding from him, what other secrets he was yet to discover.

7

COORDINATES UNKNOWN, STARDATE 57483.3

Spock floated in darkness, cloaked in the comfort of logic.

It was all he had left.

He had no concept of time. That had been stolen from him when the Reman attacker had strangled him into unconsciousness.

How long that oblivion had lasted, he did not know. But since his awareness had returned in this environment of sensory deprivation, he had counted out six standard days.

As the first webs of consciousness had been redrawn within him, he had briefly considered the possibility that he was a disembodied *katra* within the caves of Mount Seleya. But such a remnant of his personality would have no memory of his mode of death, only of the final moments leading up to the transfer of his *katra* to the chosen repository. He had undertaken such a transfer only twice. Once aboard the *Enterprise*, with McCoy, and what had transpired after he had placed that ineffable part of him within the doctor's mind he had no knowledge of. His recollection consisted of melding with the doctor in the engine room, and then slowly awakening in the Temple of Logic, with the wisps of nonbeing slowly dissipating over the months of his recovery on Vulcan.

Of his second *katric* transfer, he had even less recollection.

But in this case, he remembered the shock of his hands on his attacker's ears, the realization that the attacker was Reman, and the long fall from darkness into darkness as consciousness fled.

Yet though he floated free of gravity, without even the pressure of clothing around him, he could feel his pulse, hear his blood in his ears, sense the movement of air in and out of his mouth and nostrils. He swallowed saliva, fanned his face to feel a breeze, ran his fingers along his throat to feel swelling there, but no other sign of injury.

He was alive, mind and body joined.

Thus logic insisted that as dire as his current position was, it was not his captors' intention to kill him.

Torture was a possibility, though most intelligent species had long ago learned that it had little effect on Vulcans.

As for sensory deprivation, Spock suspected that several years in this environment might be enough to induce signs of instability. But the lessons of extended meditation developed by the first wave of Vulcan's interstellar explorers who had set out on decades-long, sublight voyages to distant stars, had been well learned by subsequent generations. Spock had more than enough accumulated data to keep his mind occupied for years, if that was what was necessary.

A more direct route to torture might simply have been removal of food and water. But Spock had yet to

detect any sign of thirst or hunger, even though his
body still excreted waste. Since he had no recollection
of ingesting anything during the time he had been conscious in this void, logic dictated one of two possibilities: Either his captors had the ability to interrupt his
awareness without his knowledge, and during those
interruptions they force-fed him; or he was being constantly supplied with water and nutrients with techniques similar to the noninvasive medical-transporter
drug-delivery systems being developed at Starfleet
Medical.

The latter possibility was the simplest explanation,
so Spock accepted it, and concluded that his captors
were supported by sophisticated technology.

That conclusion implied that though it was a Reman
who had captured Spock, the unknown planners who
had set the Reman on his mission were likely *not*
Reman.

After six days in the void, that was as far as logic
had taken him: He was in no danger of death, little
danger of torture, but with no idea why he had been
abducted, or who was responsible.

The only aspect of emotion that Spock allowed himself to contain was his hope that whatever his fate,
T'Vrel, T'Rem, Soral, and the others of his support
group had been spared it; that he, Spock, alone had
been the target of the raid. Unfortunately, given that he
had heard disintegrations, Spock feared that if he was
the target, then the others were already dead.

"Do I detect remorse, Ambassador?"

Spock listened carefully for the acoustical after-
effects of that question, to determine its likely origin
point in relation to his position. At the same time, he
created a logical decision tree, addressing the new is-

sues raised. Did the question's apt timing suggest he was in the hands of telepaths who could probe his mind without his awareness? Did that mention of remorse suggest that his assistant, Marinta, who was not present in the Soltoth Caverns, had also been captured and interrogated?

"It means everything and more, Ambassador."

Spock calmly accepted that some form of telepathy was in use, and instantly began to employ basic blocking techniques, effective even against highly trained Betazoids.

"Blocking will not be effective."

Spock decided to test the limits of his captors. He dropped into full meditation, an absolute cessation of all thought.

"I am disappointed, Ambassador. Thought never ends."

Spock moved to a new technique, created a mind-picture of the mountains near his family estate, the same ones he so often had retreated to as a youth, after arguing with his father. That powerful, looming landscape had always offered comfort to him, and he sought its towering presence now, as a pathway to total peace.

But sudden cold wind shocked him from his meditation, and as abruptly as if he had been slapped, Spock found himself on a frost-rimed ledge of the mountains of his home. He could look down past the foothills and see his family compound, ringed by a low wall of ancient red sandstone blocks, smoke threads from the kitchen chimney untwining in the breeze. All around him were the lofty, shadowed peaks of the protective mountains.

Spock gasped in the cold air; the sudden shift in perspective, the pull of Vulcan gravity, the onslaught of daylight after so long in darkness, all sensations overwhelming the meditative calm he had sought.

"Bring back memories?" a pleasant, familiar voice asked.

Spock turned unsteadily on the ledge, became aware of sharp stones crunching under his bare feet. He glanced down to check his footing, then nearly lost his balance in surprise.

His body had been transformed.

He was a youth again, lean muscles, slight build, long dark hair fluttering across his eyes.

He had on blue denim trousers and a buttoned shirt like those he had seen worn by the humans of his mother's family; an act of teenage rebellion that had inflamed his father.

"Do you know when you are?" the familiar voice asked.

Spock reclaimed his equanimity long enough to look up at the source of the voice, and even as he saw the Vulcan who stood with him on the ledge, he knew immediately that this was all an illusion.

"What if I said it was not an illusion?" Saavik asked.

Spock hesitated before answering. Illusory or not, Saavik's beauty overwhelmed him. She appeared the same age as she had been when he had first met her, when she had been an instructor at Starfleet Academy. But instead of the uniform she had worn at the time, she stood before him now wrapped in a traditional Vulcan wedding shawl, as all brides did on the third day of the ceremony, when the couple was at last left to their privacy and the blood fever.

The delicate, transparent fabric flowed around her in the breeze, making it appear as if she floated in and out of Spock's vision, here in detail, there in suggestion, alluring, enticing, shattering to all constraints of logic.

"I will ask you again," the illusion of Saavik said. "Do you know when you are?"

Spock's voice cracked like an adolescent's as he answered. "My first *Plak-tow.*" It was the only explanation for the unsettling effect her presence was having on him.

Saavik held out her hand to him, smiling in the private way reserved for Vulcan lovers. "You can experience it again."

Spock fought the fire in his blood without giving visible sign. "I recall it perfectly," he said. "And you were not my partner."

"But later," Saavik whispered, "when we had met, when we were free, did you not wish she had been me?"

"You are an illusion," Spock stated. "I am on a holodeck."

"How little you know," Saavik replied as she began to spin on the ledge and her shawl dissolved and—

—as if he had been slapped again, Spock felt the startling onset of free fall, and once again floated. But this time, he was surrounded by stars in all directions.

He looked around, quickly identifying the constellations as they appeared from Vulcan: *A'T'Pel*, the sword; *Stol*, the chalice; *Sarakin*, the crossed daggers dripping with the glowing green nebulae of *Plak Marn*. All names from deep in Vulcan's bloodstained history.

But he found no sign of Vulcan's primary, no brilliant points of light to indicate Vulcan or her system's planets.

And still he felt the breeze of his hands as he moved them before his eyes.

The holodeck had been transformed from a Vulcan mountainside to a planetarium.

"It is not a holodeck," another voice said. Not Saavik's, but the voice that had spoken earlier, from the all-enveloping darkness.

"If there is a point to all of this," Spock said aloud, "it escapes me."

He heard chiding laughter in reply.

"A Vulcan admitting defeat?"

"I admit nothing. Merely make an observation."

"But you cannot draw a conclusion?"

"I can draw several."

"Tell me."

Spock was intrigued by the question. "Can't you read my mind?"

"Telepathy is not at work here, Ambassador. Neither is a holodeck."

"Then I am at a loss to understand my position, and your motives."

"Very well, let us try another way."

Spock braced himself for another abrupt transition, but when it came, it was gentle.

First the stars slowly rolled around him as he felt gravity begin to make its influence known, giving him the sensation that he was lying on his back on a soft surface.

Then the stars rippled and smeared as if they were going out of focus. Other shapes and lights overlaid them.

One shape became humanoid in form. The gravity grew stronger.

Harsh light glared down at Spock. He tried to raise his hand to shield his eyes and see the humanoid.

His hand wouldn't move.

He was strapped to a diagnostic bed.

He looked around, moving only his eyes, saw the familiar green luminescence of a Romulan glow, decided he was in a Romulan medical facility.

He shifted against his restraints, felt a sharp pain in his inner thigh, looked down the length of his naked body to see an intravenous tube taped to his thigh. A much more primitive solution to nutrition than the transporter-based technique he had postulated.

"It is how we kept you fed," the voice said.

For the first time, Spock could determine the position of the speaker, just behind him and to the right. The specificity of that knowledge made him accept that after all the illusions he had experienced, this was reality.

He tried to look in the direction of the speaker, but his head was even more firmly held in place than his arms and legs.

"The artificial environments you created for me," Spock said. "Generated by neural pattern induction?"

He sensed movement to the left, shifted his eyes in that direction, and his eyesight had recovered enough to reveal that the humanoid standing over him was a Reman.

The pale, gray-skinned humanoid wore a red technician's smock, and angled his head toward Spock, but where he actually looked was unknowable. His light-sensitive eyes were hidden behind a pair of dark data goggles. Spock could just make out the backscatter glow of the images projected on the circular lenses. He interpreted them as basic medical scans of his body.

"Are you a doctor?" Spock asked.

"There are no Reman doctors," his unseen captor said from behind him. "At best, the Romulan Assessor allows certain trustees to be trained in basic medical procedures related to mining accidents and childbirth."

Spock made the logical assumption. "Then this is a Reman medical facility."

"To be accurate, it is a trauma care center. The only full medical facilities on Remus are for the exclusive use of the Romulan Assessors."

Spock hid his reaction at the logical conclusion that he was now on Remus, and changed the subject. "Will you show yourself to me?"

Light footsteps moved around to his right, and a female Romulan stepped into view, dressed in simple Reman garb.

For a moment, Spock was so certain it was Marinta that he had to consciously fight to keep his expression neutral.

But when the young woman stopped moving, Spock could see that though there was a resemblance, it was only general.

The woman seemed to sense Spock's misidentification. "Do I look familiar to you?" she asked.

Spock knew that whatever was going on, the Romulan was having this conversation only because she needed something from him. He decided to make her work for it.

"Should you look familiar?"

"We *have* met before."

Spock blinked. Aside from the slight resemblance to Marinta, he was certain he had never seen this woman.

"I believe you are mistaken."

"Never."

"Then may I ask where and when we have met?"

The woman shook her head. "Better to concentrate on the present."

Spock took her at her word, certain it would annoy her. "In that case, how is it that you read my thoughts without telepathy?"

His captor patted his hand. "Ambassador, you were never held prisoner in an antigrav chamber. You have been on this treatment bed for—since your capture."

Spock noted that she didn't wish to reveal how long he had been held. He set that question aside. "How is that conducive to reading one's mind?"

"I stimulated the base of your brain, specifically, the pons. You spoke your thoughts aloud. All of them."

Spock betrayed nothing of the outrage he felt. He decided that whatever was holding his head in position must be a type of induction helmet: a device capable of affecting his neural functions by focusing electrical fields at specific neurons. If any sensory input could be routed directly to the brain, then it was no surprise the false environments he had found himself in were so perfect.

"If you know everything I think, then why am I still alive?" Spock asked.

"Is that why you think I've brought you here?"

"It is obvious you require information from me."

The woman nodded. "That is true."

"Then have I not provided it?" Spock knew his thoughts had been far-ranging the past six days of his captivity.

"Not yet," the woman said.

"Have you thought of just asking me what it is you wish to know?"

The Romulan shook her head. "Information flows both ways, Ambassador. Simply by asking my question, I will be providing too much information about myself."

"Madam, I am your captive. What good will information do me?"

The Romulan thought that over.

"May I ask your name?" Spock prompted.

"You will know it when you remember it."

"Fascinating," Spock said.

"You have the same effect on me."

Spock decided he had nothing to lose by forcing the issue. "Ask your question."

The Romulan gave his immobilized hand a squeeze. "Given a choice between love and death, why do you so often choose death?"

Spock stared up at her, convinced that was only the preamble to a more specific inquiry.

But after several moments of silence, he realized that was, indeed, her question.

For the first time, Spock wondered about the mental state of his abductor, so he answered carefully.

"I am not aware of having chosen death over love in the past."

"On the mountainside, you could have chosen Saavik."

Spock narrowed his eyes. Whoever this woman was, he was beginning to suspect she wasn't Romulan after all.

"That was an illusion."

"No," the woman argued. "It was sensory input directly fed to your brain, indistinguishable from those signals processed by your own eyes and ears, pressure receptors, olfactory nerves, pleasure centers."

"Except," Spock pointed out carefully, "the situation itself was not logical, and thus unreal."

The woman shook her head as if confused. "Love *and* logic?"

Spock was utterly baffled by the conversation. "Madam, am I to understand that you have abducted me for philosophical reasons, not political ones?"

"Ambassador, I have abducted you to save you. To save Romulus and Remus. To save Vulcan. The Federation. The Klingon Empire. The four galactic quadrants, all worlds known and unknown. Life itself."

Spock's logical decision tree underwent a sudden pruning as he realized the woman was insane.

"Save us from what?" he asked politely.

She smiled sadly at him, as if she saw through his attempt to humor her. "From your loneliness. From your despair. From your . . . ignorance of the true reality of existence."

Spock had dealt with fanatics before. Indeed, it was remarkable that the unsettled conditions on Romulus had not resulted in many more irrational movements achieving prominence.

The secret, he knew, was not to challenge a fanatic's beliefs, but to gently inquire about them, showing one to be open to enlightenment, encouraging the fanatic to see a chance to bring another into the fold.

"You speak of things I do not understand," Spock said, "and it is not my intent to cause offense. But may I ask, with respect, what the true reality of existence is?"

For a moment, Spock could see that his tactic worked exactly as he had planned. The woman's smile transformed, going from a pained and solemn expression to beatific transcendence.

She reached out to stroke his cheek, as if blessing him.

Spock waited for her to define the nature of her insanity, confident he could then work within her belief system to achieve his freedom.

"Ambassador," she said softly, "the true reality of existence is everything that is around you, that you do not see."

Spock blinked as it seemed her hand, so close to his face, had gone out of focus. He concluded his eyes were dry. He made his inner eyelids slide out to better lubricate his corneas, but when his vision cleared, her hand was even less distinct, as if it were dissolving into something black and formless.

"The true reality of existence," she said, "is the *Totality*."

And with that single word, Spock *knew*.

"Norinda . . ." he said in a strangled gasp as the breakdown of the woman's hand continued, dissolving into small black cubes that dissolved again into smaller cubes, and smaller, until what had once been her flesh roiled like a cloud of dust.

"Good," Norinda whispered seductively. "You remember."

Then the living dust swept into Spock's nostrils and past his lips to suffocate him far more efficiently than any Reman soldier could, and he faced death once more at the hands of a woman he had met more than a century ago, and whatever she was, she was anything but insane.

8

S.S. CALYPSO, STARDATE 57483.3

On the cramped passenger deck of the *Calypso*, Picard
paused at the small metal door of his cabin, quickly
looked up and down the narrow, conduit-lined corridor to check for any unwanted observers, then carefully ran his finger along the edge of the door's upper
surface.

He felt the delicate ridge of the tiny thread he had
left there ten minutes earlier, when he had left to use
the shared sonic shower and head. That meant his
cabin had not been entered. He was safe from Joseph
for another day. Or, at least, another few hours.

Picard placed his palm against the security lock and
the cabin door clicked open. He stepped inside, remembering to duck his head. A week ago, on the first day of
this voyage, the first two times he had stepped inside
his cabin he had banged his head, the second time hard
enough to require Beverly to use a plaser to reduce the
swelling. But after that jarring reminder, he had finally
learned his lesson.

And the truth was, he enjoyed it.

The cabin, one of the ship's two VIP suites according

to Admiral Janeway, was barely four meters long and three meters across, and had been intended for two passengers, with fold-down bunks, a small desk and smaller wall cabinet, most of its storage space already filled with two emergency vacuum suits. And the whole cabin fairly resonated with the constant drone of the Cochrane generators only four decks below.

Even as a cadet on survival training missions to Charon, Picard had not had quarters as minuscule and as austere as this. But after decades on starships with broad, well-lit corridors, plush carpet, anti-noise technology, gymnasiums, theaters, concert halls, even social lounges, the conditions on this small ship brought back something Picard suddenly realized had been missing from his life and his career—the *romance* of space travel.

Over the years, he had undertaken the obligatory holorecreations of the early days of exploration beyond the Earth. He had spent three days in an Apollo command module and landed at Tranquility Base with Neil Armstrong. He'd spent a week—all the time he could spare one vacation—on the *Ares*, living and working with its crew on their five-month voyage to Mars. And he had hot-bunked with the crew of Jonathan Archer's *Enterprise* as that fabled ship had made humanity's first harrowing foray into the Delphic Expanse.

And each time he had emerged from those pioneering adventures, he had felt an indefinable sense of loss.

But not on this ship.

He only wished his reasons for being here were more positive. If not for young Joseph Kirk keeping all the adults on their toes, the entire voyage thus far would have been little more than a somber, weeklong funeral service.

Picard pulled his oversized civilian communicator from the pocket of his terry robe, then switched off the robe's current, making its fibers lose their repelling charge and thus collapse in on themselves so that the robe took less storage space. Children, he realized, were the force that kept death at bay. Was it wrong of him to think that this late in his life, they might still be an option for him and—

The annunciator chimed.

Picard smiled, knew who it was. "Yes?" he called out.

But instead of Joseph's voice, he heard another.

"Jean-Luc—it's Jim."

Picard tugged on his trousers and a large, burgundy sweater. "Just a moment," he said. Then he slipped his communicator under the pillow of the undisturbed top bunk, and straightened the thin blanket and sheets of his lower bunk.

The door wasn't automatic and required him to physically release its latch from the inside.

Kirk was waiting for him, one arm braced against the bulkhead. The engine noise was louder in the corridor. "Is this a good time?" Kirk asked.

"Certainly," Picard said, and stood to the side so Kirk could duck down and step in. He pointed to the small stool wedged under the desk. "Pull up a chair."

Kirk tugged the three-legged stool with its triangular seat from under the desk, was just about to sit down when Picard suddenly stopped him.

"On second thought, let me check it." Picard ran his hand over the seat, felt around the edges.

Kirk watched in amusement. "Let me guess, your enemies are everywhere."

Picard slid the stool back to Kirk, pronouncing it

safe. "Not enemies. Your son. Pressure sensors that emit certain embarrassing sounds have been known to spontaneously appear on seating surfaces."

Kirk laughed as he sat down. "What's the latest?"

"Short-sheeting is still his favorite," Picard said as he sat on the edge of the bunk. "If it's funny once, it's twice as funny the second time."

"I heard about the antigrav in the cupboard."

Picard couldn't help smiling at that one. "Very inventive." He had opened his cupboard only to have everything inside suddenly leap out at him as if mounted on springs, because Joseph had set an antigrav unit on the cupboard floor with a delay timer on the switch. "The clothes I could take. But the evac suits unfolded and came at me like very skinny alien attackers."

"I think he had help with that one."

"I think he's had help with all his pranks. Geordi and Scotty his chief co-conspirators, I would say."

"I could tell him to stop," Kirk offered.

But Picard shook his head. "And spoil my plans for revenge?"

"You're enjoying this, aren't you?"

Picard leaned back, nodded. "It's making me nostalgic for my Academy days. If I had expended half the creative thought I applied to practical jokes toward my studies, I'd probably have been Fleet Admiral by thirty-five. How about you?"

Kirk shrugged. "Actually . . . I was never really involved in, uh, extracurricular activities." He smiled sheepishly. "At least, not that kind."

"Well, your son is as delightful as he is a nuisance. You should be proud of him."

Kirk nodded. "Immensely."

The two old friends looked down at the thin beige

carpeting on the deck as the silence grew awkward between them.

Picard broke first. "I'm going to guess that you didn't come here to check on how your son was treating me."

"In less than an hour we'll be through the Neutral Zone."

Picard nodded. "And we haven't been challenged once."

Kirk chewed his bottom lip, as if judging how to proceed. "Makes me think that someone knows we're coming."

"That goes without saying. This must be the most public espionage mission Starfleet has ever launched. The Romulan Fleet has been alerted of our arrival by Starfleet Command, by the Federation Diplomatic Mission, by the Vulcan government, and our own navigation beacon." Picard saw the shadow of concern in Kirk's eyes. "What is it, Jim?"

"I came into this knowing there would be two different agendas—mine, and Starfleet's. I have no trouble with that."

"But . . . ?" Picard said.

"Admiral Janeway . . ."

"A very persuasive officer . . ."

"She left me with the strong impression that there was a third agenda. A mission I wasn't to be told about."

Picard reached back into that part of his mind that still retained the influence of Spock's father, Sarek. It helped him keep his expression composed, made it easier to lie to Kirk. "If there is, I'm not aware of it."

Kirk kept his eyes on Picard, long enough for Picard to begin to feel uncomfortable. "We've been through a lot together, Jean-Luc."

"Indeed, we have."

"My son is on this ship."

Picard forced all thought of Joseph from his mind, especially the conversation he had had with Janeway just before boarding the *Calypso*.

"As far as I'm concerned," Picard said, "and as far as Starfleet's concerned, this is a fact-finding mission. Nothing more. None of us are in danger. Otherwise, Starfleet would never have allowed Joseph to be on board."

"Then what else is Janeway up to?"

Picard tried to deflect the question. "You're certain she's up to something?"

"Haven't you ever been lied to by a superior officer?"

Picard knew he had to get Kirk off this topic soon. "Starfleet officers don't lie, Jim. They might not share all that they know, but that's a matter of security protocols and our 'need to know.' "

Kirk gave a tight smile, lightly bounced his fist on the narrow desktop beside him. "Starfleet officers don't lie . . ." He sighed. "Look at this ship we're in, Jean-Luc. On the outside, a sixty-year-old hunk of junk, with mismatched hullplates, three sensor grids down, and an out-of-balance impulse drive. But on the inside, a warp core lifted from a *Defiant*-class vessel, an undetectable, distributed phaser system that could put a dent in your *Enterprise*, and shields that could probably let us punch a hole through a main-sequence star. What is this ship but a Starfleet lie?"

"This ship is different, Jim."

But Kirk shook his head, gave a more forceful punch to the desktop to emphasize his words. "No it's not, and this is why. This ship is designed to fool people *outside* of Starfleet. So even if I accept that Starfleet officers never lie to other Starfleet personnel, can you honestly tell me that for the sake of the mission, a Starfleet officer would never lie to a *civilian?*"

Picard respected Kirk too much to argue the point with him. "Which, of course, you are."

" 'Captain' Kirk," Kirk said dismissively. "My last rank. An honorary title. A show of respect. But I'm still a civilian. And I still think I'm the only one on this ship who doesn't know *all* the reasons why we're going to Romulus."

"Jim, if there is a third mission, you're not the only one who doesn't know about it. I don't, either."

Picard could see that Kirk wasn't convinced. "Which means Starfleet somehow bypassed its greatest starship captain—" Kirk suddenly flashed a smile. "—let's make that, its greatest starship captain still on active duty, and put the responsibility of a critical espionage mission in the hands of . . ." Kirk held out his hands questioningly. ". . . Doctor Crusher? Commander La Forge? Surely not Scotty or McCoy, they're civilians now, fair game for . . . misdirection."

Picard tried another tack. "Though I have no first-hand knowledge of anything you're suggesting, I admit it is possible that Will or Worf might have knowledge of another mission."

But Kirk didn't accept that, either. "Will and Worf are back on the *Titan,* trailing us by ten light-years, with orders to stay well outside the Romulus system."

"But they are accompanying us with a cover story of their own," Picard reminded Kirk. "Since the coup, Will has served as a key negotiator in many of the discussions the Romulans have had with the Federation. The Romulans do prefer soldiers to diplomats."

"Jean-Luc, I'm going to be blunt. Have you lied to me about your mission?"

Picard kept his eyes locked on Kirk's. "No."

"Have you been instructed to lie to me?"

"Janeway would know better than that."

"Have you?"

"No, Jim."

Kirk suddenly went from displaying the demeanor of a stern officer, to that of a nervous parent hiding nothing.

"Because *I* could take it, Jean-Luc. *I* could understand. But when it comes to my child . . . my son . . . if he's put in danger by whatever Janeway alluded to, then . . . friendship aside, you're going to have to watch your back."

Picard wanted to admit everything, bring Kirk into the total mission, but like Kirk, Picard had a clear dividing line between friendship and the one thing that was more important. To Kirk, it was Joseph. To Picard, it was his duty.

"I understand, Jim. And your concerns won't be necessary."

"Okay," Kirk said. "Okay. I said what I needed to say."

"And I accept it."

Kirk stood up, held out his hand. "I liked it better when we were on vacation."

Picard ignored Kirk's hand, pulled his friend close for a hug of support. "I didn't. I still have nightmares."

"About orbital skydiving?"

"About you being eaten by a Bajoran sea monster."

Kirk's expression told Picard he was just filling time, now. He had gotten the information he required, or at least had concluded he had gotten all the information Picard was going to make available right now.

"See you on the bridge in an hour?" Kirk asked. "Should be interesting."

"I'll be there."

Kirk nodded, at once eager to leave, reluctant to go. "Thank you, Jean-Luc."

Picard patted his friend's shoulder as Kirk left. Then he closed the door, latched it, and waited in case Kirk had one last question to ask.

Picard gave him a minute.

Nothing.

He went back to the upper bunk, pulled his civilian communicator out from under the pillow, held his thumb to the battery slot till he heard an inner mechanism click, then twisted the back off the device and pried out the smaller, triangular-shaped object within.

He put the object on the deck, sat back on his bunk.

"He's gone," Picard said.

The small object leapt into the air and then locked into a fixed position, apparently floating unsupported less than two meters off the deck.

A moment later, the air shimmered as the circuitry in the tiny holoemitter came online. A moment after that, the holographic doctor, late of the *Starship Voyager*, took solid form, absolutely indistinguishable from reality.

"You heard what we discussed?" Picard asked.

The Doctor had the surprising decency to look uncomfortable. "Yes."

"I don't like it," Picard said.

The Doctor snorted. "Would you rather spend a week locked up in the back of a communicator?"

"As I understand it, you have the capacity to create

virtual environments at will. You are your own holo-deck."

"It still leaves me talking to myself. Not that I'm not fascinating company."

"What are we going to do?"

"About Kirk?"

"He obviously suspects something."

"Captain Picard, I've read his service record. The man distrusts anything that wears a Starfleet uniform. His best friend is dead. Murdered. He's concerned for his son. I heard nothing he said, detected no untoward tension that is not completely understandable in terms of the stress he's enduring. Don't worry about him. He trusts you."

"And I am betraying that trust."

"No, Captain, you are not. You are showing respect by not troubling him with . . . petty details."

"Interplanetary war is not what I would characterize as a 'petty detail.' "

"It can be," the Doctor said with unexpected compassion. *"If* you've lost your best friend. *If* you're concerned for your child."

"Is there a reason he should be concerned for his child?"

The Doctor's expression became unreadable. "We both know there is no reason at all to be concerned. And we know that Kirk will realize that in . . . I'd say forty-seven minutes. That's when we're scheduled to leave the Neutral Zone."

"And enter a war zone," Picard said bitterly.

"Only if we fail our missions," the Doctor said. "All four of us."

9

S.S. CALYPSO, STARDATE 57483.4

Even on this sorry excuse for a bridge, Kirk could feel the excitement and the challenge of how moments like this once played out on his *Enterprise*.

On one of the three forward screens, the familiar contours of the Neutral Zone glowed, with a small blue dot of color almost touching the once inviolable boundary, indicating the *Calypso*'s current position.

On the far side of the boundary, four green triangles—the best this ship's navigational computers could do in terms of representation—moved toward that same boundary, on what was clearly an intercept course. The triangles represented Romulan vessels. One lone bird-of-prey acting as scout, a few light-hours ahead of three warbirds traveling in attack formation.

Kirk stood on the raised deck at the aft of the bridge, back to the commander's office, feeling the adrenaline rise. Scotty and Bones were with him on the main level of the bridge below, ready to face whatever challenge would unfold in the next few minutes, the next few seconds. If he closed his eyes, he could see them all, miss them all: Chekov and Sulu, Uhura, even Spock watching the main screen with the pale blue glow of his science viewer washing up over him.

Then Kirk opened his eyes, and instead of the past, he was immersed in his new and unexpected present. Geordi La Forge manned the engineering stations with Scotty. Beverly Crusher sat at communications, with McCoy beside her at life-support. Jean-Luc Picard had his hands resting on the navigation console, whose glowing panels and switchplates hid the controls for the *Calypso*'s disguised weaponry. And at Kirk's side, his son, his child, Joseph, watching everything with his own unique combination of wide-eyed wonder and calculation beyond his years.

"And we are through the Zone," Picard announced. "Entering Romulan space."

Kirk became aware of Joseph looking up at him. "Dad, I didn't feel anything." Joseph seemed puzzled, as if he had expected the ship to shudder as it had passed through a physical barrier.

"It's just a line on a map," Kirk said. To himself he added, *One that's cost thousands of lives over the centuries since it was first drawn.*

Then the bridge speakers hissed as the *Calypso*'s communications system prepared to relay a transmission. Kirk had no doubt what the source of that transmission was.

"This is Commander Roil of the Praetor's Vengeance to unknown vessel. You have entered Imperial space. You will drop from warp and prepare for boarding, or you will be destroyed."

Kirk felt Joseph's hand seek his, hold it tight. Kirk smiled at his son. "Nothing to worry about. That's just how they say hello. Remember how we've talked about how the same words have different meanings to different people?"

"Like Klingons being rude?" Joseph said.

Kirk gave his son's hand a squeeze. "The Klingons think we're rude when we don't get to the point as quickly and as bluntly as possible." Then Kirk spoke to his bridge crew. "Jean-Luc, take us out of warp and drop all but navigational shields."

The *Calypso* lurched and the stars on one of the other forward screens slowed, then stopped.

"Do they really not know who we are?" McCoy complained. "Or are they being obnoxious on purpose?"

"Standard Romulan military protocol," Picard explained. "It doesn't matter that they've been told a hundred times who we are and why we're coming. Because we're a civilian ship, until they've officially challenged us and we've acquiesced, we're the enemy, and they maintain the right to blast us out of . . ." Picard abruptly stopped speaking, glanced back over his shoulder at Joseph. "Uh, the right to treat us harshly. Nothing to worry about, though."

Kirk silently thanked Picard for his valiant attempt to avoid talking death and destruction around Joseph, but from the way Joseph gripped his hand, Picard's efforts were too little, too late.

"Everything's going to be fine," Kirk whispered to his son. Then the forward screen with the map of the Neutral Zone flashed once to present a visual image of Commander Roil.

The Romulan was much younger than Kirk would have expected for his rank, likely a sign of the turmoil the Imperial Fleet was experiencing in the aftermath of the coup, so that only inexperienced officers untainted by the politics of a naval career remained eligible—and alive—for promotion. Picard had told Kirk that virtually the entire military diplomatic team Riker had opened talks with six months ago had been replaced. Some officers had apparently "retired" to farms on Romulus. Others, like Commander Donatra, who had helped save Picard's *Enterprise* from Shinzon's last, desperate attack, had simply disappeared from the diplomatic lists and the participants' memories. No news of her whereabouts, or even continued existence, was available. For all the upheaval Romulan society had undergone in the past half-year, Romulan intrigue, it seemed, was alive and well.

"*Identify yourself,*" Roil commanded from the screen.

Kirk's response to the Romulan's threatening manner came from a lifetime of facing down belligerents. There was no fear, no hesitation, no indication that Kirk thought Roil was anything other than a speck of space dust to be pushed out of the way without thought.

"I'm James Kirk. This is my private vessel, the *Calypso*. If you do not already have that information, which has been provided to your Fleet command through several sources, and which is being broadcast by my navigational beacon, then may I assume that your communications systems are in disrepair and you require my assistance?"

Kirk saw the Romulan actually flinch at his insulting reply, a sign of his inexperience. But he quickly recovered, a sign of his expert training.

"*The Imperial Fleet is well aware of the ship and crew the Federation claims is to visit our space. We are also well aware of the spies and enemies who would seek to capitalize on the empire's generous permission for that ship and crew to continue their journey in Romulan space. You will now drop all shields and allow your vessel to be scanned.*"

Everyone on the lower deck of the bridge looked back at Kirk, except for Picard.

"Lower shields," Kirk said.

It was time to find out how well Starfleet had managed to disguise the presence of the *Calypso*'s distributed phaser system, overpowered warp engine, and other hidden armaments.

"We're being scanned," La Forge announced.

"Aye," Scotty confirmed. "Nothin' special. Single sweep . . . och, they're boosting power on the engine room. Comin' back for another scan."

Kirk betrayed nothing, knowing that even though the sound from his bridge was not being transmitted, his image was. A powerful warp engine on a small private ship could be easily explained. The ship's sophisticated weapons could not.

"Sweep is complete," La Forge said.

On a forward screen, Commander Roil looked over to the side, obviously listening to a report from his own bridge crew, whose voices were also blocked from transmission. Then he settled back in his chair, and Kirk could sense that the Romulan was controlling his reaction to what the sensor sweep had discovered as much as Kirk had controlled his own.

"Your warp engine seems outsized for such a small vessel," Roil said.

"Life is short," Kirk replied, making it seem as if he were annoyed by this interruption. "I prefer to spend as little of it as possible traveling between destinations."

Roil considered that statement for several long moments, then seemed to reach a decision. *"Understandable."* Another one of his bridge crew, unseen except for a single arm, handed Roil a small green padd that appeared to be badly scuffed. He read it, then spoke again. *"Mister Kirk, you and your vessel will remain at these coordinates until your escort arrives to take you the rest of the way."*

Kirk didn't have to feign annoyance as he responded. "Our charts are up to date. I don't need an escort to Romulus."

Roil stared across space, from his bridge's visual sensors to Kirk's screen, as if he didn't care what Kirk needed. *"No,"* the Romulan enigmatically agreed. *"You don't need an escort to Romulus. And none will be provided."* He held up a hand, about to give an order. *"Fair warning. If you leave these coordinates, you will be destroyed."* He brought his hand down, and the communication ended, his image instantly replaced by the schematic of the Neutral Zone boundary, showing the *Praetor's Vengeance* withdrawing at warp speed.

"Does anyone know what he was talking about?" McCoy muttered. "We're supposed to wait for an escort they're *not* providing?"

"There are still three more Romulan ships approaching," Picard reminded everyone on the bridge. According to the schematic, the warbirds were only a few minutes away from rendezvous, well within subspace range. "We could be witnessing the results of fractured lines of communication within the Fleet. But I believe it's more likely that we're being subjected to some type of test."

Kirk had been thinking the same, but had one key objection. "Jean-Luc, the way we're being treated doesn't play like typical Romulan tactics. At least, not the kind I'm familiar with. It's almost . . ." Kirk shrugged, tried to think of a species this pattern of delay and obfuscation might fit. "I don't know . . . Tholian?"

"This Commander Roil's attitude is certainly unusual," Picard agreed. "But then, these are unusual times for the empire." He turned in his chair to look back at Kirk. "However, this is your mission, and your call."

Kirk grinned. "I'm supposed to ignore the advice of a captain of the *Enterprise?*"

"I haven't given any advice," Picard said.

"I know how to read between the lines, Jean-Luc. We'll hold this position. But raise navigational shields."

Picard nodded and with a faint hum of circuitry, the navigational forcefields were reestablished, offering the ship protection from random dust and the occasional molecule of interstellar hydrogen, but not from weaponry.

Kirk felt a tug on his shirt, looked down at his son. "Are we in trouble again?" Joseph asked in a quiet voice.

Kirk shook his head, and hoped Joseph could sense his lack of concern over their present situation. "The Romulans have special rules for visiting their space, and we don't know all of them. So we're just going to wait until we find out more about what rules we have to follow."

Joseph accepted that, nodded sagely. "And then you'll figure out how to change them," the youngster said.

Kirk heard the echoes of someone else's words coming through his son, reminding him of the time Joseph had spent several weeks with the learning programs in the holosuites on Deep Space 9. The dabo girls working the bar there had taken Joseph under their wings—and in the case of one female, a Velossian, those wings were literal. After leaving Bajoran space, Kirk and Joseph had had many discussions concerning the appropriateness of certain words and phrases, and under which circumstances, if any, they could be used.

"Who says I change the rules?" Kirk asked.

The child stuck out his lower lip and held up his empty hands as if expecting something to drop into them. "Everybody?"

Kirk could see there was another topic he'd have to craft some careful discussions around. "I don't change rules all the time. Some rules shouldn't be changed at all."

"Uncle Scotty says you keep trying to get him to change the rules of physics."

"That's only because Scotty *can* change the rules of physics . . . *if* you ask him the right way."

Joseph looked down the length of the bridge at Scott, working at his engineering station. "Wow . . ." the child said with respect.

Kirk glanced ahead at Scotty, too, grateful for the kindness and forbearance the engineer showed his son, happy that he was shaping up to be a considerable influence on the child. And then he noticed the middle screen on the forward bulkhead flash from its display of the boundary schematic to an extremely dark visual image, again from what appeared to be the bridge of a Romulan ship. The warbirds had arrived.

"The demand is made: Where is Kirk?" a rough voice growled over the bridge speakers. It apparently belonged to the figure who was little more than a dark silhouette on the screen, backlit by a dim cluster of ready lights.

"Which ship is that coming from?" Kirk asked. He needed to know if he was speaking to the commander of all three Romulan vessels, or to another intermediary.

"And can we do anything about the image quality?"

"No hailing frequencies," Beverly Crusher said from her communications console. "They just started transmitting."

"Tholian courtesy and Klingon manners," McCoy said. "Reminds me of a Vulcan I know."

Kirk refused to think Spock, reminded himself he was on, essentially, a diplomatic mission, and replied appropriately. "I'm James Kirk of the private vessel, *Calypso*. Whom do I have the honor of—"

The commander on-screen didn't bother to wait for Kirk to finish. *"The demand is repeated. Where is Kirk?"*

Kirk looked ahead to communications. "Doctor Crusher, are our transmissions getting through?"

"You have ten seconds to comply," the commander snarled.

"Wonderful," McCoy said. "On top of everything else, they took diplomacy lessons from the Borg."

"Put this on all channels, Doctor Crusher," Kirk said, trying to keep the urgency from his voice. "The demand is met. I am Kirk." And then, in what he hoped was an appropriate tone, he added, "Who are you?"

"No indication that weapons are powering up," La Forge said.

"But th' three of them are still in attack formation," Scott added.

"Adjust that image, please," Kirk said. "I'd like to see who's threatening us." Then he felt Joseph's hand tugging his shirt again, and he regretted his word choice. He looked down at his son, mouthed the words *It's okay,* then held his finger to his lips to signal silence. Joseph was well trained and immediately pressed his lips together.

Static lines flickered across the small forward screen, and for a moment the background of ready lights seemed to flare up as if they had exploded. But the speaker, if indeed he was the speaker, remained a silhouette.

"That's the best I can do," Crusher said. "They've stripped the visual information out of their signal. There's nothing there to enhance."

"Jean-Luc?" Kirk asked, trying to decide on his next step. "Could this still be part of a test?"

"Your guess is as good as mine," Picard said. "But in the final analysis, keep in mind that we can always outrun them."

The last thing Kirk wanted to do was to close the door on finding justice for Spock. But he also had a responsibility to the people on this ship, and to his son. He made his decision.

"Jean-Luc, full power to shields. Mister Scott, Mister La Forge, prepare for full warp on my order, on a reverse course back into the Neutral Zone." Then Kirk addressed the screen again. "The demand is repeated. Who are you? *You* have ten seconds to comply."

For eight seconds, the only sounds in the bridge of the *Calypso* were mechanical. Then the speaker answered.

"*Our demand is* not *met. You are not Kirk.*"

Kirk didn't understand, called out to McCoy. "Bones, prepare to transmit my complete medical records, including DNA sequence."

McCoy began working with the medical tricorder on his belt.

Kirk spoke to the screen again. "I am transmitting my full medical and genetic profile, proving that I am—"

"Not you," the speaker interrupted angrily. *"Your blood. T'Kol T'Lan Kirk. The demand is repeated for the third and final time."*

Kirk felt a sudden disconnect with his surroundings, as if a holodeck had suffered a brief programming hesitation in its re-creation of an ancient event. For a moment, he told himself he couldn't possibly have heard what he thought the speaker had said. But then he saw that everyone else on the bridge had turned to look at Joseph.

As carefully as if he were defusing an antimatter bomb, Kirk took control of the situation. "Scotty," he said quietly, "I want those engines ready to go instantly."

The chief engineer nodded once, his expression grim, and turned back to his board.

"Jean-Luc, prepare to coalesce distributed phasers."

Picard didn't object, even though the instant the widely dispersed sections of the *Calypso*'s disguised armaments slipped along the hull rails to assemble themselves into functional phaser cannons, the ship's usefulness and her mission would be at an end. "Standing by," he said.

Kirk prepared himself for the split-second decisions he knew he would have to be ready to make. He didn't risk looking at Joseph beside him. Then as arrogantly as he could, he replied to the speaker.

"By what right do you dare make this demand of my blood?"

There was no delay in the response. *"By the right of all Imperial subjects to reclaim their birthright and their heritage."* There was a slight, though distinct, change in the speaker's inflection, then, as if it had suddenly come to his attention that he was addressing an alien unaware of the topic under discussion. *"Your line is honored, James Kirk. Your blood is welcome. As consort to Teilani of the* Chalchaj 'qmey. *As sire of T'Kol T'Lan . . ."*

And then the speaker on the viewscreen leaned forward, slipping into a pale band of illumination on his bridge, at last revealing his features and the answer to so many questions.

Tholian courtesy. Klingon manners. Borg diplomacy. All in Romulan space.

The commander of the warbird was a Reman.

"James T. Kirk, we welcome your child as our own. . . ."

10

REMUS, STARDATE 57485.7

Watchful, ever watchful. Those were the words the slaves whispered in the mines, down through the generations, from the time of the Clans, from the legends of the Old Ways. Watchful like the stone. Watchful like their world itself, forever keeping one face turned to the sun, the other turned to the night, never blinking, never shirking, waiting for the time when change at last would come, and the slaves would be free, and the free, enslaved.

So Remus orbited its sun. So the *Calypso* orbited Remus.

It was one small ship, alien and alone, flanked protectively—or threateningly—by massive warbirds painted not with the plumage of Romulan raptors, but with the harsh script of the forbidden language of those who worked the stones.

Vast orbital refineries that would make Terok Nor look like a shuttlecraft wheeled above the *Calypso,* spewing clouds of superheated rock vapor, bringing pollution to the pristine vacuum of space. Ion freighters driven by thrusters venting light-speed streamers of plasma rose past the *Calypso* with holds overfilled with raw dilithium ore. Their blistering exhaust would devastate the surface of any other world. But Remus was beyond devastation.

It was a resource to be exploited, its veins of exotic minerals no different from the individual lives of the Remans who toiled within its caves. A rock crushed. A Reman life expended. Both had equal meaning to those who ruled from the sister planet.

Most Remans never saw that world to which they gave their lives. But for those few thousand trustees picked from among the buried millions, who crewed the freighters and the orbital refineries, who built and maintained the surface domes and structures, who had a chance to see the sky—that sister planet was more often than not a glittering green star, the brightest in the heavens.

But other times, as it was now, when the resonant orbits of the two worlds came into opposition, approaching within a million kilometers of each other in an echo of the single world they once were before they were shattered, Romulus was a disk that grew until its bands of green vegetation and soft white billows of clouds filled the sky like a window into Paradise.

Some Remans held within their hearts the secret wish, the secret dream, that Romulus was where their souls would be reborn after death, their reward for the punishment of their lives in the mines.

But other Remans knew that their only chance for reward was in this life, and that reward would come only when the inhabitants of Paradise—their Romulan brothers—were punished for their transgressions.

Shinzon had not been the first to arise from among the oppressed to fulfill the ancient legends of change and revolt.

But he had been the first to gain the ear of the Romulan Senate.

He had been the first to be given the ship and the soldiers to pursue his dream. And the truth that was known to those who had supported him, guided him, directed him, was that if only Shinzon had kept his word and pursued the one pure goal of Reman freedom, then Shinzon would have succeeded.

But Shinzon did not keep his face turned to the sun. He was not watchful.

As he accumulated power, he forgot the legends of the Old Ways, the lessons of the Clans. He allowed himself to be distracted by petty personal desires, and those distractions brought his downfall.

But those who had supported Shinzon were not defeated by his failure.

They had armed one surrogate to fight their battle, and they could arm another.

As many as it might take to bring the inevitable day of change.

Not the change the Remans dreamed of, but something even more satisfying, more welcome, more peaceful, more in accordance with the true reality of existence.

"I say we tell him everything." Visual sensor implants glistening, Geordi La Forge looked around the narrow galley of the *Calypso*, as if daring anyone present to object to what he had so plainly stated.

But Picard couldn't argue with his engineer. Indeed, he appreciated the irony that the one member of his crew who had been blind since birth was often the one person who saw a problem's solution most clearly.

However, Picard was also very much aware of the

holographic doctor studying him, awaiting his decision. And given current circumstances, there was only one decision Picard's orders allowed him to make.

"That's out of the question," Picard told La Forge. He nodded at the Doctor, who stood at the side of the ship's tiny galley. He was the only one present who wore a Starfleet uniform, and he apparently preferred not to crowd in with the others at the small table. The Doctor gave a tight smile and folded his arms as if acknowledging victory. "At least, at present," Picard added, and enjoyed seeing the Doctor's smile change to a frown.

"Well, I agree with Geordi," Crusher joined in. "The whole point of this mission was to get to Romulus. Being sidetracked to Remus puts everything at risk."

"We are merely delayed," the Doctor said, giving a wonderful holographic impression of being exasperated. "Not derailed."

"But for how long?" La Forge asked. "The longer we're stuck on Remus, the greater opportunity there is for evidence to disappear on Romulus. And if we can't find out who's responsible for Ambassador Spock's murder, then . . ." La Forge frowned in frustration.

Picard turned to the hologram. "Doctor, believe me, I understand what Admiral Janeway's orders require of us."

"That's quite a relief," the Doctor said without waiting for Picard to finish.

"But I also agree with my crew's assessment. Conditions have changed, and I believe we, and the mission, would be better served if we brought Jim, and Doctor McCoy, and Mister Scott into our confidence."

"Absolutely not," the Doctor said flatly. "The

renowned Captain Kirk is a maverick. A lone wolf. He barely functioned within Starfleet's chain of command when he was officially in service, and now, as a civilian, with a child who is the focus of his concern, there is not the slightest chance that we can rely on him to put the needs of the Federation above his own."

Picard tapped his finger on the narrow galley table, which looked like polished wood, but clicked like metal. The small room with its so-called gourmet food replicators was only large enough to hold ten people at a time, and under normal circumstances with a full crew and passenger load, people aboard the *Calypso* would have to eat in shifts. On the first day of this voyage, Picard had explored the ship and quickly decided it would be a safe place for private meetings with his fellow co-conspirators. It was far enough forward and away from the engine room that anyone approaching would be revealed the moment the turbolift doors opened in the quiet corridor outside. "Doctor, it was you who said that Kirk's child would not be in any danger on this mission."

The hologram looked offended. "That was Starfleet's determination and I support it. We're not monsters, Captain. No one at Command would even *consider* placing a child in harm's way. And, in point of fact, it seems young Joseph is to be treated as an honored guest by the Remans."

"Guest?" Crusher repeated in surprise. "I'm at the communications console, remember? From the messages flying back and forth, I'd say Joseph is considered to be a long-lost child at last returned home."

The holographic doctor wasn't convinced. "I fail to see how that translates into the possibility of harm."

"Doctor," Crusher said earnestly, "now that he's

here, I don't think the Remans have any intention of allowing Joseph to leave."

Before the hologram could reply, Picard added, "And if that *is* the case, then what do you think Jim's reaction will be?"

But the Doctor took Picard by surprise, reversed the question. "What do *you* think his reaction will be?"

"The same as any other parent's, with the added complication that Jim has more than enough skill and experience to reclaim his child from any Reman authorities rash enough to keep father from son."

"Exactly," the Doctor said, as if delivering the last unassailable word in the argument.

But Picard didn't understand what point the hologram was making. "You'll have to be clearer than that."

For better or worse, the Doctor never seemed averse to talking in detail. "If you think our mission is in difficulty now, what do you think the repercussions will be for us if Kirk goes on a parental rampage on Joseph's behalf, stirring up a diplomatic incident at the least, or an act of war at worst?"

"Don't you think that it falls to us to prevent that?" Picard asked. "As a group."

The holographic doctor looked up at the low ceiling of the galley, and Picard was struck by how convincing the artificial life-form's emotional subroutines appeared to be. He felt a pang of loss as he thought of Data, and wished that the android and the hologram had had a chance to discuss their similarities and their differences. *There's never enough time*, he thought. *Not for any of us.*

"Captain Picard," the Doctor began sternly, "must I remind you that what passes for the current semblance of order in the Romulan Empire is so precarious, that the slightest provocation from an outside entity, such as the Federation, could ignite the civil war that is already within weeks, if not days of beginning."

La Forge shook his head, his earlier frustration growing. "You really believe that Captain Kirk defending his child is enough to start a war?"

"Commander La Forge," the Doctor argued, "there is no question that the forces of civil war are already in place at the heart of the Romulan Star Empire. If Shinzon hadn't attempted to make his ill-fated attack on Earth, that war would already be upon us."

"It would be upon the Romulans," La Forge insisted.

"No, no, no, no," the Doctor sighed. "These aren't the days of Captain Jonathan Archer blundering through the galaxy from one isolated star system to the next, learning on the job as he goes. It's not even the fragmented mosaic of independent political entities that Kirk and his contemporaries began to knit together. Those early explorers did their job, Commander, and today we truly are an intergalactic community, each system linked to the other through trade and commerce, despite our cultural differences.

"A civil war between Romulus and Remus can not—and will not—be considered a 'local disturbance.' The Romulan Fleet is arguably the third strongest in the Alpha and Beta Quadrants combined, which means they can tip the balance of power by aligning themselves with virtually any other political assemblage."

"Not if they're caught up in an internal war," La Forge said. Picard knew the engineer well enough to see that his anger was rising. Since Data's death, the engineer had seemed to lose his capacity for patience, as if now he must do everything in a hurry, as if untimely death stalked him, as well.

"But how long do you think that conflict would *remain* internal?" the Doctor countered. "How long do you think it would be before the losing side allied itself with the Breen? Or the Tholians? And then the winning side would counter by making overtures to the Klingons. Do you believe the Federation will stand by while the Romulans and Klingons form a new alliance?"

The holographic doctor gestured grandly as he listed his objections.

"We're still rebuilding from the Dominion War. Millions of Federation citizens killed. Thousands of ships lost. It's only now that the first Starfleet Academy class not affected by the war is graduating. And even the four full graduating classes between the end of that war and today did not come close to producing enough officers to replace all the ones lost during the conflict.

"The Federation would *have* to take action to prevent that alliance of two old enemies, and inevitably, the Romulan Civil War would become a galactic one."

Picard could see that the Doctor had succeeded in making his point. There seemed to be little that La Forge, Crusher, or he could say in response.

But once again, Picard realized he should never underestimate his engineer.

"Look, Doctor, if a Romulan civil war is inevitable, then it really doesn't matter what we do, does it?" La Forge spoke quietly, now, hands folded on the table, his impatience in check. "So why don't we at least do the honorable thing?"

"Honor has many definitions, Commander. Klingon. Romulan. Human. Which would you suggest?"

La Forge didn't hesitate. "Human. The fact remains that Starfleet is using Kirk and his son as window dressing for a covert operation. I won't argue about the propriety of that. During a normal tour of duty, we have children on the *Enterprise*. But obviously Starfleet didn't research this specific situation thoroughly enough. No one predicted the Reman response to the presence of Kirk's son."

"Well, how could they?" the Doctor protested. "The mother of the child was Romulan, not Reman."

"Teilani was a Romulan-Klingon hybrid," Crusher clarified.

La Forge wasn't concerned about details. "The fact remains we're in orbit of Remus. Because Starfleet *failed*."

Picard was surprised by the power of those three words as they hung in the awkward silence.

Everyone in the galley had dedicated his or her life to Starfleet and its ideals. There were always opportunities for improving it. Cadets were taught to recognize the wide-ranging conditions under which orders could be questioned and commanders asked for clarification of intent.

But to hear the word "failed," stated so baldly.

No one was comfortable with that.

Except, Picard could see, the holographic doctor.

"As Admiral Janeway's representative on this mission," the hologram said firmly, "it is my directive that we continue as planned, *without* informing the civilian members of the party."

La Forge began to object, but the Doctor wouldn't yield the floor.

"*However*, Commander—and everyone else—we will revisit this decision once we have additional information concerning the Remans' intentions for Captain Kirk's son. I suggest we leave it there."

La Forge and Crusher looked to Picard, and he gave no indication of disagreeing with the Doctor's pronouncement.

The discussion was over. For now.

"Very good," the Doctor said, sounding quite proud of himself. "It is all for the best, you'll see." He stepped beside Beverly Crusher. "Doctor Crusher, if you'll do the honors."

"Of course, Doctor." Crusher held out her hand, palm up. The holographic doctor nodded his head in farewell, and then seemed to melt into thin air. Picard could almost believe the doctor's smile was the last to go, leaving him with the impression that he and his crew had just spent twenty minutes debating Starfleet policy and Romulan politics with the Cheshire cat.

The dull metal badge of the doctor's holoemitter dropped into Crusher's hand, and now there were three people in the galley instead of four.

"Sorry to be so contrary," La Forge said to Picard. "But how can he expect orders written weeks ago on Earth to apply to what we've just encountered out here?"

Picard reached across the table to take the holoemitter from Crusher, held it up for La Forge. "I'm sure the doctor will be more than happy to explain that to you when he reappears."

La Forge narrowed his artificial eyes at Picard. "You mean . . . he can still hear us, even when . . . he's not switched on?"

Picard snapped open his bulky civilian communicator, revealing the hidden compartment inside. "How else could he come to our rescue if things go badly? As he puts it, he keeps an ear open." Picard snapped the communicator closed.

La Forge stood up, stretched his back, went to the replicator. "So what constitutes 'continuing as planned' under current conditions?"

Picard attached the communicator to his belt, stood up as well. "Doing what soldiers have always done so well," he said. "Wait."

Crusher rose from the table, and Picard could tell from her sly smile she had something to say that would probably annoy the holographic doctor and amuse everyone else. But before she could speak, someone else did.

"Wait for what?"

Joseph stood in the doorway, a small figure with dark eyes wide and innocent beneath his Klingon brow. He had obviously arrived on this deck through the engineering ladders and not by turbolift.

Picard had no idea what to say next. He could converse with Joseph if he had time to prepare himself. But unanticipated meetings with any child invariably left him feeling as if he had met an unknown alien after leaving his Universal Translator pinned to his other uniform.

Crusher smoothly took the burden of a reply from Picard. "We're going to wait for dinner, sweetie." Picard imagined that this was how she had once talked to her own son, Wesley, when he had been Joseph's age. "Are you having dinner with us tonight?"

Joseph nodded, and stepped into the galley.

Picard wanted to know how long the child might have been in the corridor, how much he might have heard, how much of that he might have understood. But even to ask the question would be to make the moment too important—something he might describe to his father.

"What would you like now?" Crusher said. She took Joseph's hand and moved along the wall toward the replicators. La Forge was just removing a coffee drink from one of the wall-mounted machines, a sweeping spiral of something white rocking back and forth on the surface of the liquid. "Chocolate milk?"

Joseph shook his head. "*Tranya*," he said.

Crusher peered at the drink replicator, peering at the fine print on its instruction screen. "Let's see if that's programmed. . . ."

As she read, Joseph looked back at Picard, pointed at him with one of his three perfect fingers. "One," he said earnestly. Then he looked at La Forge. "Two," he said. He pointed at Doctor Crusher beside him. "Three."

Picard wasn't sure what a correct response would be, so he covered, "Very good, Joseph," as if counting to three was an arduous task.

And then Joseph innocently added, "But where's number four?"

That's when Picard knew they had a problem.

11

PROCESSING SEGMENT 3, STARDATE 57485.7

As the Reman transporter room resolved around Kirk, his first impression of this new world was a twinge in his lower back—the pull of high gravity.

Then he realized how dark the room was. Of course, he'd just come from the daylight-bright transporter bay of the *Calypso*, and his eyes had not yet adjusted.

He decided it would be wise not to step off the transporter pad until he could see where he was going, and could trust his legs to take him there.

"Welcome, James Tiberius Kirk."

The voice was rough, the words half-whispered, the greeting the kind that children dread in nightmares.

A silhouette moved toward him, its presence defined by the glowing transporter equipment controls it eclipsed.

"Thank you," Kirk said reflexively, feeling, sensing the silhouette halt before him, at the base of the transporter pad platform. Waiting.

Most probably Reman, Kirk reasoned, perhaps two and a half meters tall.

Kirk did not move.

"Are you in need of assistance?" the silhouette asked.

Kirk knew he should mention the dim lights and the heavy gravity to explain his hesitation. But decades of Starfleet training and experience made him give a different answer. There was no need to voluntarily reveal weakness to a potential foe.

"Not at all," he said. He stepped forward, gritting his teeth as his legs almost buckled in their efforts to keep him balanced. Only his peripheral vision kept him from pitching off the steps at the edge of the platform. By looking to the side, he could just glimpse them like a low-magnitude star at the limits of perception.

He stood before the silhouette, close enough to make out the upward sweep of batlike ears, the gleam of small, deeply set eyes, even the glint of fangs.

The Reman held a fist to his chest, nodded his head in a graceful movement that was surprisingly deferential—and Romulan, Kirk noted.

"I am Facilitator."

Kirk returned the salute, careful to nod his head to the same angle and for the same duration as his greeter. But he had no knowledge of what he was expected to say in return. The *Calypso* did not have a Starfleet databank filled with details of alien protocol. So he reverted to what would be expected on Earth. "It's a pleasure to meet you."

The Reman stiffened, angled his head as if trying to see Kirk from a new perspective. A moment later, recovering, he pointed to the side. "Please, your hosts await."

Coinciding with the Reman's gesture, a door slid open, and against one dark wall Kirk caught the glow of a corridor. The light was pale green.

Facilitator led the way and Kirk followed. The silence of the place was almost refreshing after the annoyingly loud environment of the *Calypso*. Although after the first few days, as always, even the constant noise of ship's machinery had faded to the background for Kirk. Still, the Reman corridor was remarkably quiet, as hushed as a Bajoran temple.

The corridor curved a few hundred meters from the transporter room to a second door.

Facilitator paused, slipped a small object from the long leather cloak he wore, then placed it over his eyes. A moment later, the Reman gestured again, and the door opened.

Kirk looked into a dark antechamber. Something about its small size made him think of an airlock.

As Kirk and Facilitator left the corridor, the door behind them slid shut and a third door opened on the far side of the antechamber.

The light was blinding. Bright as a summer day in Iowa.

Kirk reflexively held a hand to his eyes, blinked as his challenged vision adjusted yet again. He turned to Facilitator to see how he was handling the onslaught of light, but the Reman was now wearing the object he had taken from his cloak. It was a light shield for his eyes.

Then Kirk was surrounded by a chorus of greetings, each slightly different, but all some variation on, "Welcome, James Kirk," together with the words *"Farr Jolan."*

Without a Starfleet combadge with its Universal Translator, Kirk had no way of comprehending the phrase's meaning. The language the words belonged to, however, was not unfamiliar.

As his eyes grew accustomed to the light, they confirmed that his hosts were all members of the same species: Romulan, not Reman, as Kirk had anticipated.

The first to present himself to Kirk was one of the oldest. He began by placing his fist on his chest, as Facilitator had done. But then the Romulan awkwardly held his hand out to Kirk, as if he'd been told—but never seen—how humans greeted one another.

Kirk shook the proffered hand, and the Romulan identified himself as Virron, Primary Assessor of Processing Segment Three, and fourth cousin to the second removal of Teilani of Chal.

Teilani? Kirk stared at the man, realizing why this preliminary meeting was taking place. This was a *family* reunion. Teilani's family.

Over the next few minutes, Virron made all the introductions while Facilitator remained silent, standing to one side.

Each Romulan present announced his or her name, position, and some variation of the phrase *Farr Jolan.*

The sheer number of new faces and names and complex associations began to bury Kirk. By the tenth introduction, he was struggling to keep up even with the memory tricks that Spock had taught him. By the twentieth introduction, he had resigned himself to the reality that he could not keep up, and so concentrated solely on those who claimed direct family ties to Teilani, and thus to Joseph.

Kirk had no illusions that Teilani's child was the purpose of this meeting, and that he, Joseph's human father, was merely being tolerated. The Romulans were flattering him with what was on the surface a grand reception so he would relax and allow Joseph to accompany him on his next trip here.

The truth of it came after the final introduction had been made. As if some telepathic signal had been given, the assembled Romulans began to leave the room. In less than a minute, Kirk was alone with Virron, two other Romulans, and Facilitator, the Reman.

"Please," Virron said, indicating a cloth-covered chair in the elegantly furnished room, "sit down, Kirk. I know this world's gravity can be tiring to offworlders."

Kirk hoped the sweat on his brow didn't give him away. The brightly lit room with polished wood panels and sparkling-green lightglows was hot enough to make Spock happy. "I hadn't really noticed, but it does feel a little stronger than Earth's." The chair Virron offered was a welcome respite, and as Facilitator helped the other Romulans arrange other chairs around Kirk's, as if creating an alien version of a Starfleet officer's lounge, Kirk tried to keep the look of relief from his face.

The other two Romulans were also part of Teilani's extended family, though after so much time had passed, their connection seemed tenuous at best, at least as far as Kirk's understanding of Romulan methods of calculating relatedness.

Sen was an elderly female, whose short white hair had an odd green highlight from the lightglows. Nran was a young male, with a curious band of gold under his left eye. Kirk couldn't decide if it was some sort of applied decoration, an enhancement implant, or even a metallic tattoo. Whatever it was, he had never seen a Romulan with facial ornamentation, so while noting it, he was not too obvious in his examination.

Sen and Nran both deferred to Virron, and he led the conversation.

"I trust you are not feeling too beleaguered, Kirk, meeting so many of us at one time."

Feeling the weight of another agenda descend on this new, smaller gathering, Kirk reverted to his earlier cautious approach, and so ignored the question that was asked. He asked his own instead.

" 'Of us'? All of those people were related to Teilani?"

Virron regarded Kirk calmly as if he knew exactly the tack Kirk was taking, and subtly acquiesced. "Not formally, as we are." He gestured to include Sen and Nran. "But in spirit, yes."

When in doubt, Kirk thought. "I don't understand," he said bluntly.

"Everyone in this room—" Virron held out his hand to Facilitator, who remained a silent presence at the side. "—*everyone,*" he emphasized, "is part of a larger family." Virron looked at Nran, as if giving him permission to continue.

"The *Jolan* Movement," Nran said. Kirk heard the respect, almost the awe, with which the young Romulan spoke those words. Strictly by instinct, and by nothing rational, that tone of voice put Kirk on alert.

"*Jolan,*" Kirk repeated, and he was even more concerned by the reflexive way in which the three Romulans smiled at the word. "I heard many of the people here say that. *Farr Jolan,* I believe."

"It is our way of greeting," Sen said.

"A blessing, really," Nran added.

"Though we don't emphasize that nature of it," Virron explained.

"Because . . . ?" Kirk asked.

Nran and Sen looked to Virron, and he answered, choosing his words with care. "The *Jolan* Movement is from another age, Kirk. Indeed, it arose on Romulus at the same time Teilani's parents were taken from Remus to become the first generation of the *Chalchaj 'qmey.* A time of impending war and uncertainty, as you know."

Kirk moved directly to what he thought the conclusion would be. "A peace movement?"

"There is no need for war," Nran said. The young male's voice was fervent.

Kirk read the guarded expressions on each of his hosts. It was painfully obvious that they were holding back information from him. So he responded to the challenge by deciding to see how much he could draw from them. "A peace movement within a military society at a time of impending war . . . it can't have been easy for the movement."

"Dark times, indeed, Kirk," Virron agreed. "On Romulus, the movement was a failure. Today, only an echo of it remains. *Farr Jolan,* said in greeting. *Jolan True,* said in parting. What once were meaningful blessings are now empty rituals, their true meanings forgotten. Which is the only reason the government tolerates their use."

"What are their true meanings?" Kirk asked.

Virron shrugged, as if the answer were inconsequential—something Kirk did not believe. *"Farr Jolan . . .* 'peace awaits' . . . the truth is near . . . a greeting among those who believe a better time is to come. *Jolan True . . .* 'find peace' . . . may your day be filled with peace. . . . Each follower finds his own meaning, her own meaning. Surely on your world there are similar sentiments expressed, whose meanings have changed over time?"

Kirk was aware his probing was being deflected, but chose not to press the issue with his reticent hosts. Once he returned to the *Calypso,* he could get a coded message back to the *Titan.* That starship's language databanks would shed more light on the *Jolan* Movement and its rituals.

"On every world, I would think," Kirk said. Then he deflected the conversation himself. "So how is it the *Jolan* Movement came to survive on Remus?"

"I think what you mean to ask," Virron said, "is how did the Movement come to survive among *Romulans* on Remus?"

Kirk gave him that one. "Fair enough."

"It must come as no surprise to learn that we Romulans 'assigned' to Remus are outcasts from the homeworld."

"I know very little of Remus," Kirk said truthfully.

"Then you are like most Romulans." Sen spoke without bothering to hide the bitterness she obviously felt.

"The Remans are a slave population," Virron said gravely. "At the time of the Arrival, the First chose their own worlds for their own reasons. Romulus, as a world to build homes, plant crops, live a free life. Remus, as a source of riches. To fuel the creation of a new society.

"Those among the First who chose to come to Remus—the engineers and the miners—they did so believing they would give a portion of their time and their lives to the common dream of freedom, then share in the fruits of their labor on Romulus with the others.

"It was a difficult time—the first years of any colonization project always are. Transport ships between the two worlds were small, limited. Travel time could take weeks and life-support requirements, of course, diminished the amount of ore that could be returned. The First found they could not return to Romulus as frequently as they had hoped. Inevitably, as the years went on, families formed here. And the Divide began."

Virron clasped his hands together, leaned forward in his chair as if imparting a critical secret. He even dropped his voice to a whisper. "On Romulus, Kirk, all the ancient records have long been purged. But in the oral tradition of the Remans, the tale is told that perhaps two or three generations after the Arrival, there was a war between the two worlds. The government on Romulus today would never permit this discussion to take place, but we were Vulcans then. Fierce, proud warriors. And unlike the world of our birth, we did not have the weapons that could eradicate ourselves, and thus there was no brake on the savagery we could unleash on one another.

"But those who would become Romulans controlled the spacelanes, the high ground. Those who would become Remans were starved. The war lasted little more than a year, from one planetary opposition to the next. And in the end, what had begun as a partnership had become, instead, the relationship between the conquerors and the conquered. We were Vulcans no longer. We were master and slave. Romulan and Reman."

For all that Kirk distrusted Virron and his unstated purpose for this meeting, he heard the anguish in the old man's voice as he related the secret, tragic history of his people.

Kirk did not hide his compassion. "Even on my world, this is not a unique story, Virron. I know that can bring no comfort, except, perhaps, the knowledge that other worlds and other species have faced similar horrific situations, and have, in time, risen above them."

"It is rare to have such an honest conversation with an alien," Virron said.

Kirk sought to capitalize on the moment of rapport. "You were telling me you were outcasts on this world."

"The correct term here is 'Assessor.'"

"And that, you said, was your function on Remus. Primary Assessor."

The Romulan's face tightened. "It's a clinical term, Kirk. The one preferred by our masters on the homeworld. In any other language, it would mean what it is—slave driver. Overseer. Monster."

Virron settled back in his chair, as if he had surprised himself with the anger Kirk had teased from him.

"You must forgive him, Kirk," Sen said. "These are not easy times for us. Since Shinzon . . ."

Kirk suddenly saw a connection. "Were you involved in Shinzon's coup?"

Nran's words tumbled from him. "There was not supposed to be a coup! For generations, we have had no voice on the homeworld, and Shinzon was to speak for us."

Kirk had been briefed on Shinzon's rise and his coup—at least, he had been told as much as Starfleet knew, which admittedly was not complete.

"The day Shinzon set foot on Romulus," Nran continued with undisguised pride, "as a guest officially invited to address the Senate . . . it was such a proud day for all Remans."

"Yet, Shinzon was a human," Kirk said.

"No," Virron said. "No matter what their species, those who are consigned to Remus *are* Reman. Whether like Facilitator, their family's roots stretch back to the time of the Arrival. Or, like ours, are only a few generations removed from the homeworld. Or, like Shinzon, an alien brought here as a child. In truth, there are no aliens on Remus. The moment any being is sent here to work the rock, they *are* Reman."

Kirk saw the threads of Virron's story come together then. "Virron, I apologize if I'm straying into a subject you'd prefer not to discuss, but am I right in thinking that your family was exiled to Remus because of its involvement in the *Jolan* Movement?"

Virron squared his shoulders like a soldier. "To not believe in war was considered a crime. One night, they came for us. The Tal Shiar. We were rounded up. Some families simply ceased to exist. Some were torn apart, as was ours. Your wife's parents were sent to Chal to be experimented upon. My side of the family was banished to Remus. And generations later, here we remain."

Kirk saw how closely the three Romulans watched him now, and he knew the final question he must ask. At the same time, he was afraid because he knew what the answer would be.

"Virron, I am learning a great deal from this discussion, but I feel the purpose of your invitation to me has not yet been mentioned. What is your interest in Joseph?"

All three Romulans sighed in relief, as if Kirk had finally opened the door to a subject they had been forbidden to mention first.

"He achieved the dream of our people," Virron said.

"T'Kol T'Lan—your Joseph," Sen added, "is of Remus, yet has a life beyond the rock."

"The legends of the Old Ways speak of him," murmured Nran. "From the time of the Clans, he has been called He Who Returns."

Kirk felt the bristling of hairs on the back of his neck.

Sen's expression was blissful. "The Reman who found freedom, and brings it as a gift to all."

Kirk gripped the arms of his chair to keep his hands from trembling.

"Your son has come to end our suffering and unite the Clans," Virron said with conviction. "He is our liberator, Kirk. Our savior.

"Your son is our new Shinzon."

12

S.S. CALYPSO, STARDATE 57485.9

Had he been younger, Picard knew he would like nothing more than to put his fist through a bulkhead of his cramped cabin.

All of Starfleet's careful plans, all of Admiral Janeway's precise implementation . . . none of it meant anything now.

Kirk wanted out of the mission.

And the hell of it was that Picard couldn't fault the man.

"They think Joseph is their *savior*," Kirk raged. He was the sole person standing in Picard's cabin. Doctor Crusher sat on the desk stool. Picard and La Forge sat on the bunk. "The Remans have legends about one of their own kind, born free, away from Remus, someday returning to end their suffering and unite their clans."

Picard saw that Crusher and La Forge had nothing to say. They clearly understood Kirk's dilemma and decision, and Picard suspected they felt they could no more offer a valid counterargument than he could.

But still, he was their captain, the ostensible leader of this mission, despite the invisible presence of Janeway's personal representative, the Emergency Medical Hologram.

So Picard tried to defuse Kirk and bring him back onside. "Jim, surely they understand that Joseph's not Reman, so how can they—"

"The Remans have a very inclusive outlook on those who share their suffering. Shinzon—" Kirk looked briefly apologetic for raising the name of Picard's clone. "—the first Shinzon, was human. But the moment he was condemned to Remus, even he became Reman in their eyes. Virron told me there are political prisoners on Remus from dozens of species. But they are all considered Remans, just as the Romulan outcasts are."

For the moment, Picard put aside any discussion of Reman identity, and focused instead on the chilling statement Kirk had just made. "What do you mean by 'the *first* Shinzon'?"

Kirk appeared to realize his mistake at once. "Shinzon is a name title. 'Liberator.' He was served by 'Viceroy,' another name title. Just as I was escorted by 'Facilitator.' It seems the public names Remans go by are all related to their function. They have personal names, but those are only shared among equals. At least, I think that's how it works."

Kirk looked in appeal to Picard. "Sorry, Jean-Luc, I didn't mean to suggest there's another clone of you on Remus."

Picard allowed himself a moment of relief, then tried once more to save the mission. "Jim, is there anything—*anything*—that you can imagine doing that would enable you to continue our primary mission to Romulus, without endangering Joseph?"

Kirk held his arms open in helplessness. "Don't you think I've tried to think of a way? Spock is dead,

Jean-Luc. Murdered. Maybe I *do* have a chance here to discover who's responsible, and why. But now . . . I have to balance justice for Spock against the safety of my child. How can I do that?"

La Forge leaned forward so Picard sat back, fervently hoping his engineer had seen some opening that had escaped the rest of them. "Captain Kirk," La Forge asked, "what do you think the Remans' next move will be?"

"What they've proposed is that I return to Virron's segment headquarters tomorrow, with Joseph. There's a ceremony they'd like to perform."

"What kind of ceremony?" Crusher asked.

"A . . . christening, I suppose. They want to give him his formal, family names. And his function name, as a Reman."

Picard frowned because he knew what that name would be. Shinzon.

"Jean-Luc," Kirk said earnestly, "I know the moment Joseph sets foot on Remus, I've lost him. They will not let me take him back."

There was only one thing Picard could say to that, and he said it. "Then we will not let Joseph set foot on Remus."

Kirk took a deep breath, as if he had been expecting more of a confrontation. "Thank you. Then the sooner we break orbit, the—"

"We're not leaving," Picard said. "We *have* to get to Romulus. We *have* to investigate Spock's assassination."

Kirk regarded him in astonishment. "Jean-Luc . . . you've heard the stories, about the kind of fighters Remans are, the savagery. If we stay in this system, this ship can't outfight them. Our only chance is to outrun them."

"Exactly," Picard said. He knew as well as Kirk did

that the Remans had warbirds to guard their orbital processing platforms, and those ships were staffed by Reman soldiers who served in the Dominion War. "We can outrun them to Romulus."

Kirk's shoulders squared for battle and Picard's instincts told him why. For too long, Kirk had been a starship captain, a man whose every word was respected, whose every order was immediately carried out. He was unused to taking part in arguments he could not win simply by claiming command authority.

"We don't have clearance for Romulus," Kirk said angrily. "And given the relationship between these two worlds, how do you think the Romulan government is going to respond when they find out we're carrying the Shinzon who's someday supposed to free the Reman slaves?"

Picard nodded, no argument possible. "You're right. We're a civilian ship. They'd blow us out of space. Worry about the diplomatic repercussions later." He glanced at La Forge beside him, Crusher at the other end of the small cabin, could see that both of them were silently urging him to break Janeway's orders and bring Kirk into the full mission.

Picard hesitated, weighing his options.

That hesitation did not go unnoticed.

"What's going on, Jean-Luc?"

Picard stood to face his friend. "Jim, I respect you too much to say 'Nothing.' Or 'I don't know what you mean.' Obviously, there are other considerations at work here."

The cold fury that leapt into Kirk's eyes surprised Picard.

"When you asked for my help, did any of you know what the Remans wanted with my son?"

The awful betrayal that drove that question made Picard's heart ache for Kirk. And made him eternally grateful that this was at least one question he could answer with absolute honesty.

"No, Jim. On that you have my word. We all expected to be on Romulus now, investigating Spock's murder. No one—me, my crew, the planners at Starfleet—none of us had the slightest thread of information to suggest the Remans would become involved."

Picard could see that Kirk was replaying each word he had spoken, as if searching for the smallest indication of falsehood.

" 'Other considerations,' " Kirk said in an ominous, quiet way. "Starfleet desk jockeys, you mean. Putting me in this position. Putting my *son* in this position."

Picard hadn't thought it would be possible to feel any worse about having lied to Kirk. Now he regretted ever agreeing to Janeway's plan.

"Jim . . ." Picard began, trying to find a way to bridge the divide between them.

But Kirk shook his head with an angry snap. "Just don't. Don't say a thing. I *asked* Janeway point-blank, and she denied to my face that there was a third mission. I asked *you*, and you lied to me, too."

"Need to know, Jim. Operational security." Picard hated each word as he spoke it, but there was nothing else his orders permitted him to say. Wisely, La Forge and Crusher remained silent, adding no more fuel to the incendiary standoff.

Kirk made fists of his hands, tried to pace but there was just no room. "Even now . . ." Whatever else he was going to say was swallowed by a harsh laugh of disbelief. "All right . . . you needed me on this trip. You thought maybe Joseph would be protective coloration.

After all, what sane father would risk his own son in a covert Starfleet operation?"

Picard remained silent, let Kirk say whatever he needed to make sense of the terrible decision he was facing.

"And now you're asking," Kirk continued, seething, "if there's anything I can imagine doing that will let you continue your primary mission to Romulus." Kirk pointed his finger at Picard. "Getting my son the hell out of Romulan space. *Now.*"

Picard straightened his jacket, mentally seeking as he did so some way to keep the dialogue going, even though he knew he could not accept Kirk's terms. "The *Calypso* can probably outrun the ships in this system. But we'd be at risk of interception before we reached the Neutral Zone. And our primary mission to Romulus would be lost."

But Kirk shook his head. "No. You keep the *Calypso.* You keep your mission. But the other thing you do is get the *Titan* in here to take Joseph out."

La Forge whistled, which was as an effective way of commenting on the impossibility of Kirk's request as anything Picard thought he could say.

"Problem?" Kirk asked sharply.

"Several," Picard reluctantly said. "And they're significant."

"That's not the right answer, Jean-Luc."

Picard prepared to make one last attempt to follow Janeway's orders, before taking the initiative himself.

"Jim, the *Titan* is on a diplomatic mission to Latium Four."

Latium was one of the first Romulan colonies to be established by the fledgling empire. To limit the number of potentially hostile ships traveling to their home system, the Romulans had established Latium IV as a centralized location for alien trade and diplomatic missions. It was far easier to obtain clearance to travel to Latium than to Romulus. So Starfleet had created a minor diplomatic inquiry to justify Will Riker's presence only ten light-years from Romulus.

"That's less than ten hours away for the *Titan*," Kirk said. "And that's why she's there, isn't it? To come to our rescue?"

Picard knew this was as far as he could go. One more chance. "To come to *our* rescue, Jim. To save the *mission*."

Picard waited, in hopes that Kirk would seize on what had not been said.

"You mean, to save the mission, but not my son." Kirk's voice flattened, as if the anger and betrayal roiling within him had suddenly given way, too great to exist. "Damn you."

With that, Picard knew he had gone far enough. Janeway had given her orders under one set of circumstances, but those circumstances had changed. So the orders must change, too.

It was time to tell Kirk everything.

Picard reached up to the upper bunk, pulled his civilian communicator free of the folded blanket there just as the annunciator chimed, followed by a familiar knock.

"That's my son," Kirk said.

He opened the door and Joseph barreled in, hugging him wildly, excitedly saying, "Daddy, Daddy!"

McCoy remained out in the corridor, giving Picard a shrug as his comment on Joseph's inexhaustible supply of energy.

"Slow down, son," Kirk said quietly.

Joseph broke away from his hug, looked around at

the others crowded into Picard's cabin. "Is the ghost here?" he asked, wide-eyed.

"The ghost?" Kirk repeated.

"Seems the ship is haunted," McCoy volunteered. "We've been looking for 'the ghost' on every deck."

Kirk tapped Joseph on the nose. "What did I tell you about ghosts?"

"There's no such thing," Joseph said. "Except on this ship."

"We take the blame for that," Crusher said before Kirk could ask his son to explain. She got up, went to Kirk and Joseph. "He heard us talking in the galley, thought he heard another person."

"I did," Joseph insisted.

Kirk glanced at Picard, and there was no question that the gentle acceptance he showed his son did not extend to Picard and the others. "Did he?" Kirk asked.

Picard snapped the battery cover from his communicator. "Not exactly," he said.

The *Calypso* shuddered.

Everyone in the cabin braced themselves. Kirk pulled Joseph close. Instinctively, they waited for some indication that the problem was due to the artificial gravity, which would be an inconvenience, or due to collision, which would be a disaster.

Scott's voice came over the PA system, shouting over bridge alarms. "All personnel t' the bridge! A cloaked ship has just grappled onto our hull!"

"Bones!" Kirk was closest to the door, pushing Joseph toward McCoy in the corridor. "Get to an escape module!"

McCoy reached in to take Joseph's arm, when suddenly a flash of disruptor fire threw the frail doctor to the side.

Instantly, Kirk pulled Joseph back from the door, looked around. "Who has a weapon?"

But an intruder was already in the doorway, hand disruptor held out to fire.

In the instant it took for Picard to charge forward to drive Kirk out of harm's way, Kirk had wheeled and kicked the intruder, forcing him back.

Who or what the intruder was, Picard did not know. The figure was in full combat helmet with mask, and the sealed uniform concealing the rest of him was all black, devoid of markings. Picard had just enough time to register it as a special operations pressure suit—one that allowed its wearer to survive explosive decompression—before he collided with Kirk.

By then two other intruders had appeared in the doorway, pushing forward, shouting in static-filled voices from exterior speakers on their helmets, warning everyone to step back.

As Picard and Kirk leapt to their feet, La Forge fired a palm-sized phaser, but the energy blast ineffectually shimmered over the first intruder's suit, dissipated by the attenuation armor.

A heartbeat later, La Forge crumpled as the intruder returned fire.

Kirk slammed the disruptor from the first intruder's hand as the second intruder jumped through the door. Picard slowed him down with a solid punch to his midsection.

The ship shook again, gravity shifted, and now the deck angled down, throwing everyone off balance.

But that didn't stop Crusher from swinging the desk stool at the first intruder as he tried to reach for his fallen disruptor.

He fell back into the second intruder, and both slipped to the deck.

The victory was short-lived, though. A third intruder was in the doorway, disruptor rifle leveled, well out of reach of a punch or kick.

"Send out the child." The harsh, mechanical voice was frightening in tone, and in intent.

Eyes wide, Kirk glanced back as did Picard, to see Joseph cowering against the far bulkhead, beside the wall cabinet.

At once, Picard pulled himself forward against the growing slant of the deck to stand at Kirk's side, ready for Kirk's forward move to block the third intruder's line of fire. He had no doubt Joseph's father would sacrifice his life for his child. But, together, perhaps one of them could draw fire while the other continued the fight.

Instead, Crusher started swinging the cabin door closed and Kirk grabbed the edge of it, pulling it faster as he kicked at the tangled bodies of the first two intruders that blocked it.

The disruptor rifle fired and the door blew back against Crusher, sending her to the deck beside La Forge. Kirk pulled his hand to his chest, clearly in pain.

"The child! Now!" the intruder demanded.

"Never!" Kirk answered.

The intruder lunged forward, expertly flipping his rifle to strike at Kirk with its stock.

Kirk slammed back into Picard, who staggered with the impact. The angle of the deck was too steep now for either of them to stay upright.

As he crashed to the deck, Picard heard Joseph begin to cry with fear.

Kirk swore and scrambled to regain his footing.

The third intruder pulled himself through the door, braced himself against the metal frame, and held out his hand to Joseph. "Come here or I'll kill your father!"

Joseph wailed with terror now as more of the enemy appeared in the doorway. The ship was overrun.

"Come here or I'll kill them all!"

Kirk leapt at the intruder.

The intruder leapt at him.

And then, as if the *Calypso* had fallen into a wormhole, all action in the cabin ceased as the golden light of a transporter beam flickered over everyone, accompanied by a soft musical tone.

Kirk and the intruder turned in mid-fight as both looked for the source of the beam.

Picard found it, as well.

A shimmering curtain of light enveloped Joseph, his tearstained face fading, even as his last cry for his father did the same.

"Joseph!" Kirk's disbelief tore at Picard. But the child was gone.

An instant later, the intruders leveled their disruptors. Picard saw the flash of their emitters and then . . .

Nothing.

13

Consciousness returned to Kirk in a series of memories, melting one into the other, each of them different, each of them the same.

They were memories of pain, stiffness, the burning of a sudden reflexive breath. The symptoms came from different causes: a Klingon fist, an Andorian knife, an alien kiss. But as it had so many times before, the return of consciousness was accompanied by one all-too-familiar sensation: the hum and sparkle of medical equipment, and by McCoy's stern scowl above him, as the ship's doctor worked his miracles on him as surely as Scott worked his miracles on the *Enterprise*.

"Bones . . ." That single word came out as a bark. Kirk coughed, cleared the postdisruption congestion in his chest. "You're all right."

"My few remaining original parts are just fine." McCoy moved away from Kirk, and as Kirk struggled to raise his head and squint through the dim lighting, he saw his friend hobbling away, leaning heavily on a cane of pale green metal, like weathered copper. "Unfortunately, they're not the important ones these days," McCoy groused to himself.

The doctor came back to Kirk's medical bed with a strange instrument—what appeared to be an uncut ruby the size of a lemon with something silver and gleaming embedded within it.

But medical instruments weren't Kirk's concern. "Joseph?" he asked.

McCoy's expression was unreadable. "What do you remember?"

Had any other person in the galaxy dared refuse his question by asking another, Kirk would have grabbed him by the throat and squeezed until he had satisfaction. But McCoy had always had reasons for everything he did. Most of the time, those reasons even made sense.

Kirk sank back on the medical bed, closing his eyes as he rapidly arranged his last memories in coherent order. "Scotty said something over the speakers about a cloaked ship grappling the hull. Gravity went out of alignment. The *Calypso* was boarded. Humanoids in combat environmental suits. No identifying insignia. But they used disruptors." He opened his eyes, looked at McCoy. "Since you're still with us, they weren't set to kill. But whoever boarded us, they wanted my boy. They threatened to kill all of us if he didn't go with them."

Kirk took a deep breath, and his chest relaxed. Whatever the instrument McCoy was using on his chest, the pain of disruption was lessening. But there was no cessation of the agony of losing his son far too close to the agony of losing Spock.

"And then what?" McCoy asked briskly.

"Joseph was beamed away. Starfleet signature."

That was the only reason Kirk wasn't tearing apart

wherever he was in order to find his son. However improbable, Joseph had been rescued by a Starfleet transporter. "Was it the *Titan?*"

McCoy put the odd medical instrument on a narrow tray. "Here's the thing, Jim. What you remember is what Picard remembers. Both of you say that Joseph was transported by Starfleet technology."

Kirk felt his stomach churn, but forced himself not to interrupt. *McCoy has his reasons,* he told himself. *Don't push him.*

"But the mystery is," the doctor continued, "that there are no Starfleet vessels on orbit of Remus. In fact, we're the only Federation ship within ten light-years of this system."

Kirk had to sit up then. The sudden movement made him dizzy, but it was impossible to remain still in the face of this news. "Then where did he go?"

"I don't know."

"But it *was* a Starfleet transporter," Kirk insisted.

"No argument from Picard."

"Bones, could there be another Starfleet Q-ship near us?"

McCoy leaned against a counter, hooked his green metal cane over the countertop, and stretched his arm. "Well, there's the other mystery. Scotty maintains that when we were attacked, our full navigation shields were up. There's so much junk and mining debris on orbit here, seems that's standard procedure."

Kirk saw the problem at once. "So how could Joseph have been beamed through the shields?" Then he saw the solution. "Intraship beaming! He was beamed from one part of the ship to another, inside the shields."

Kirk's heart beat wildly. Joseph could still be on the ship.

But McCoy dashed that hope quickly. "No such luck. Apparently the *Calypso*'s transporter bay doesn't have that kind of capability. It only has a single transporter array and can't be backfocused. Besides, Scotty was the last one of us shot. He says he would have seen the transporter system come online. And it didn't."

"Then where's my boy?"

Kirk swung his legs off the edge of the medical bed. It was only then he realized how high off the floor he was, and knew he was where he had never wanted to be again—back on Remus. This was a Reman medical facility. He'd hoped this infirmary might have been on a Reman ship or ore-processing platform, still on orbit. But the room was too quiet, just as the corridor leading to Virron's rooms had been.

Kirk had another thought. *The intruders—different size, different height.* Whatever they were, they hadn't been large enough to be Remans.

"Picard did see one positive sign in what happened," McCoy said. "If you think about it, Joseph was *rescued* from a group of people who were determined to kidnap him at gunpoint. Picard says that means whoever has Joseph, he's likely not in danger. And I'd tend to agree with that."

Kirk squeezed at his temples to ease his headache. If Picard was right, then there was one way the situation could make sense.

"The intruders, Bones . . . they were too small to be Reman. So let's say they were Romulans, determined to keep Joseph from becoming the new Shinzon."

McCoy nodded grimly. "Picard told me about that, too."

"Then it's possible Joseph was 'rescued' by the *Remans.*"

"Well, that would cover the motivation." McCoy looked thoughtful, then shook his head. "But not the physics. It still doesn't explain how Joseph was beamed through shields by a Starfleet transporter."

But Kirk had thought of a way to make the puzzle's pieces come together. "Remember, there're dozens of Reman ships orbiting with us. Even three warbirds. Odds are one of them—maybe all of them—are outfitted for covert operations. They could easily have modulators to change the appearance of their transport beams."

"But what about the shields, Jim? How did the beam get through the shields?"

Kirk had spent enough time analyzing what had already occurred. He needed to take action, plan for the future. He jumped down from the table, nearly keeling over in the unexpectedly rapid drop. "I don't care how they did it, Bones. It only matters that somehow, it was done. The *Calypso* isn't a starship. All its systems are simpler. Give Scotty ten minutes to run a diagnostic and he could probably pinpoint exactly how our shields were defeated."

Kirk abruptly realized that he and McCoy were the only two people in the infirmary. "Where *is* everyone else?"

McCoy frowned. "Scattered to the winds for all I know. I woke up in another infirmary." He waved a thin hand toward a closed door. "Somewhere down the corridor out there."

"Woke up?" Kirk asked, wondering why his next question had taken him so long to ask, hoping the delay was not an indication of mental confusion he could not afford. "How *did* we get here?"

"A Reman doctor . . . that is, a Reman whose name,

apparently, *is* 'Doctor,' could only tell me that we also had been 'rescued' from the *Calypso*, which is now adrift without power."

McCoy looked around the dimly lit facility, its only apparent source of illumination the soft glow from the displays and controls of a few banks of unfathomable medical equipment. "So, welcome to Processing Segment Three."

"Do you know how long we were out?" The more time had passed, the farther away Joseph could be.

McCoy shook his head. "No Starfleet communicator, no easy way to compare units of time. And the Remans don't use stardates. I suspect the disruptor victims were out less than an hour or two, but—"

Kirk had to interrupt. *Another delay in my responses,* he thought, troubled. It wasn't like him to forget to inquire about the others who'd been with them. "What are the injuries? Who's affected?"

"La Forge was already conscious when Doctor brought me round. When La Forge pointed me out as another physician, I was next to be revived, to help the Reman. Picard was out, worse than you. He'd been shot at least twice. Scotty got banged up on the bridge. They stunned him but he caught his head on a console on his way down."

McCoy had missed one of their party. "What about Doctor Crusher?"

McCoy replied with a haunted expression. "Not good at all. Jim, do you remember what hit her?"

Kirk replayed the fight on the *Calypso*. "The cabin door. It was blasted straight into—" Kirk looked at his hand—the one burned when the door had been shot. "I could have sworn . . ."

"You did," McCoy said. "Not as bad as the last time,

but you had first- and second-degree burns on your thumb and palm."

Kirk's hand was unblemished. "Good work, Bones."

"Don't thank me. It's good old Reman medical science at work. At least, Reman trauma care. They're extremely sophisticated when it comes to treating industrial accidents. That's why they're treating Crusher and Scott."

"What about Picard and La Forge?"

McCoy waved his thumb at the door. "As far as I know, still back in that first infirmary. They brought you and me to this one for the regeneration equipment to treat your hand."

"So . . . we're here. Jean-Luc and La Forge are someplace else. And Scotty and Crusher are in . . . intensive care?"

"Something like that."

Kirk knew his only hope for getting Joseph back was to have a full team. But the team had been separated. A chance occurrence? Or deliberate manipulation?

He stepped closer to McCoy, leaned back against the counter beside him, carefully checking the infirmary for surreptitious audio and visual pickups. He guessed any infirmary intended to treat Reman slaves would be subject to observation by a Romulan Assessor.

"This doesn't feel right to me," he said in a low voice.

McCoy snorted. "Then I pronounce you fully recovered."

"Seriously, Bones. My son's gone. We don't have a ship. And we've been split up."

McCoy unhooked his cane from the counter, tapped it decisively on the floor. "My first duty was to my patients. I've discharged that. So you tell me: What do we do next?"

There was only one answer to that as far as Kirk was concerned. "Get Picard and La Forge. Strength in numbers."

McCoy gave him a quizzical look.

"What?" Kirk asked.

"Something about the way you said that. You know, when Joseph and I barged in on you in Picard's cabin, I got the sense that . . . things weren't going too smoothly?"

Kirk wasn't about to reveal to an unseen observer what Picard had confirmed about there being a third mission. "Later," he said, looking up at the ceiling. "When we don't have an audience."

"Like that'll ever happen." McCoy pointed to the door with the tip of his cane. "You first, hero. In case there's a sniper."

Despite everything, Kirk smiled. "So comforting to know that someone's looking out for me."

There was silence then, as both of them immediately thought of someone else who should have been there to share this moment of action, and danger, and confronting the unknown.

Kirk's throat tightened.

"Yeah," McCoy said with a shake of his head. "Me, too."

Kirk headed for the door out of the infirmary.

It didn't slide open at his approach.

He pressed the door control, tried several toggles. "Locked," he said.

"Are we surprised?" McCoy asked.

Kirk looked around. "See anything that looks like a communications screen?"

McCoy pointed to a wedge of green metal on a wall beside a medical console. The wedge was about a third of a meter tall, no more than ten centimeters across. There were several controls arranged in a precise grid on one angled face. A blank display screen and speaker grille were on the other.

Kirk went to it, peered closely at the controls. "These controls . . . they're all the same color, none of them marked."

"Tells you what it's like to live on Remus. If you haven't been specifically instructed in how to use something, then you shouldn't be using it. I didn't see any directional signs in the corridor, either."

Kirk took a moment to contemplate the paranoia that must exist on a world with millions of slaves held in thrall by only a few thousand Assessors. "If you don't know where a corridor goes, then you shouldn't be in it." He flexed his fingers. "I don't suppose they wire these to explode." He pressed some controls at random.

Nothing happened.

He touched the screen, spoke into the speaker grille, punched several controls multiple times. But still no response. Kirk turned back to McCoy. "Moving on. Anything in here we can use to get through the door?"

McCoy led Kirk to an equipment stand and selected several ultrasonic scalpels. Like the instrument McCoy had first used on Kirk, each scalpel appeared to have two parts—a gleaming, metallic operational part, sunk deep into an uncut gemstone that made a heavy, though secure handle.

Kirk held up the egg-sized emerald that held the scalpel McCoy had given him. "Is this some kind of power source?"

"I doubt it," McCoy said as they returned to the door. "More of a tradition, I think. Maybe dating back to a time when the Romulans wouldn't provide *any* medical care to the Remans. It's not unusual for primitives to believe the nonsense that raw stones contain some sort of unexplained power."

"Raw stones like . . . uranium and dilithium?" Kirk asked.

"Don't me get started," McCoy grumbled.

They examined the infirmary's door, and even in the shadows of the dark room, the key locking points were simple to locate.

Kirk pointed to the first site. "Doctor . . ."

McCoy expertly switched on his scalpel, and the blade disappeared in a blur of rapid motion.

Kirk was impressed as McCoy smoothly inserted the invisible blade into the narrowest of cracks between the door and its frame. McCoy made a one-finger adjustment to the blade's setting control, lengthening the blade's reach.

After a few seconds, there was a satisfying *pop*, and a wisp of smoke curled out from the door frame. "That's one," McCoy said.

Now that Kirk had seen the technique demonstrated, he used his own scalpel on the other half of the door. The *pops* of severed locks sounded every minute or so, until nine had been defeated. With so many locks, it was clear the door was designed to operate as a pressure seal. That raised the possibility that the corridors beyond could be open to the virtually nonexistent Reman atmosphere. Decompression would be a brutal and effective method for containing any potential revolt.

Kirk braced his hands against the door, then began to force it to the side.

It was like trying to get a recalcitrant horse to budge, but slowly the door began to move.

When it was open enough to enable the two of them to squeeze out, Kirk slowed his effort. He felt no resistance that indicated the door would slide shut again, but he had McCoy ease through first while he braced the door open for him. A second later, Kirk escaped behind McCoy. Together, they slid the door shut again.

"Now which way?" Kirk asked.

McCoy pointed to the right and they started off.

The corridor was almost identical to the one Kirk had walked through on his first visit to Remus. Again he was struck by the fact that there were no other doors or intersections, until they came to what McCoy called the first infirmary.

Kirk tried the door controls. No response.

He withdrew his ultrasonic scalpel and McCoy did the same.

Again, they began to probe for locking points to attack, but then Kirk noticed the door rocked slightly in its frame.

"Bones . . . step back for a second."

McCoy complied and Kirk easily slid open the unlocked door.

The infirmary beyond was dark, lit by controls and displays, but empty.

"Looks like Jean-Luc and La Forge beat us," Kirk said. "I suppose I shouldn't be surprised."

But McCoy didn't share Kirk's assessment of the situation. "Smell that?" he asked.

Kirk sniffed the air. In truth, each world he had visited had its own distinct smell, some more pleasant, some less so. He had judged Remus as having an

industrial bouquet: a unique combination of lu-
brisols, machinery, dry dust. The Romulan Assessors
and Remans had their own particular scents as well.
The Romulans, musty. Remans, sharp. Kirk knew it
was a combination of diet and the differing life-support
systems they lived in. But the odors of each new
world and species were part of the overall experience
of exploration, and Kirk had never been bothered—
or offended—by them.

And then he understood what McCoy wanted him
to notice.

The sharp, ozone scent of ionized air. The underlying trace of heat and smoke.

"Weapons fire," Kirk said. He held the scalpel as if it
were a knife, one finger ready to switch on its blade.
"Stay here," he told McCoy.

"Say that again, I'll hit you with my cane," McCoy
answered. He stayed at Kirk's side as they moved
through the infirmary.

"Over there." Kirk pointed to an overturned equipment tray, its contents spread across the floor.

The smell of burning grew stronger the closer they
approached, and Kirk recognized an odor that, in the
end, was one of the few that was the same on every
world.

Charred flesh.

Kirk rounded an equipment console, nearly gagged
as the stench hit him full force.

The body was on the floor directly in front of him,
chest open and smoking, organs within it still glistening with green blood and gore.

"Doctor," McCoy said in shock. He started forward,
but Kirk held him back. There was no hope for the
dead Reman.

"He was a healer," McCoy said in dismay, "not a guard. This isn't right."

"Jean-Luc didn't do this, Bones. Neither did La Forge."

Kirk crouched by the body, refusing to look into the open, staring eyes of the Reman. Instead, he searched the blood-sodden pockets of his cloak, the pouches on his belt.

"What are you doing?" McCoy hissed.

Kirk's fingers touched rock. He pulled out a metal card punched by a series of square holes and then a small, smoothly polished black stone, no larger than the tip of his thumb. The stone had a small hole drilled through one end, as if at one time it might have been strung on a thin chain or leather strip, to be worn as an amulet.

Kirk examined the metal card more closely in the light from a display screen on a medical monitor. "The Remans authorized to work in this area have to have some way of getting around. This might be a key to access communications and at least some of the doors."

McCoy seemed unable to take his eyes off the Reman's corpse. "But if this poor devil still has his key, then how did Picard and La Forge get out?"

To Kirk, the answer was obvious. "They were taken out, Bones. By whoever killed the doctor."

"Taken prisoner?" McCoy seemed unconvinced. "By who? Who else is there here except Remans?"

"The Romulan Assessors."

"But they're Reman, too, Jim. You said so yourself. Anyone condemned to Remus *is* a Reman." McCoy leaned more heavily against his cane, and Kirk could see that Reman gravity was taking its toll on him. "You know what I think?"

"I know you're going to tell me."

"I think there's a war going on down here. And I think we've landed smack in the middle of it."

"The third mission," Kirk said, deciding to speak freely. It was unlikely this infirmary was under observation. Otherwise, someone would surely have come to deal with the Reman doctor's body and determine what had happened.

"Jean-Luc, La Forge, and Crusher . . ." Kirk said as he saw McCoy's look of incomprehension. "They had another reason for coming on this trip."

McCoy's confusion grew. "What reason?"

"I don't know. It's what we were . . . 'discussing' in the cabin when you and Joseph arrived."

"Before the attack and our 'rescue.' "

"Before all that," Kirk agreed.

"Well, I'm sure it'll be fascinating to learn what everyone's really been up to—later—but for right now, what are you and I supposed to do?" McCoy asked.

Kirk turned the metal card over and over in his hand, thinking through his options. "If there *is* a war under way, you and I are involved. And that means we have to choose a side."

"Whatever happened to neutrality?"

"If there is a war, then one side has my son, and the other side wants him. I *have* to choose a side, Bones. It might be the only chance I have to see Joseph again, to take him home."

Another time, Kirk knew, McCoy might have pointed out that he didn't have a home. But the sentiment was understandable, and McCoy didn't challenge it. He did, though, add an important note of caution, even as he made clear his continued support.

"Let's just hope the side we choose is the same one Picard and La Forge are on."

"Let's just hope," Kirk repeated, as he stared down at the body of the fallen Reman doctor.

Because anyone standing between James T. Kirk and his child would be on the wrong side.

14

"We have to find Jim and McCoy," Picard said.

La Forge nodded his agreement, but like Picard, kept close watch on the Reman doctor on the other side of the darkened infirmary. The two men stood beside an oversized examination table that was fitted with a pallet of autonomous medical devices. "Do you think we're too late?" the engineer asked.

Picard held his hand over his mouth, as if covering a cough. "To stop the civil war?"

"If that's what's really going on," La Forge said. For a moment, his eyes turned to Picard.

Picard returned his gaze without discomfort. The fact that the engineer's eyes were artificial implants no longer registered with him. He had enjoyed friendship with a wholly artificial being in Data. He was presently taking direction, if not orders, from a holographic entity. More than any other person, Picard knew that the shell of an intelligent being had no bearing on what was truly important: the spirit that animated that shell.

"I've been wondering that myself," Picard said,

before he, like La Forge, returned his attention to the Reman.

"The third party," La Forge said, and Picard knew the words La Forge wouldn't say to identify that group. Words too dangerous to speak aloud in this system.

"Deliberately provoking a civil war," Picard added. To him, that was the questionable theory that had driven this mission, but that now fit the facts. If custody of Joseph had truly been the sole reason for the attack on the *Calypso*, then why was the ship's crew allowed to live? The intruders could just as easily have set their disruptors to kill. Surely, if the *Calypso* and all hands aboard had simply disappeared, the resulting situation would have been far more stable. As it was, with survivors to raise the alarm and push for an investigation, and with a father like Jim Kirk who could be counted upon to attempt to rescue his son without regard for consequences, it seemed the people responsible for this outrage could not have done more if they had wished to create further tension.

But with the Romulan Empire already on the path to war, why undertake a side mission to attack the crew of the *Calypso*? Picard still could not fathom the strategy involved, nor the purpose behind it.

"Can you see what he's doing over there?" he asked La Forge.

The engineer blinked.

Picard waited patiently for his response. Blinking meant La Forge was shifting the frequency sensitivity of his implants, perhaps to look into the infrared.

"I'd say he's preparing spray hypos."

"Not an encouraging development, I'd say."

La Forge folded his arms. "We could take him."

"We might have to," Picard agreed. "But what then?

Beverly and Mister Scott are in whatever passes for surgery around here. And Jim and McCoy are in the burn unit."

"Captain, this might not be the most welcome suggestion, but we are outnumbered down here. I think the best course of action might be to get back to the *Calypso* and call for the *Titan*."

Picard was uncomfortable even considering that possibility, but knew he must. "It means leaving our friends behind."

"The way they've been treating us so far, I don't think they'd be in danger."

Picard couldn't argue that point. It was exactly what he had said to McCoy about why they shouldn't fear the worst for Joseph. The boy had been beamed away by people determined to save the child from kidnapping. It did not stand to reason that Joseph's rescuers would then wish to cause him harm.

"And with the *Titan*'s sensors," La Forge went on, "we could find Kirk and McCoy, and Doctor Crusher and Scotty in . . . under a minute. Beam them aboard, and be gone."

"What about Joseph?"

"Do you really think he's still here?"

Picard had gone back and forth on that one, and in the end had decided the most likely outcome was that Kirk's son *was* on Remus. He shared his reasoning now with La Forge.

"Whoever boarded the *Calypso,* they were too small to be Remans. Which means they were likely Romulans. Which makes it almost a certainty that Joseph was beamed out by Remans."

"With a Starfleet transporter," La Forge said skeptically, "through full shields."

"When we resolve this situation and we're safely back home, I look forward to your engineering report," Picard said crisply. And that was all the time he wished to devote to thinking about the physical impossibility of what had happened to the child.

"Here he comes," La Forge warned.

The Reman doctor, whose name was the same as his function, approached with a green metal tray, made of the same oxidized-copper-color substance as the cane he had given to McCoy. Picard could just make out the small cylinders of two spray hypos resting on it.

"I have prepared a medicinal compound for you," Doctor said. His voice was an improbable cross between a Klingon growl and an Andorian hiss. Quite impossible to analyze for signs of threat or lies, or so it seemed to Picard.

"It will help your liver metabolize the waste products created by your bodies' stress response to the disruptor blasts."

"Thank you," Picard said, trusting the nuances of his voice were equally impenetrable to the Reman. "You are showing us a great kindness."

Doctor hesitated, giving Picard a measured look. Picard returned it, wondering if Federation Standard did not easily translate into the Reman language.

La Forge's intervention began as he stepped up to one side of the Reman, who towered over him by a head. "Should I roll up my sleeve?" the engineer asked, even as he began to tug up on the arm of his jacket.

"Here, let me hold that while you give us the shots," Picard said, reaching for the tray as he approached Doctor from the other side.

The Reman was momentarily flustered by their double approach. "No, it is not necessary to remove clothing," he said to La Forge. "Not necessary," he said to Picard, withdrawing the tray, stepping back.

But the Reman's withdrawal came too late. La Forge swung his already raised fist into Doctor's face just as, from the other side, Picard used both his hands to swing the tray up and smash it into Doctor's head.

With a shrill hissing shriek, the Reman stumbled back, and La Forge and Picard pressed their advantage, wrestling him to ground.

If the Reman had been a Klingon, the battle would have been over in seconds.

But the Reman had been born on a high-gravity world. The Reman had been raised tearing ore from rock with no tools but bare hands.

Once the surprise of the attack was over, two puny humans did not present a challenge.

From flat on his back, Doctor threw a single closed-fist punch upward at La Forge, knocking the engineer backward into a medical cart. Then, even as Picard, astride him, tried to close his hands around the Reman's throat, Doctor swung up his knee to strike Picard's back, sending him flying forward.

The Reman was on his feet in a single, fluid movement, growling, spittle dripping from his fangs.

With a console for leverage, Picard struggled against gravity and pulled himself up to see La Forge slowly getting to his feet a few meters behind the Reman.

The two of them moved as if they shared the same idea: Their only hope was to renew the attack, keeping it constant from two sides. This time they would not miscalculate their foe's strength and fighting prowess.

As if reading their minds, the Reman abruptly spun

and darted between two medical beds to the far side of the infirmary, forcing his pursuers to press their attack together.

Picard and La Forge immediately gave chase, but then Picard called out for La Forge to hold back—the Reman was heading for an equipment cabinet. They had no way of knowing what kind of medical instruments might suddenly be turned against them.

La Forge immediately lifted a tray by its wheeled stand, turned the stand sideways for use as a quarterstaff.

The Reman hissed, his large, pointed ears seeming to crinkle closed, as the tray and its contents clattered to the floor. Testing what he took to be a sign of possible Reman weakness, Picard grabbed a narrow cylinder from a workbench. A mouthpiece dangled from it—emergency oxygen, he guessed. The cylinder became his club as he approached the doctor warily, banging his weapon noisily against whatever hard surface was at hand.

But the Reman was not deterred by noise.

He whirled around from the cabinet with a small disruptor in hand.

"Get back!" he snarled.

La Forge and Picard slowed their advance, but neither of them stopped. In Picard's experience, it was one thing for a noncombatant to draw a weapon, quite another to fire it at another living being. All it would take was a moment's hesitation, and together he and La Forge could subdue their adversary.

His warning disregarded, the Reman quickly made an adjustment to his weapon, took aim at a workbench between Picard and La Forge, and fired.

Picard and La Forge ducked for cover as the workbench split in two, lab equipment shattering and flying in shards.

"Consider carefully, humans," the Reman spat at them. "After I destroy you, honor demands I will have to destroy your companions, as well."

After all the opportunities there had been to kill the crew of the *Calypso*, someone was finally making a death threat.

Picard motioned to La Forge not to advance again. Picard knew that neither he nor the engineer was willing to risk the safety of their friends. After the workbench demonstration, the Reman's weapon was clearly set to kill.

Picard took a chance that even an alien doctor would be reluctant to cause harm if it were not absolutely necessary. He dropped the cylinder, held his hands up and open.

"No one needs to get hurt," Picard said.

The doctor swung his disruptor at La Forge.

Picard nodded and La Forge tossed his tray stand away, then also raised his hands.

"But we need to see our companions," Picard said. He wondered if his analysis of their situation was correct. Were they being kept alive to guarantee there would be further complications? Or were Reman motives simply too alien to predict?

"They are being treated."

"We can help."

"You are not medical personnel."

Picard considered his options. If the doctor was not part of whatever conspiracy brought them here, then perhaps he could be an unwitting source of information. *At least we have a dialogue going,* he thought. "We are concerned that we and our companions are being held prisoner," Picard said, hoping that the doctor might confirm or deny that supposition.

Instead, the doctor looked at him with an expression of confusion so strong that it easily crossed the divide between their species. "You are on Remus. *Everyone* is a prisoner here."

"But we're Federation citizens," La Forge said, picking up on what Picard had started. "When we've been treated, won't we be allowed to return to our ship?"

The doctor shook his head, as if he couldn't understand what La Forge had said. "You are on Remus," he repeated.

Picard tried again. "But can we leave?"

"No one leaves."

Picard couldn't decide if the doctor was referring to some decree concerning the kidnapped crew of the *Calypso* or if he were simply incapable of understanding that not everyone on Remus *had* to remain there.

Yet among the Remans, the legend of Shinzon was grounded in the almost religious belief that someday freedom would be obtained for all Reman slaves. Picard essayed a new approach.

"Can we leave once the new Shinzon comes to Remus?"

The doctor's stern expression became beatific, the change accompanied by a slight shift in his body, as it relaxed.

Picard exchanged a glance with La Forge, recalling Kirk's mention of the reverential attitude that had come over the Romulan Assessors as they discussed what seemed to be their religion—the *Jolan* Movement.

"When Shinzon comes," the doctor murmured, "all Remans shall have freedom."

"Doctor," La Forge said suddenly, "what is 'freedom'?"

The engineer had noticed something in the doctor's answer. *Something important. Something I missed,* Picard thought.

The Reman's bliss faded. "It is what we will have when Shinzon comes."

"But what is it?" La Forge pressed him. "What will your life be like when you have freedom?"

The doctor took a long time to answer, and even then all he said was "Better."

Picard was suddenly overcome with sorrow, then anger, because this alien being, so long a slave, so long crushed beneath Romulan oppression, was unable to even grasp the concept of freedom. How could any so-called intelligent species force another into such abject servitude?

For a moment, he wondered if a deliberately manipulated civil war might actually be what the Romulan Star Empire needed, and for just that moment, Picard's thoughts matched his emotions. *If so, let them reap the destruction that they've sown here. Let the Romulans suffer as they have made their Reman brothers suffer.*

But the rational side of Picard knew better.

A Romulan civil war would not remain the problem of the empire alone.

Another way had to be found.

"Doctor," Picard said calmly, remaining absolutely still and nonthreatening. "My companion and I apologize for attacking you. I thought you were trying to hurt us."

The doctor regained his troubled expression. Picard guessed there was no Reman equivalent for the concept of "apology." And on second thought, Picard decided that it *was* likely the doctor had intended to harm them in some way with whatever had been in the spray hypos.

"Will you resist the medication?" the doctor asked.

"Let us see our companions, and then . . . we will accept the medication."

The doctor carefully readjusted his disruptor, taking it down to a lesser setting. "Conditions are resistance."

Picard saw that the doctor was determined to follow his orders. He and La Forge would be stunned, and then the medication would be administered without need of their cooperation.

Faced with an intractable problem, with both tactical alternatives leading to the same unwanted outcome, Picard found himself considering how Kirk would face this dilemma. It was one thing to say, "Change the rules," but there were precious few rules at work. Unless . . .

"Doctor," Picard said quickly, "we do not resist the medication. It is not necessary for you to stun us. But we are concerned that the medication is not suitable for humans. It might render us unable to perform our work here. That would be a waste of resources which the Assessors would notice."

The doctor appeared distressed by such a possibility. He was obviously prepared to take action against the prisoners left in his control, but Picard guessed that the Assessors were equally prepared to take action against any Reman slave who interfered with productivity.

"Has the medication been tested on humans?" Picard asked. He gambled that if it had been tested, the doctor would have dismissed his earlier question.

"I do not know," the doctor admitted.

"Take us to McCoy. He is a doctor."

"I know," the Reman said, distraught.

Picard remained calm, offering his conflicted captor a way out of his predicament. "Tell McCoy about the medication, and he will know whether it will allow us to perform our work, in accordance with the Assessors' orders."

The doctor looked from Picard to La Forge, his eyes hidden in the deep shadows of his prominent brow and the darkness of the room, keeping his thoughts equally unknown.

Then he reached a decision. "As we walk," the Reman said, "you will remain two meters in front of me. If you attempt to escape, I am authorized to kill you."

"So you will take us to McCoy?" Picard asked.

"So you may perform your work for the Assessors."

As the doctor reached behind his back to close the equipment cabinet door, Picard took that moment to look over at La Forge. The engineer gave him a look that said, Good work.

And then the infirmary door shuddered and slid open with a squeal of torn metal. A small dark humanoid silhouette stepped into the doorway, outlined by the green glow of the corridor.

Picard and La Forge moved as one as they dropped to the floor. The silhouette was far too similar to the intruders who had boarded the Calypso.

But the doctor swung his disruptor toward the figure.

"Escape will not be permitted!" he shouted.

In response, the figure raised its weapon, convincing Picard that he and La Forge were right. This was just like the Calypso.

The doctor fired first.

But his disruptor's low-power beam flashed harmlessly over the intruder's armor.

Then the intruder fired and a bolt of lethal energy slammed through the space above the doctor just as he ducked and ran for cover.

Picard and La Forge could only watch as the doctor scurried through the lab and the intruder called out, *"Down! Down! Down!"*

Two more blasts of energy singed the air.

Then Picard saw the doctor jump up from behind an equipment console, taking aim once again.

Too late. The intruder's final shot seared into the doctor's chest and the Reman died at once. The choking smell of disrupted flesh spread through the infirmary.

Picard and La Forge rose shoulder to shoulder to face the doctor's killer.

The intruder was already before them, his weapon held to the side, pointed at the floor. Picard had remembered the other intruders were smaller than Remans. But this one was smaller still. The top of his helmet was barely up to Picard's eye level.

"Follow me," the intruder said, his words still generated by his external helmet speaker. The artificial voice brought back memories of the attack on board *Calypso*.

"What about our friends?" Picard demanded, though he had no means to force a reply.

"If you help us, we can save them all. But we must hurry."

The intruder started to step away, but Picard persisted, grabbing his shoulder, and then was shocked by the speed of the intruder's response—instantaneously wheeling and grabbing and twisting his arm, so that the slightest move on his part would result in a fractured arm at best. At the same time, their captor aimed his disruptor point-blank at La Forge.

Picard's frustration boiled over. Nothing made sense here. People were missing. And people had died. For what? "Why should we believe you? We're here *because* of you!"

"*I did nothing to bring you here, Picard. But there are others who will think nothing of killing you and your friends. And that we must not let happen. Do you agree?*"

Picard could hardly believe an answer was necessary, but the intruder did not lessen his grip or lower his weapon. Waiting.

"I agree!" Picard said.

The intruder let go, turned away from both of them. "*Move quickly, stay close.*" He sprinted toward the open door.

Picard and La Forge exchanged a baffled look before they followed their liberator. *Our own personal Shinzon,* Picard thought wildly.

The figure in black armor ran swiftly to the left, then stopped in front of a blank section of corridor wall. He placed a hand on one spot indistinguishable to Picard from any other spot, then tapped his black-gloved fingers.

Amazingly, as if a holographic curtain were in place, a sharp line appeared in the wall, then grew wider—a hidden door opening.

The intruder jumped through, Picard and La Forge right behind him.

There was another, narrower corridor on the other side of the hidden door. The intruder moved to close the door behind them.

More like an engineering passage than a corridor, Picard thought as he checked out their surroundings with some difficulty. The glow here was even duller than in the main corridor. One wall was completely covered with pipes and conduits—nothing labeled, everything the same drab green-gray color.

He found La Forge watching the door close as both sides came together to form a single vertical line, and then the line vanished as if the door had never existed.

It was then that Picard noticed the intruder had not just used his hand to control the door. He was holding a small mechanism. And right now, he was looking down at his equipment belt, opening a small pouch, apparently trying to put the device back inside.

Picard had worn enough environmental suits to know how difficult it was to look directly down in a helmet. For precisely that reason, most critical controls were placed on a suit's forearms.

For just these few moments, their captor was vulnerable, distracted, especially since he would not expect his two captives to offer any more resistance.

Surprise, Picard thought.

He brought both fists down on the back of the intruder's helmet, counting on the impact doubling as the force of the helmet struck the back of the skull, and the faceplate rebounded to slam into the intruder's nose.

La Forge jumped to help, snapping the intruder's disruptor from its adhesion patch.

The intruder sagged to the floor, and for a moment, Picard heard an odd hissing noise, almost as if he had broken an air-pressure seal on the intruder's suit.

He had a moment of panic as he suddenly feared the intruder might require a different atmosphere. But there was no way to predict how long the intruder might remain stunned. He had to act now.

"Quickly," Picard said, and together he and La Forge

rolled the intruder onto his back, propping him against the wall.

Picard felt a twinge of unease. The intruder seemed too light, almost as if he weighed little more than his armor.

La Forge popped the seal on the helmet, Picard pulled it free, and both of them gasped in shock as they saw *nothing* within the helmet—*nothing* past the shadow of the helmet's pressure-seal ring—*nothing* as the suit slowly settled like a deflating balloon, completely, inexplicably, empty.

"All right," La Forge said as he got to his feet. "Now I'm worried."

Picard's mind raced as he sought rational explanations for what they'd just seen. Had the occupant of the suit been beamed away by a silent, instantaneous transporter? Was the suit somehow equipped with miniature forcefields and actuators to create the illusion of an occupant? Could it contain a holoemitter, and a holographic being like the *Voyager*'s doctor, who had simply switched himself off?

Or were he and La Forge somehow still captives, held prisoner in a holodeck in which reality could be effortlessly controlled?

The answer came to him in the form of the sweetest voice he had ever heard.

"Jean-Luc . . . Geordi . . . honestly . . . I'm so disappointed in the both of you, I don't know what to say."

Picard and La Forge slowly turned to the source of that voice.

"Leah . . . ?" La Forge whispered.

"Jenice . . . ?" Picard said.

For in the pale glow of the passageway, a woman approached them.

Picard didn't understand why his stomach fluttered, his pulse quickened. But then he realized what his subconscious must have already known: the woman was unclothed in the half-light, her body so familiar, so alluring.

Beside him, La Forge took a half-step forward, as enraptured by the vision of what approached as he was.

That realization broke through the enchantment of the moment for Picard. No vision of his own lost love could similarly affect La Forge.

Vision . . . illusion . . . whatever they saw, none of it . . . of her . . . was real.

But she kept moving toward them, and Picard knew he'd been mistaken. This wasn't Jenice, his first true desperate love at the Academy, merely someone who resembled her. Or rather someone who *had* resembled her in the shadows.

And neither was she without clothing, another misperception. Easily explained, Picard realized, given the extreme formfitting clothing the woman was wearing.

Beside him, Picard heard La Forge give a sigh of what sounded like relief. "I thought it was . . . but how could it be?"

Then the woman was before him, and she no more resembled Jenice than she did Beverly. She was Romulan, though her forehead was not as prominent as most, and the graceful sweep of her pointed ears was halfway between the straight line of a Romulan and the curve of a Vulcan.

"You don't recognize me, do you?" the woman asked. Her voice was like a teasing song.

"No." Picard resisted the desire to sweep her into his arms, having no awareness of where such an inappropriate thought had come from.

La Forge cleared his throat, as if he struggled with the same impulse.

The woman smiled at the engineer as if she had waited all her life to meet him. "How about you, Geordi?"

La Forge was reduced to shaking his head.

"Good," the woman said with a small clap of her hands. "I would have been worried if you'd said yes, because we have never met. Until now, of course."

She held out her hand, and to Picard it was exquisite. Delicately small, a precious object to be protected from all harm.

"I am Norinda," she said.

The name seemed familiar to Picard, though he found it difficult to think, to remember where he had heard it. If he had heard it.

"And I have come to save you," she said.

15

"Evacuate?" Will Riker said, astounded.

On the small screen on his ready room desk, Admiral Janeway looked ten years older than he had last seen her. She was no more pleased with the order she had given than Riker was to receive it.

"Every Federation mission and consulate on Latium," Janeway said, continuing her orders from her office at Starfleet Headquarters. "Their respective governments will transmit directly to them the proper instructions for the destruction of all sensitive data and equipment. The diplomatic corps will have special baggage allowances for the removal of cultural artifacts. But consular personnel and support staff will be strictly limited to a single piece of luggage—basically, whatever they can hold in their arms when you beam them aboard."

Riker still couldn't believe what she had told him. "Admiral, is it really that bad? To have us abandon all the progress we've made with the empire these past six months?"

Janeway had the grace to look apologetic. "I know

how close you are to what's been going on there. I
know half the Romulan initiatives we've developed
since the coup are because of your efforts—your special
relationship with the Romulan Fleet commanders. But
we've lost them, Will. Do you understand? Jean-Luc
and Kirk and everyone with them. Because of Kirk's
child."

Riker sat back in his chair. He had brought it from
his cabin on the *Enterprise,* as he had most of the deco-
rations and mementos in this room, including Data's
idiosyncratic painting of Spot, the cat. He looked at that
painting, remembering Data, the word Janeway had
just used resonating within him: *Everyone . . .*

That meant she had lost the holographic Doctor, too,
and Riker had no doubt the loss to Janeway was as
great as Data's loss had been to those who knew him.

"How did Starfleet Intelligence miss that?" Riker
asked. He wasn't really expecting an answer, but still,
the simple, inconsequential presence of a child seemed
such an unlikely detail to have derailed the Federation's last-ditch effort to prevent a Romulan civil
war.

Janeway rubbed the side of her face and Riker
guessed she hadn't slept for days. "We have so little
available data on Remus. But the one thing we do
know is that there are no families. Do you believe that?
The way the Romulans . . . 'manage' the Remans—
breed them is more like it—they don't keep familial
records. At one time, Kirk's wife was a Federation representative for her colony world. We have a complete
diplomatic dossier on her. But there's nothing in it that
connects her to Remus. Nothing."

Nothing ventured, Riker thought. He leaned forward,
folded his hands on his desktop, tried to sound casual.

"It will take a few days for the personnel on Latium to prepare for evacuation, so why don't—"

Janeway interrupted, smiling wryly through her exhaustion. "So why don't you just take a joyride into the Romulan home system and poke around?"

"At this point," Riker said, trying to sound completely neutral and reasonable, though he was neither, "with all reports saying war is inevitable, would it hurt?"

"I'll be honest with you, Will. From the reports we're getting out of Romulus, we could probably send in the Seventh Fleet and the Romulans would be too distracted to notice. But what you *must* keep in mind, and why you *must* follow these orders, is that you're the only lifeline the people on Latium have. Without the *Titan*, they have no way home. So when hostilities start, they'll be trapped behind enemy lines, to become prisoners, political hostages, or . . . victims. There's a strong xenophobic streak in Romulans, and we can't rule out an attack on the diplomatic quarter by a vengeful mob. The *Titan has* to stay put."

But Riker felt there was something missing from Janeway's insistence that the *Titan* stay at Latium. "Admiral, I understand the importance of giving our people a way home, but if the *Titan* is in no danger in the Romulan system—"

Janeway didn't let him finish. "No danger as far as we can tell, Will. But we missed Kirk's connection to Remus, and Starfleet's not willing to risk your ship on the assumption that we haven't missed anything else."

"With respect, ma'am. The *Titan* and her crew can handle themselves, even against the Romulan fleet. And if we're delayed in our return to Latium—"

"You want me to say it?" Janeway jumped in. "Because I'll say it. The *Titan* is the only ship in the sector capable of handling the evacuation of so many people."

Riker felt his face register his confusion. "Admiral . . . we're talking about a star system a stone's throw from the Neutral Zone. There is a constant Starfleet presence along the boundary. Five starships at least."

Janeway sighed. "You didn't hear this from me, but something else has come up. There's some emergency meeting being convened at Starbase Four Ninety-nine."

Riker didn't see the relevance. Starbase 499 was essentially a subspace relay station, part of Starfleet's communications net, but by no means one of the most critical components. "That's almost the other side of the quadrant."

Janeway nodded. "As far as I can tell, it doesn't have anything to do with the Romulan situation. But Meugniot and half the admiralty are heading out there at warp nine-point-nine. And they've taken the fastest ships we have available this close to home. So the *Titan* is it."

There was only one other option Riker could think of, and he decided to keep it to himself.

Janeway noticed his silence, guessed the reason for it, and fortunately for Riker, guessed wrong.

"I know what Jean-Luc means to you, Will. He's the finest captain in the Fleet, and the only reason he's not back here running the show is because he's too damn valuable out there, facing the things that . . . no one has ever faced before. But in the end, our duty as Starfleet officers has to take precedence over our obligations to our friends. There are twelve hundred women, men, and children on Latium, counting on you to take them home. You know you can't put their lives at risk for only one man."

"Understood, Admiral. The *Titan* will not leave orbit of Latium, as ordered."

Janeway's weary smile was tinged by sadness. "Thank you, Captain. I know what that means. And what it's cost you."

Riker nodded, nothing more to say about the matter. But he did have one last question. "Admiral, if I may, a point of clarification."

Janeway took on a slightly defensive posture, as if she were uneasy about whatever topic he might raise next.

"Is there truly no chance that the civil war can be averted? Is Starfleet Intelligence convinced that they missed nothing that might offer hope?"

Janeway relaxed. It was a reasonable question, and apparently not the one she'd expected. "All right, Will. By my authority, I'm letting you into the circle. And this is not to be shared with any other member of your crew."

Riker couldn't resist smiling. "Uh, I do have a Class Four security exception."

Janeway hesitated, then smiled in return. "Of course, Deanna. You're married to a Betazoid. Very well, the exception is noted. You *and your wife* are forbidden to share the following information with the rest of your crew."

"Thank you, Admiral." Riker declined to point out that Troi was half-Betazoid, and that her empathic abilities were limited to sensing emotional moods, and not full telepathy. But Starfleet Intelligence had ruled that was grounds enough for the Class Four exception, so Riker was comfortable he was abiding by the rules.

Janeway took a moment to collect her thoughts, and when she began to speak, Riker heard the cadence of an experienced Academy lecturer.

"A lot of this you already know, because you were at the forefront of the Federation's initial diplomatic contact with the Romulans, after the coup. You're aware of all the different groups vying for political power in whatever new government arises from the current chaos."

"Very much aware," Riker said. At times, some of the diplomatic meetings he had chaired had reminded him of refereeing a crowd of unruly children fighting over who got the best slice of birthday cake.

"What you might not have known is that one of the groups working behind the scenes is the Tal Shiar."

Riker felt as if a jolt of transtator current had flashed through him. The Romulan Tal Shiar had been among the most brutal secret police organizations in the galaxy, eclipsing even the hated Cardassian Obsidian Order. Romulan citizens lived in fear of ever speaking against the Tal Shiar, because those who did often ceased to exist, along with their families. Even the Romulan Senate had not dared to act against them, and so the Tal Shiar had operated outside even Romulan dictates of honor and tradition.

Several years before the outbreak of the Dominion War, a disastrous attempt to launch a preemptive strike against the Founders resulted in the near-collapse of the organization, and the almost total loss of their influence and power. So little had been heard from them in the years since that most intelligence reports concluded they had been effectively disbanded, left to the trash pile of history where they belonged.

Given all that, Riker had never sensed any indication that the Tal Shiar were among the power brokers striving for a say in the formation of a new Romulan government, and he had never seen any report, formal or otherwise, that had suggested the same.

"I see you're as surprised as we were," the admiral observed.

"Incredibly so," Riker agreed.

"Starfleet was understandably worried. If the Tal Shiar were to gain control of the new Senate, within a decade, we would be facing an expansionist Romulan Empire armed with cloaked, *Scimitar*-class warships and thalaron weapons, with absolutely no moral reservations about using them. It would be as if a nest of Borg had sprung up in our midst, intent on destruction instead of assimilation."

"That is a frightening scenario," Riker said, and he meant it.

"So as we watched the chaos continue to spread throughout the Romulan power structure, it became more and more apparent that what we were seeing was not predictable political confusion, but the result of someone deliberately spreading dissent. As combative as the Romulans are, they also have a pragmatic side. You've seen that in their Fleet commanders."

"I have," Riker said. Romulans were tough negotiators, no question. But Riker had learned to respect them because at some point they would always concede that the other side needed a reason to accept an agreement, and so, eventually, would make concessions—something that Klingons rarely did, and Andorians, never.

"Eventually, it became obvious to Intelligence what was going on. The Tal Shiar knew it could never legitimately take power in the Senate. So the only path open to it was to create even more chaos."

"A civil war," Riker said.

"Romulus against Remus. Two thousand years of racial hatred deliberately inflamed, then unleashed."

"I don't understand why they would take the risk," Riker said. "They had to know the destruction would be devastating."

"To Remus, yes. But the Imperial Fleet is dependent on singularity drives, not dilithium. The empire's balance of trade would take a substantial loss, but it wouldn't affect their military preparedness. And if they needed trade credits, they could always license mining rights to any interested party willing to rebuild the Reman mining communities. Then, once reestablished, those communities could be nationalized again."

"That sounds . . . very Romulan," Riker said.

"Doesn't it, though."

"So, knowing this, doesn't that put us in a position to tell the admirals what the Tal Shiar has planned?"

"Which admirals?" Janeway asked in return. "Can you say which ones aren't already working for the Tal Shiar?"

"So . . . we just stand back and let this happen?"

"No, Will! Not at all. At least, we were working to ensure that that was what we wouldn't do."

Riker could see the emotional toll of this for Janeway. Since her triumphant return from the Delta Quadrant, she had been hailed as a miracle worker— the admiral to go to when the problem was insoluble, when there was no hope and no way out. Because Janeway would always bring her people home, would always find a way to win.

It was no surprise that the Romulan situation had become her primary assignment. But perhaps in taking it on, Janeway had met the one problem that could defeat her.

"Admiral, I couldn't help but notice that you used the past tense. 'Were working.' "

Janeway's face darkened, with anger or with frustration, Riker couldn't tell.

"We came up with a plan, Will. At the highest consular levels, working with Starfleet Intelligence, the Vulcan diplomatic corps, the psychohistorians at Memory Alpha, every resource we had available to us."

Riker could hear the distaste in Janeway's voice, knew she didn't approve of the plan that had been developed, and that had evidently been given to her to implement.

"What was the plan?" Riker asked.

Janeway's jaw clenched. "We were prepared to make a deal with the Tal Shiar."

Riker's mouth dropped open in shock.

"That was my reaction, too," the admiral said.

"What . . . what kind of deal?"

Janeway took a long slow breath, then spoke quickly, in a rush to get the distasteful words behind her. "We were prepared to support the Tal Shiar in their reconstitution of the Romulan government. Arms, trade credits, technical personnel, whatever they needed."

Riker felt his face redden and he took a deep breath before responding.

"Who the hell could ever think that was a good idea?"

Janeway shrugged. "You understand why it's necessary for you to give up a chance to search for Jean-Luc, in order to save the twelve hundred Federation citizens on Latium. How is that different from making an offer to the monsters of the Tal Shiar in exchange for sparing the citizens of the Romulan Empire from a devastatingly brutal war, and sparing the Alpha and Beta Quadrants from an even more destructive conflict that could lead to the collapse of galactic civilization? The Romulans aren't the only ones who can be pragmatic, Will. And we were prepared to do things even more reprehensible when it seemed we were losing the Dominion War."

Riker shook his head, ashamed he could be even the smallest part of this outrageous plan that held in contempt every ideal on which the Federation had been founded, and which Starfleet served. "Admiral, tell me there's more to it than that."

"Oh, there is. If it makes you feel better—and truly, this was the only reason I accepted the plan and didn't resign my commission—our offer to the Tal Shiar was never intended to be more than a way to buy time. If the Tal Shiar didn't feel threatened, then we estimated we could have upward of a decade to rebuild our fleet, design and test thalaron defenses, learn new ways to defeat their cloaks. At the same time, a formal connection between the Federation and the Tal Shiar offered many opportunities for infiltration and intelligence gathering."

"On both sides," Riker said, reluctantly beginning to see the logic in what Starfleet had planned.

"It was a risk, but one we felt was preferable to the risk of galactic war."

Then Riker saw the contradiction in the plan. "Admiral, a few minutes ago, you pointed out how impossible it would be for me to know which Romulan admirals might be aligned with the Tal Shiar. So how were you planning on making this offer of cooperation? How were you going to make contact with them?"

Janeway closed her eyes as if making a silent prayer for forgiveness. "That was Jean-Luc's assignment," she said. "His third mission."

Riker felt as if he had been stunned by a phaser. For Captain Picard to agree to make such an offer to an unspeakable enemy, the danger to the Federation, to both the Alpha and Beta Quadrants, had to be even worse than Riker could imagine.

"How?" Riker asked quietly, overwhelmed by what Janeway had revealed. "Who was he supposed to contact? How would he know?"

"Picard was to follow and support Kirk's investigation into Ambassador Spock's murder. And once the murderers had been identified—"

"No," Riker said, truly shocked. "He wasn't going to bring those murderers to justice, was he?"

"All our intelligence points to Spock's having been assassinated by the Tal Shiar. Once Kirk had made the identification of those responsible, Picard was to take Kirk out of the picture, then contact the murderers with the Federation's offer of support."

Riker couldn't believe what he was hearing. "And the captain went along with this? Betraying his friend? Dealing with murderers?"

"One of the Vulcans who helped develop this plan, a Doctor T'Vrel, explained that the Vulcans have a principle they follow in matters like this, where no humane solution is logically possible. " 'The needs of the many outweigh the needs of the few, or of the one.' "

Janeway wiped at her eyes, banishing sleep or tears, Riker didn't want to know.

"We all wish there had been another way, Will. But with billions of lives at stake, how can one life . . . or seven lives . . . be held in the balance?"

Riker had no answer, couldn't speak.

"In the end," Janeway continued, "for all we were willing to compromise our principles, for all we were willing to sacrifice to ensure our survival . . . it turns out it doesn't matter.

"Jean-Luc's mission failed. The Tal Shiar will plunge the Romulan Empire into civil war. And for the next ten years, we will be fighting for each day of our existence, thinking back with nostalgia to when the only thing we had to worry about was the Dominion."

"It might be grasping at straws," Riker said with difficulty, "but until that civil war starts, I think I'll keep hoping for a miracle."

Janeway offered Riker a hollow smile. "I have great experience with that particular tactic. And you know, sometimes it works." On the screen, she reached to the side of her own desk. "Welcome to command, Will. The view isn't pretty, is it?"

"Not today," Riker agreed. "Thank you for your candor, Admiral."

Janeway nodded once, and the subspace connection ended, her face replaced by the symbol of the Federation. Riker tapped the switch on his desk to shut it off. He didn't want to see it.

He sat back in his chair, closed his eyes, trying to process all that Janeway had told him.

"I know what you're thinking," Troi said from the corner of the ready room where she had sat in silence through the whole exchange. Technically, her presence was a breach of regulations. But Starfleet recognized that some of their personnel would inevitably enter into romantic commitments with telepaths, and thus the Class Four exception existed. Had Troi not listened in to the conversation between Janeway and her husband, she would still end up knowing its contents as well as Riker did. Her presence was simply a more efficient way of managing the *Titan*'s resources, and Riker would be willing to argue that before a disciplinary hearing at any time.

"You're not supposed to know what I'm thinking," Riker said, and just the act of speaking to the woman he loved brought a measure of peace to him, despite what he had just learned. "You're only half-Betazoid."

Troi stepped behind his chair, rubbed at his stiff shoulders. "But I'm all yours."

Riker sighed as her fingers dug into complaining muscles. "Do you know what I'm thinking now?" he asked with an effort at playfulness he didn't feel.

She leaned down, kissed his ear. "Yes, but there's no time, because of what you were thinking before."

"And that is . . . ?"

"I heard how you parsed the admiral's orders."

Riker reached up to hold Troi's hand, anticipating what she was about to tell him, amazed anew that she knew him so well.

His wife's voice continued, full of unshed tears and love. She knew what her husband had to do and she wanted him to know she accepted it.

"Technically, she told you that the *Titan* has to remain at Latium. She said nothing about what *you* have to do."

16

PROCESSING SEGMENT 3, STARDATE 57486.9

"Give me your cane," Kirk said.

McCoy stared at him. "So you can leave me here in the corridor?"

"I will if you don't give me your cane." Kirk held out his hand, and McCoy slapped the curved handle into his grip. "Thank you."

"You're welcome. Now what?"

Kirk stared at the blank wall of the shadowed corridor, the fourth such passage they had encountered since leaving the infirmary and the body of the Reman doctor. All the corridors had been linked to each other by empty rooms, most of them small and dark like the antechamber of Virron's brightly lit meeting room. The last chamber that he and McCoy passed through, however, had been some type of storage area, and they had helped themselves to a couple of Reman dark-leather cloaks. Now their civilian clothes were less evident and their alien features were hidden within hoods.

"Do these corridors make sense to you?" Kirk asked.

"Nothing on this planet does," McCoy answered.

"But the corridors, Bones. There should be a pattern to their layout."

"They all look alike," McCoy said. He tugged back his hood to look up and down the corridor. "All of them. The same curve. No signs. One useless light every ten meters. Always one door at one end and a second door at the other. It's . . . it's . . ."

"Go ahead, say it."

McCoy sighed. "It's illogical."

"Exactly. And it *can't* be. This is a mining operation. These corridors have to handle thousands of people moving back and forth. Which means there's something here we're not seeing."

"In this light, I guarantee there's plenty we're not seeing."

Kirk waved off McCoy's complaints. "So let's try this," he said. He swung the green-metal cane over his head and smashed it against the corridor wall as hard as he could.

Kirk's entire arm vibrated with the force of the strike.

Startled, McCoy jumped, looked up and down the corridor again as if hordes of Reman security guards were going to charge them any second. "What're you doing?!"

Kirk regarded the cane with surprise. Its rigidity was unusual. He ran his hand over the wall, felt the indentation where the cane had struck. "Prospecting," he said.

He moved a meter along the wall, swung again. This time, now that he knew what to look for, he could see the faint shadow of the new indentation.

Kirk kept moving along the wall, McCoy shuffling beside him.

"How long before you think someone's going to come and investigate the racket you're making?"

Kirk hefted the cane in his hand, determined to ignore the tingling in his elbow. "Listen to how quiet this corridor is. It has to be soundproofed. Probably with antinoise. No one's going to hear this." He struck again, looked at the wall. "Now we're getting someplace," he said.

"Mind telling me where?"

"Look at the wall, Bones. See where I hit it?"

McCoy peered up in the general area of the strike, shook his head. "No."

Kirk ran his hand over the unmarked wall, smiled as he felt the indentation and saw the tips of his fingers appear to melt into the wall's surface. "Holographic screen."

McCoy actually smiled. "You're kidding."

Kirk reached under his cloak and into his jacket for an ultrasonic scalpel. "Are you amazed because there's a holographic screen, or because I'm right?"

McCoy held out his own scalpel, thumbed it on. "I'll reserve judgment for now." He began to run his hand along the wall beneath the area Kirk searched.

Then Kirk felt what he knew had to be there—the vertical indentation of a doorway. "Doctor, if you please . . ."

McCoy found and traced the indentation, then with superb skill, slipped his ultrasonic scalpel along it.

Kirk marveled at the sight of the scalpel appearing to move through a solid wall. There was a familiar metallic *pop*, and a puff of smoke suddenly bulged from the smooth wall. A moment later, the wall shimmered and two sliding door panels were clearly revealed.

"Well, I'll be." McCoy was positively grinning now.

Kirk handed him back his cane. "And to think you doubted me." Kirk began to push, and the door panels slid open, more easily than the ones connecting each corridor to its linking rooms.

On the other side of the concealed door was another narrow passageway, lined along one side with pipes of various sizes but identical gray-green color.

For a moment, Kirk wondered if they had only escaped to another frustrating loop of corridors. But then he heard something new. Noise.

"You hear that?" Kirk asked.

McCoy listened intently, pointed to the left. "Machinery? Coming from that direction."

"Very good," Kirk said, starting forward, anxious to move on.

"And that's because . . . ?" McCoy asked, awkwardly keeping pace with his cane.

"Remans live in darkness, Bones. They rely on sound. Their ears are sensitive, so the corridors they use are soundproofed. But this passageway isn't. So chances are we're in an area restricted to Romulan Assessors."

McCoy understood what Kirk had concluded. He began to shuffle forward faster. "So if we're headed toward machinery which only Assessors have access to, there might be a control room."

"A control room with communications . . . maybe even a transporter."

"On a slave planet?" McCoy asked. "You honestly think they'd allow a transporter down here?"

"There has to be one," Kirk said with conviction. "Someone used a transporter to save my boy."

McCoy fell silent and concentrated on his walking, asking no more questions.

After another two hundred meters, it wouldn't have mattered if he had. The groans and shrieks of heavy machinery made the passageway so noisy conversation was impossible. And the din was increasing the farther they walked on.

After four hundred meters, McCoy was holding his cane under his arm so he could limp on with both hands pressed tightly over his ears. Kirk shielded his as well.

After six hundred meters, the passageway ended.

But what lay beyond seemed endless.

Ahead of them was a large viewport looking into an enormous black-rock crater.

By Kirk's first estimation, the crater was at least two kilometers across, with sides perhaps five hundred meters high. Above its rim, there was a tenuous glow that held a scattering of pale stars. *Perpetual dusk*, Kirk thought. *The boundary between perpetual day and perpetual night.* The crater was located on the permanent terminator of Remus.

But the crater's location was less important to Kirk than what was in it. No more than fifty meters below the viewport, on the crater's smoothly excavated rock floor, Kirk saw spacecraft. At least five different classes, from enormous robotic ore haulers constructed from spiderweb lattices of open scaffolding, to sleek, eight-passenger atmospheric shuttles. Some of the craft were illuminated with running lights; others were dark. Some were connected to umbilicals and attended by workers in environmental suits, and others were isolated with no one near.

"A spaceport," McCoy exclaimed.

"More like a cargo station," Kirk amended. But terminology didn't matter. He was a starship captain. He

knew without doubt that he could tame any of the
spacecraft on the crater floor. And once he had a spacecraft to command, he could do anything.

"We have to get down there," Kirk said.

"Here's a better plan," McCoy suggested. "We have
to get down there without being seen."

Kirk held out his hand. "Give me your cane," he
said once more. It was time to go hunting for pressure
suits.

It was too easy, and Kirk knew it. He didn't even
need McCoy to say it, but McCoy said it anyway.

"They have to know we're here, Jim. It's a setup, and
I don't need logic to tell me that."

Kirk double-checked the power connections on the
Romulan environmental suit he wore, then looked at
the rack of helmets on the wall. The suit itself, along
with its life-support pod, was bright yellow, scuffed
here and there, stained with streaks of black and brown
dust. The helmets were the same color, with visors that
were little more than narrow slits instead of the full-
face visors Kirk was used to. Again, there was nothing
in the way of insignia or even safety and maintenance
labels on any part of the equipment, except for the front
of the helmets. Where a full visor would normally be,
each helmet carried in green the symbol of the Romulan Star Empire—the raptor in flight grasping two
worlds in its claws.

"So, what, you're ignoring me now?" McCoy asked.

"No," Kirk said as he took a helmet from the shelf,
eyed the pressure ring to see if it was a match for his
suit. "I agree with you. Except for the workers out in
the crater, we haven't seen anyone since we left the infirmary. That's impossible."

McCoy stood up in his own suit, needing only a helmet and gloves. "So what are they up to?"

Kirk had thought about nothing else since he and McCoy had stepped into the bright equipment room and found forty-five pressure suits hanging on the wall, much too conveniently. There wasn't one empty suit stall.

"I can think of two reasons," Kirk said.

"Enlighten me."

"This is some kind of Romulan game. They're toying with us. Either the suits are faulty, or they're going to beam us back to the infirmary or a prison cell as soon as we step into the airlock." Kirk selected another helmet from the shelf, handed it to McCoy.

"Or . . . ?"

"They want us to go, Bones."

McCoy snapped his helmet into place, turned it to seal it, and when he spoke, it sounded as if he were shouting up from a well. "Why would they want that?"

Kirk found it harder to voice the words than to think them. "Because it means I'm abandoning Joseph."

Kirk pulled on his helmet sideways, felt it click into place, then rotated it to snap the seal. Through the high narrow visor—which was even more difficult to see through than he'd anticipated—he saw McCoy standing directly in front of him. The doctor leaned forward so their helmets touched and they could speak without shouting. "You're not abandoning him," McCoy said, his voice muffled but louder than before. "Your boy knows you'd never do that."

Kirk simply nodded in reply, tried to smile at his friend and hoped his visor let enough of his expression of gratitude show through. But the truth was for all that Joseph was precocious in some ways, at heart he was still a child. And though Kirk had never let a day go by in his son's short life without telling him how much he was loved by his father and his mother, that young innocence and trust was threatened.

Kirk tried not to dwell on what Joseph's rescuers . . . captors . . . might be telling him now. How his father had abandoned him—proof that he had never been loved. How they were the only ones whom Joseph could rely on, because, after all, they had saved him where his father had failed. Kirk shrank from imagining the insidious whisperers laying siege to Joseph's impressionable mind, ultimately convincing him he was their savior, their Shinzon, the answer to the Remans' prayers.

Kirk had experienced the siren call of rank and privilege, had succumbed to it in his youth, knew better in his maturity. But what defenses were there for a child, with no experience in the ways of the world?

He feared for his son. Even as he twisted on his suit's gloves and prepared to leave this world and Joseph, Kirk condemned himself for what he might be condemning Joseph to.

McCoy held up his gloved hands and Kirk suddenly heard a static crackle in his helmet. *"Hey, Jim . . . has your helmet display switched on?"*

Kirk blinked as his helmet filled with light and he suddenly saw the reason for the awkwardly constructed visor. It wasn't intended for sight. Instead, built into the lower four-fifths of his helmet was a virtual screen, one that allowed him to see his immediate surroundings as clearly as if he wore no helmet at all.

At the bottom of the virtual image floated a series of symbols, which Kirk vaguely recognized as Romulan status indicators. As his eyes focused on them one by one, each smoothly expanded in size, and smaller figures appeared. The smaller figures were definitely Romulan numbers, and these Kirk could read. He just didn't know to which suit functions they applied.

"Can you interpret the status lights?" Kirk asked.

"No," McCoy answered. "But since they're all red, and one of the Romulan danger colors is a vivid green, I'm going to say that all my systems are functioning properly. How about you?"

Kirk ran his eyes along the symbols, almost feeling dizzy as they expanded and contracted. "Nothing that's vivid green—or a skull and crossbones." Then the virtual screen seemed to flash. "Did you just get an image flicker?" Kirk asked.

"Jim, look!"

Kirk turned to see McCoy pointing to something on the wall above the rack of helmets. Colored light panels were flashing—amber, purple, amber. "I see it. Can you hear anything?"

"I don't know how to switch on the external audio. Might be a time signal."

"Or a warning," Kirk said. "Maybe they think we've gone far enough."

"Jim! Behind you!"

Kirk turned as quickly as he could in the cumbersome suit, in time to see the door he and McCoy had entered through slide open again.

A crowd of Romulans was entering, all dressed in simple jumpsuits. Work uniforms! Kirk thought. He looked back at the flashing lights, suddenly realized what they meant. "Bones, that's a shift change! We must have come in here on their rest cycle. That's why no one was around."

Kirk looked back at the Romulans. They had to be

Assessors. He recognized at least three of them from the gathering in Virron's chambers. Another one waved at Kirk and McCoy, said something to the Romulan beside him, as if making a joke. *Let's hope they're laughing at the guys who went to work ahead of schedule.*

"Bones," Kirk said, and though it made no sense under the circumstances, he found he was whispering. "Let's get to the airlock as quickly as we can. And radio silence after this. We can't let them hear us."

McCoy didn't reply, but he did give Kirk a small wave of acknowledgment. The airlock's massive door was at the far end of the room, and McCoy determinedly hobbled for it. Kirk followed, quickly catching up, wishing McCoy could move faster.

Then he heard another burst of static in his helmet. A voice spoke in Romulan, then another. Kirk slowed, turned clumsily, looked back. And saw ten Romulans half-dressed in their suits, some already wearing helmets. More Romulans entering.

And then Kirk's gaze stopped on a single Romulan holding McCoy's cane, regarding it suspiciously. The rest happened almost in a blur of motion as another Romulan ran his hand over the shelf holding the helmets, clearly upset that something was missing, then turned to say something to the Romulan beside him, as the Romulan with the green-metal cane lifted it and pointed it straight at Kirk and McCoy.

Kirk was galvanized into action. *So much for thinking it was a setup,* he thought. He turned and grabbed McCoy's arm, started pulling him toward the airlock.

Then something slapped his shoulder and he let go of McCoy, who continued on his own.

Kirk half-turned to see an angry Romulan waving McCoy's cane and shouting at him, though the voice seemed distant through his helmet. Kirk pointed at an ear through his helmet, shook his head. Another Romulan stepped up behind the angry one, and pulled on a helmet. Now Kirk could hear someone shouting at him in Romulan over his internal speakers.

Kirk moved his hands in a meaningless gesture, said the first thing that came to mind. *"Farr Jolan."*

The shouting stopped at once. The Romulan with the helmet touched the Romulan with the cane, bent close, saying something that wasn't transmitted. Then Kirk heard a Romulan voice over his speakers, *"Farr Jolan."* Then another, and another.

Kirk bobbed his head in his helmet, trying in vain to recall any hand gestures or body language from the gathering he'd attended. Then he had it. *The salute!* At once, he clenched his fist, brought it to his chest in the Romulan style.

The Romulans close enough to see the gesture actually took a step back. *Three possibilities*, Kirk thought. *I've just committed a grave social blunder; I'm a high-ranking official; or I'm just insane.*

Kirk decided not to give them a chance to make up their minds. Acting on their confusion, he grabbed McCoy's cane from the surprised Romulan's hand, saluted again, said, *"Jolan True,"* then wheeled about and hurried to the airlock, where as he'd hoped, McCoy already had the thick door open.

Kirk at once pushed through to join McCoy, then swung the armored door closed, pulled the lever handle, and wrenched it as hard as he could.

As a babble of excited Romulan voices exploded within his helmet, Kirk felt McCoy tap his arm, looked to see that he was pointing at the airlock's second door. Beside it a display screen had come to life.

This time, the symbol was simple to interpret. An amber lozenge shape began to fade to a transparent green on a purple screen. Kirk glanced at the symbols on the bottom of his virtual screen, and sure enough saw another amber lozenge, obviously the symbol for atmospheric pressure.

Kirk moved to stand before the second door, waiting for the lozenge to stop changing color, at which point he presumed the airlock cycle would be finished.

He gave McCoy a thumbs-up sign, and McCoy replied with the same, then reached for the cane, but Kirk held it back. He pointed to the second door, opened his hand in a questioning gesture.

There were now a great many urgent Romulan voices transmitting back and forth. If he and McCoy had inadvertently gone this far because their movements had coincided with a rest cycle or shift change, then another shift of returning workers might be waiting outside.

The lozenge on the screen reached its palest color, then flashed as the floor beneath their feet began to vibrate. Kirk didn't hesitate, deciding its most likely cause was that the safety interlock was being released from the second door.

He reached out, pumped the door lever. His assumption was confirmed. The door moved easily.

He pushed it open.

There were three towering figures waiting inside the rock-walled chamber beyond, wearing thick red vacuum suits with heavy armor plating.

Remans.

Now there was no way back and no way forward.

Kirk and McCoy were trapped.

17

JOLAN SEGMENT, STARDATE 57486.9

"Farr Jolan," the elderly Romulan said. "Welcome, Jean-Luc Picard. Welcome, Geordi La Forge. I am Virron, Primary Assessor of Processing Segment Three, follower of the *Jolara*, the name which means 'She Who Leads Us.' "

Picard bowed his head, remembering what Kirk had said about these people, seeing for himself the near-trance state they were in. *"Farr Jolan,"* he replied.

Beside him, La Forge said the same.

And then there was silence in the bright, wood-paneled chamber. At least twenty Romulan Assessors, transfixed by expressions of adoration, along with Picard and La Forge, stood in breathless anticipation, waiting for what the *Jolara*—Norinda—might say.

She passed through the Romulans, as graceful as a dancer, and they, just as gracefully, moved from her path.

There was a small dais of polished green marble in the center of the room to which Norinda had brought Picard and La Forge. Now, beneath the domed ceiling from which the brilliant light of day poured down, she stepped onto the central dais to be bathed in that radiance.

For a moment, Picard was almost certain the haloed figure on the dais was not Norinda, that another woman had somehow taken her place as she glided through her crowd of worshippers. His eyes narrowed to sharpen focus.

A trick of the light, Picard decided, remembering how in the darkness of the passageway, for only the briefest of instants, he had first thought Norinda might be a lost love from his youth. And then how her body had seemed to be without . . . Picard felt his cheeks flush. But it was true that her jumpsuit had been unnecessarily tight.

His next conclusion had been that she had Romulan ancestry, softened by finer, almost Vulcan features. But here in this chamber, he could see that she was most certainly full-blooded Romulan. Her forehead was high, her short hair space-black, her fringe of bangs cut with laser precision.

Like the others encircling her, Picard gazed at Norinda standing above them, and decided that his imagination had made more of her clothing than reality revealed. What he had thought was a too-formfitting jumpsuit was, in light of day, a standard-issue Assessor uniform, though crisp, and finely tailored. The uniform merely hinted at her alluring form. It did not expose it.

"*Farr Jolan*," Norinda sang.

Before Picard had even time to think, he found himself replying with the same phrase, as did all the others, including La Forge.

Norinda clapped her hands like an excited, happy child. "We welcome guests today." She held out her hand and all eyes turned to Picard and La Forge as a chorus of welcomes in Romulan and Standard swelled.

Norinda smiled beneficently at the guests, as if in the entire universe, only they existed, only they deserved her devotion.

To Picard, it felt almost as if the warmth of the sun above was being directly transferred to him through her, and he longed to be closer to her, to feel that warmth skin to skin, no uniforms, no barriers, no—

Norinda was speaking in Romulan now, her attention turned to others in the crowd. Picard wiped at his forehead, felt the drops of moisture there.

"Captain? Are you all right?"

Picard looked at his engineer, saw the sheen of sweat on his face. He tried to think of a way to phrase the question. "Geordi . . . are you . . . having unusual thoughts?"

La Forge nodded. "I'll say." He glanced over at Norinda, who sang now in Romulan. "All about her." He blinked several times, resetting his vision, Picard knew. "She keeps looking different to me, but I can't pick up any trace of a holographic screen, or optical camouflage. I think she really is changing as we watch her."

How did I miss that? Picard chastised himself. There were many life-forms like that in the galaxy. Allasomorphs and chameloids that could change shape, sometimes even according to the unvoiced wishes of those around them.

Picard stared at the shining figure before him. But there was more to Norinda than just her physical appearance. Her force of personality was overwhelming. Even over communications channels, she could—

Picard rocked back on his feet and La Forge caught his arm as if fearing he was about to fall.

"Captain!" La Forge whispered.

Picard looked around, but none of the Romulans were paying attention to their new guests. All were looking at Norinda, only Norinda.

"Jim Kirk told me about this woman," Picard whispered in reply.

"He knows her?"

Picard nodded as it all came back to him, as if whatever influence Norinda had exerted on him, to draw him to her, had also worked to block his memory of the story Kirk had told him last year on Bajor.

"He encountered her years ago, in one of his first missions as captain of his *Enterprise*. There was a contest. The Romulans won. And Norinda . . . was the prize."

Kirk had told the story as the two captains had trekked across the Bajoran desert and faced death and mystery and, perhaps, the Prophets of the Celestial Temple themselves.

In the first six months of Kirk's original five-year mission, Starfleet had tracked an alien vessel entering an unexplored system at an inconceivable warp velocity. The craft had come into range of deep-space sensors on a trajectory that was extragalactic.

Whatever the craft might have been—crewed vehicle or robotic probe—it was a technological marvel that Starfleet wished to study.

So the *Enterprise* had raced to the Mandylion Rift, and there had discovered Norinda and her ship, and many other suitors—Andorian, Orion, Klingon, and Tholian. Starfleet had not been alone in tracking the alien vessel's arrival and rushing to claim it.

But Norinda made no claim to be master of her extraordinary vessel. She and her people, the Rel—whom Kirk was never shown—were refugees, she said. Escaping a dire threat they called the Totality, which was somehow responsible for the fate of the Andromeda Galaxy. Picard was aware that at the time, Kirk and Starfleet had no way of knowing that that part of Norinda's story was true. But as Kirk would later discover for himself, Andromeda *was* dying in an onslaught of rising radiation levels, and other refugees—most notably, the Kelvan—were also seeking escape to the Milky Way.

Faced with so many demands for her amazing ship's technology, Norinda had organized a bizarre and deadly competition among the assembled starship captains, offering herself, her ship and its secrets, to whoever could triumph over all others.

Spock said her tactic was logical. Norinda feared the Totality and claimed it would come to this galaxy next. Her goal was to identify the spacefaring culture that could best use her ship to develop defenses against that threat.

But Kirk freely admitted to Picard that logic and an unproven alien menace had little bearing on his interest in Norinda's contest. He'd viewed Norinda as much a prize as her ship. And a Klingon was his rival.

Years later, on the Bajoran desert, Kirk labeled this response of his as wrong and typically egocentric to Picard. But more important now, he had also described at length the disturbing physiological effect Norinda had had on every male on his *Enterprise,* including Spock.

Doctor Piper, the ship's surgeon on that mission, had hypothesized that some remarkably effective form of low-level telepathy was at work. Norinda could influence male minds even over subspace channels, though recordings of those communications had no effect at all.

In the end, facing certain defeat, and for the first time losing a crewman as a direct result of an order he had given, Kirk felt driven to enter the contest himself. He won. But he could not claim victory.

Norinda had one last surprise for him, and while he had played the game within the rules she had set, she had apparently changed those rules altogether.

Kirk's victory in the contest was hollow.

Norinda gave herself and her ship to an opponent the *Enterprise* could not detect, nor could Kirk see.

A few years later, after Kirk had become the first Starfleet captain to make visual contact with the Romulans, Starfleet analysts determined how Kirk had lost his prize. At the time of Norinda's competition, a cloaked warbird had been in the Mandylion Rift, completely unnoticed.

The analysts deduced that Norinda saw the cloaking device as evidence of superior capabilities and awarded her ship and its technological secrets to the culture that had developed it: the Romulans.

But as more years passed and Starfleet detected no truly startling or unexpected advances in Romulan technology, the matter of Norinda and the mysterious *Rel* and their ship faded further into the background, eventually becoming yet another unexplained event of the past with no connection to the present.

Until now, Picard realized.

After the ceremony—and Picard felt certain that was what the gathering with Norinda and her followers had been—Picard and La Forge were invited to a private audience with the leaders of the *Jolan* Movement.

They were ushered into yet another large chamber, once again featuring a dazzling cascade of light spilling down from an immense ceiling dome.

This chamber was hot, and extremely humid, filled with near-forests of lush purple-green plants and towers of large and elaborate blooming flowers.

"I expect you have many questions," Virron said pleasantly.

"That is an understatement," Picard said. He drew a deep breath with some difficulty. The perfumed air was heavy, cloying. "And if I may, my first question is where can I find a subspace transmitter?"

As if Picard hadn't spoken, Virron introduced to him and La Forge a white-haired female Romulan, Sen, and a younger male Romulan, Nran.

Norinda, who had somehow found an instant of time to change from her Assessor's uniform into a daringly sheer white gown, required no introduction. Nor did she seem to have any interest in the discussion between Picard and the others. Instead, she moved along the banks of flowers, and Picard could almost swear those blossoms moved to follow her, as if she were the sun.

"Is there a problem with me using a transmitter?" Picard said crossly. He was running out of diplomacy. As impossible as his mission might be under current conditions, until the Romulan civil war actually started, he refused to give up.

Virron looked apologetic and actually answered him this time. "Ah . . . communications within the home system are . . . erratic, Picard."

Picard was beginning to get the man's measure: He was a senior bureaucrat with no power to agree to anything.

"That's not the only thing that's erratic," Picard said. It was definitely time to be forceful, to push Virron into going to the next in command—someone who *could* make decisions. "My friends and I came to this system to visit Romulus. Instead, we were 'escorted' to Remus, held on orbit, viciously attacked by unknown intruders, then held captive in a mining compound, until Norinda somehow rescued us and brought us here, where we still feel like prisoners."

All three Romulans looked appalled by the anger Picard displayed.

"As a Federation citizen, I demand the right to contact the consulate on Latium," Picard added for good measure.

"And that is where you give yourself away, Captain."

At the sound of Norinda's voice, Picard felt all anger leave him. He didn't need to contact Will. He didn't need to call for the *Titan*'s assistance. He didn't need to find Jim and McCoy and Beverly and Scott. He didn't even need to stop the Tal Shiar from provoking a Romulan civil war that would engulf the galaxy.

There was only one desire that filled him.

Picard swept Norinda into his arms, crushed her lips against his, felt himself melt into her embrace, losing himself, losing—

Picard gasped with sudden pain as La Forge's fist slammed into the side of his ear, crushing the cartilage. He spun around to see his chief engineer and three cowering Romulans staring at Norinda.

"*Stop it!*" La Forge shouted.

Norinda faced La Forge calmly, opened her arms to him, and even through the pain of his mashed ear, Picard felt a terrible pang of jealousy.

"Stop what, Geordi?" she asked.

Picard couldn't understand how anyone could be so angry with Norinda. Didn't La Forge understand? But all he seemed to be doing was blinking rapidly, as if resetting his vision, over and over.

"You know perfectly well what I mean," La Forge yelled out, no sign of his outrage abating. "Telepathy, pheromones, direct stimulation of the amygdala—I don't care what you're doing, just stop it now!"

"Geordi . . . Geordi . . ." Norinda crooned soothingly.

Picard stared in fascination as her sheer white gown evaporated, leaving her exposed and achingly beautiful as she offered herself to La Forge. And then his fascination became unease as her straight black Romulan hair moved as a living thing, changed to brown and took on waves and grew longer to spill enticingly over her naked shoulders, as her flawless skin kept its perfection, but deepened slightly in shade, and her pointed ears rounded and her forehead grew smaller until Picard knew he was looking not at Norinda, but an exact, idealized replica of Doctor Leah Brahms, the woman La Forge had long loved from afar.

La Forge pressed his fingers to his temples as if contending with severe pain. His eyes watered, as if crying. But he did not look away from the vision before him. Neither did he move toward it.

"*Forget it!*" he screamed. "*Deal with us as we are or let us go! No more deception!*"

By now, the three Romulans were on their knees, fists to their chests, eyes averted, murmuring as if reciting prayers, urgently and repeatedly.

The creation that had been Norinda, that was now Leah Brahms, shifted again, to become the slender Jenice from Picard's memory, then Beverly, as she'd been when he'd first met her, and fallen so desperately, improperly, and completely in love with her.

With a force of will that seemed to spring from that Vulcan echo of Sarek still within him, Picard followed La Forge's lead and raked his nails down his aching ear. The shock of pain brought tears to his eyes and his stomach knotted into nausea, and though it had been a day since he could last remember eating, he brought up bile and gagged.

But when he could look up again, there were no more visions to torment him. Instead, before him stood a gray-skinned, large-eared Reman female whose eyes were hidden behind a visor of solid black. Her long leather cloak shimmered with iridescent colors like the shell of a scarab.

"Very well," the Reman said. Her voice was harsh and guttural. But even then Picard knew she was Norinda. At last in a guise that elicited no unwanted response. "Ask your questions, Picard. Whatever you want to know, I will tell you."

18

PROCESSING SEGMENT 3, CARGO TERMINAL, STARDATE 57486.9

Kirk had been prepared to launch a full assault on any Romulans outside the airlock, but the presence of Remans made him reconsider.

One Reman would be challenging. But three of them—when he was handicapped by an environmental suit? Rushing out, fists flying, no longer seemed appealing. So Kirk changed tactics on the fly. Quickly motioning to McCoy to stay put, he marched up to the first Reman, gave the Romulan salute, and then, because he knew that saying anything in Federation Standard would give the Remans reason enough to attack, he began cursing them out with every word Joseph had brought back from Quark's holosuites on Deep Space 9, heavy on the references to Tellarite anatomy, and taking great pains to growl in the back of his throat on the appropriate Klingon syllables, all the while waving the green-metal cane.

The unorthodox approach had the proper effect. The Remans remained in position, making no move against Kirk or McCoy. Their helmets had no visible visors at all, but from slight changes in their posture, Kirk could see that they were all engaged in a conversation, though on a com channel his helmet wasn't picking up.

Successful as the tactic was, Kirk knew it was vulnerable to a more forceful set of orders from the Assessors on the other side of the airlock. It was time for his next diversion.

He fell into the rhythm of the swinging cane, keeping it flashing hypnotically, he hoped, until he raised his other hand and the cane became his *bat'leth*. Without missing a beat of his recitation of words Joseph was not allowed to say, Kirk slashed the curved handle of the metal cane into the helmet of the first Reman in his best approximation of the *k'rel tagh* stroke of major severance.

The first Reman staggered back, gloved hands on his helmet, and even as the second Reman began to lunge for Kirk, he used the momentum of his first strike to deliver a partial *k'rel meen* blow to the second Reman's chest, knocking him off balance.

Then, in a move that had no name in the catalogue of ritual *bat'leth* combat, Kirk let the cane slide through his glove until it was at full extension, and used the curved handle to catch the second Reman's boot and yank it forward, making him fall back into the third Reman.

The need for caution gone, Kirk yelled at McCoy to run, then spun the cane up into a rifle grip, and used it like a pole to punch the first Reman in the gut, forcing him into a crouch, making it easy for Kirk to swing the cane around and bring it down like a club on the back of the Reman's helmet.

The last Reman standing dropped limply to the metal deck beside his struggling companions, and Kirk saw self-sealing pressure foam bubble up from a hairline crack in the helmet.

Surprised at first that he had been able to crack a vacuum helmet with only the strength in his arms, he realized a moment later that Remans would not necessarily be outfitted in the most robust of equipment, the result of some Romulan Assessor's cold and cruel calculation of the balance between the worth of a Reman slave's life and the cost of a properly reinforced helmet. At least the helmet had a self-repair capability.

Kirk swung at the other Remans with all his might, until they, too, remained on the deck, pressure foam swelling to encase their own damaged helmets.

Less than a minute after the airlock door opened into the rock chamber, Kirk tossed the metal cane to McCoy and together they rushed out into the crater itself.

In the distance, red-suited Remans and yellow-suited Assessors stopped their individual activities— staring at the two interlopers who had suddenly appeared on the crater floor.

But Kirk was still confident of reaching the spacecraft he'd already selected as his first choice. The Remans and Assessors were just far enough away that he and McCoy still could make it.

The small transport shuttle with an attached warp pod was only one hundred meters distant, and it was still unguarded. Kirk had seen the craft from the observation window, parked in a landing ring marked with the Imperial emblem, connected to power and air umbilicals.

The small craft's warp pod was too small to contain a Romulan singularity drive, or hold enough antimatter for a trip to the nearest star, so the shuttle was most likely a VIP transport used to ferry Romulan inspectors to and from the homeworld in short bursts of warp speed. But as a VIP transport, Kirk was counting on it to be fully equipped. For what he had planned, the shuttle's range was a secondary issue.

But as he and McCoy headed for the shuttle— McCoy's breathing becoming more and more labored and his awkward cane-assisted gait threatening to topple him to the ground—Kirk saw he hadn't considered the ramifications of one feature of the craft.

It was so small that, like a Starfleet shuttle, it had no airlock. But Kirk had not asked himself why it was parked in the open, deadly atmosphere.

The question and the answer collided in his mind as he saw the small transport slowly begin to descend into the crater floor.

The shuttle was parked on an elevator pad, one that would drop down to an airlock chamber. If he couldn't reach the craft before the chamber roof closed over it, he and McCoy would lose their best—perhaps only— chance for escape.

Telling McCoy to keep moving as quickly as he could, Kirk broke into a sprint and forged ahead, challenged for breath himself by the twin burdens of Reman gravity and the bulky environmental suit.

By the time he reached the edge of the crater floor, the landing pad had dropped two meters.

Kirk knew he had no choice, and so he leapt without hesitation, fully aware that the extra mass of the suit would be no friend to him. Plummeting with unnatural speed, bending his knees and hitting the pad as if he were coming down on a fast orbital parachute descent, Kirk rolled onto his side to spread the energy of impact over the largest surface area he could.

Despite his best efforts, the landing was hard. So

hard Kirk's chest went into spasm and he couldn't breathe.

But neither could he wait until breath returned to him. McCoy could never make that jump. And if the shuttle reached the airlock chamber below . . . Kirk knew he'd never be able to climb back up to the crater floor to try for another craft.

It was this shuttle, or nothing.

Black stars flickering at the edge of his vision, Kirk forced himself to his feet, scrambling for the shuttle's hatch.

He pulled the release switch. The hatch wasn't locked. It swung open in a cloud of normal atmosphere venting from within.

Kirk pulled himself inside, checked quickly to be certain there was no one in the passenger cabin, then forced himself into the pilot's chair and at last gulped down air, able to breathe again.

The shuttle was powered up, the controls familiar. He had flown Romulan craft before and the basics remained the basics.

Kirk dispensed with any type of preflight check. Either this would work, or it would not.

He looked out through the main viewport. He could see the airlock chamber roof was at eye level, already beginning to close. He estimated he had twenty seconds. After that, the shuttle would have descended far enough that the roof could close over it.

Twenty seconds, Kirk thought rapidly. The plasma thrusters weren't charged. The impulse engine was cold. There was no way he could get off the ground in time.

But there had to be a way.

The roof sections were above his eye level now,

moving closer, coming together like a night-blossoming flower closing at dawn.

Kirk's hands felt heavy moving over the controls. He had looked forward to adjusting gravity in this shuttle, so that—

The idea came to him at once, fully formed, and he didn't stop to consider if it was even possible.

Kirk threw on the primary shields, and because they were designed to respond instantly to navigational hazards, there was no delay. The overlapping force-fields sprang to life around the shuttle, violently disconnecting the suddenly severed umbilicals, and forcing the shuttle to suddenly pop up a meter into the air. The shields were treating the landing pad as a navigational hazard to be avoided.

Kirk grinned as he threw more power to the dorsal shields, setting them at maximum deflection. The dorsal shields forced the shuttle straight up from the immovable deck, making it bob like a child's toy on a string, twenty meters above the crater floor.

Then Kirk fired the RCS thrusters to make the shuttle spin around.

McCoy, at the edge of the open pit, stared up and waved at him. The Remans were seconds from reaching him.

Kirk swiftly adjusted the shields again, forcing the shuttle to roll toward McCoy, pass over him, and flip as if about to crash directly on the Remans charging for him.

The Remans scattered.

Kirk checked his controls again. The thrusters were charged.

He put his hands on the flight controls, and the shuttle was his.

Kirk eased the craft down beside McCoy. The hatch

was still open and McCoy fell through it, wheezing with exhaustion.

"*I have no idea how you did that,*" he gasped, "*but I'm glad you did.*"

"Strap in," Kirk told him. "Now it's going to get rough."

"*Now?*" McCoy said. But he dragged himself to a passenger chair behind Kirk's, pulled the restraint web over his chest. "*Strapped in.*"

Kirk had already picked out his target.

He brought the shuttle around, flying on plasma maneuvering jets instead of the now available impulse drive, merely to spray exhaust and cause general confusion.

He flew over as many exposed spacecraft as he could, scorching their hullplates, and scrambling their ground crew, who ran for cover.

But the fun was almost over. Kirk saw other shuttles lifting off. At least two, he recognized, were military craft, likely outfitted with disruptor cannons.

Kirk assessed his resources. The small VIP transport shuttle had no weaponry. But it did have a warp drive, complete with a miniature warp core, perhaps less than half a meter in length. And warp cores could go critical at the touch of the proper button.

He sped for the inside wall of the crater, picking up speed, drawing the other shuttles after him.

A disruptor blast flashed over the small craft's viewports, which meant the shields had held. Kirk gave thanks to the VIP who flew in this craft. The shields were probably several levels of power higher than usual for a standard transport this size.

A collision alarm began to sound as they neared the crater wall.

"Switching to internal gravity," Kirk warned McCoy. He tapped the control that activated the shuttle's artificial gravity, keeping it set for Remus normal so the change would not be abrupt.

Then, with gravity established and inertial dampeners online, Kirk engaged the impulse drive—*in full reverse*.

The plasma jets were no match for the impulse engine and the shuttle *instantly* shot backward, its gravity and dampeners keeping Kirk and McCoy from being thrown from their seats and through the hull with the violence of the maneuver.

But the pursuing shuttles were at a disadvantage. They didn't have pilots with Kirk's skill.

One pulled up so abruptly that it fishtailed out of control, rising in a spiraling motion, then stalling and plunging for the crater floor. Kirk guessed its operator had not taken the time to switch on dampeners, gravity, or impulse engines. The unfortunate result was what would happen in a primitive twentieth-century fighter jet. No hope of making a ninety-degree turn.

Another shuttle didn't pull up in time, and slammed into the crater wall, as if the pilot had hoped to duplicate Kirk's maneuver, but wasn't fast enough to activate the necessary systems.

Two other shuttles avoided collision and loss of control, and Kirk knew they'd be back on his tail in less than a minute. He was also certain that by now the Reman warbirds had been dispatched from their orbital patrols to deal with the hijacked shuttle.

"Not to be a backseat pilot," McCoy said, "but wouldn't this be a good time to think about getting out of here?"

"One last pass, Bones." Kirk brought the shuttle around on its final approach. "We're going to give them a little something to keep them too busy to come after us."

Kirk activated the warp core.

Purposely, he set the fuel mix to maximum imbalance, and ignored the sudden flash of a green warning light and wail of a siren.

"What kind of alarm is that?" McCoy asked.

"Warp-core imbalance," Kirk said. He held his finger over the emergency separation control, watching the Romulan numbers flash by on the warp systems status display.

"We're going to warp this close to a planet?" McCoy asked.

"We're not," Kirk said reassuringly. "But that big ore hauler is."

He pressed the separation control and the shuttle lurched gently as the explosive bolts holding the warp pod to the hull blew free. The pod tumbled toward a fully loaded ore hauler just rising from the crater floor.

Kirk pulled the shuttle into a ninety-degree climb, then touched the controls that brought imagery from the rear visual sensors online.

At first, the warp core was too small to be seen.

Then it exploded.

And then it ignited the fuel and engines of the ore hauler.

The crater terminal resembled a volcano, blazing with fire.

"My God, Jim . . . how many people did that kill?"

"With luck," Kirk said, "none. The atmosphere's too thin for there to be much of a shock wave, and our first couple of passes should have driven most workers to shelter."

He found the controls for the hatch, closed it, began

the pressurization cycle. Next he tried to find the gravity adjustment settings, but suddenly the shuttle shook with thunderous vibration as the viewport flared with blue fire.

Kirk checked the tactical display. As he had expected, a Reman warbird was closing, and VIP shuttle or not, he knew the small craft's shields couldn't withstand an all-out attack.

But since the small VIP transport was as fully equipped as he'd hoped, Kirk knew it wouldn't have to withstand an attack.

He veered to the right, activated the shuttle's cloaking device, then instantly cut speed and veered to the left.

A few seconds later, the massive, double-hulled warbird streaked past, launching a spread of torpedoes in the wrong direction, indicating that its crew had lost their prey.

Kirk set the shuttle to climb to a standard orbit, then finished adjusting the gravity, setting it to eighty percent of Earth normal.

For the first time in days, he felt he could truly breathe again, and just before he took off his helmet, he heard McCoy sigh with the same welcome relief.

The cabin air was still cold, but life-support was working, and when Kirk took off his gloves, he could feel heat blowing from the circulators.

"You're a hell of a pilot," McCoy said so wearily that Kirk went back to help him with the rest of his suit. "How're you holding up?" McCoy asked.

Kirk shrugged out of his own Romulan suit, let it fall to the deck. "Nothing finding my son couldn't cure."

McCoy stared at him. "You have a plan, don't you?"

"Most of one," Kirk admitted. "But you rest now. I'll let you know when we get there."

"Get where?"

There was a fully armed, overpowered, heavily shielded Starfleet vessel in orbit of this planet, and as far as Kirk was concerned, it was time he made use of it.

"The *Calypso*," he said.

19

Norinda had given the Romulans her ship, yet neither she nor they achieved what they wanted. Norinda had had to confess that she could not explain the functions of the vessel she had stolen from the Totality, and the ship's alien technology baffled the Romulan engineers.

"But I did teach them something," Norinda told Picard as they walked among the flowers. "The supremacy of the most important power in the universe: love."

"And that was the start of the *Jolan* Movement?" Picard asked.

"There were other peace movements on Romulus at the time. I brought them together, the best of each."

I'll bet you did, Picard thought. By visually re-creating herself moment by moment, Norinda could become a perfect mirror for the desires of her audience. Yet there was no truth in her appearance, whatever shape she took.

Even now, discussing a philosophy of love with a shapeshifting being who only looked like a Reman threatened Picard's own concept of reality. Only the bloody cloth he kept pressed to his torn ear kept him focused on what he really needed to get from Norinda. It had taken La Forge to realize there was one force stronger than love—pain.

For years, the engineer had been plagued by constant headaches brought on by his first artificial sight system: the Visual Instrument and Sensory Organ Replacement. When his VISOR had been replaced by ocular implants, La Forge's headaches had all but disappeared. But through the inevitable experimentation with his new vision system's settings, the engineer discovered certain optical frequencies able to reproduce those early headaches with stomach-churning precision. That was how he had managed to block whatever signal Norinda was transmitting into his nervous system, by burying it beneath an even stronger one.

Picard's means had been far less elegant, and bloodier, but the end result was the same as for his engineer. Norinda had ceased her attempts to control the two of them as she did everyone else, and had opted for a more novel approach: open discussion.

"And so, when you grew too powerful," Picard said, "you were banished to Remus with your followers?" He looked across the chamber to see La Forge keeping a watchful eye on him. The three Romulans who had been so distraught at the way the two humans had treated their spiritual leader had left immediately after Norinda's transformation into a Reman.

"I am not powerful," Norinda said lightly, though as a Reman, the words came out with a deep rumbling undertone, like a felinoid purring. "It is my message which the war-makers fear, because it is true, and in their hearts they know it."

Picard stopped walking, looked up at Norinda with

no fear of losing his ability to concentrate. From what she had just said, he finally had his opening, knew the argument that would convince her.

"Norinda, we must work *together*, because your goals, the goals of the *Jolan* Movement, they're my goals, too."

From her lofty Reman height, Norinda gazed down at him, her Reman eyes a mystery to him, still protected by her visor from the bright light of this greenhouse chamber. "You believe in the supremacy of love?" she asked.

"I believe in stopping war."

"But through the supremacy of love?"

Picard had to get her off her one-track approach, open her eyes to other strategies. "Through whatever means possible," he said.

Norinda smiled at him, Reman fangs glistening. "That is what I intend to do."

"I'm sorry," Picard said, puzzled. "I don't know what you mean."

"The reason you're here, Picard. It's because of the civil war."

The pain in Picard's ear suddenly vanished in his surprise. "You know about it?"

"I have been trying to stop it."

Picard was stunned. There was no need to convince Norinda that a war was coming. She was ahead of him.

"How do you know?" he asked.

"The followers of *Jolan* are everywhere in the empire. We know the Tal Shiar's plans firsthand."

Picard's pulse quickened with new hope. If the *Jolan* Movement had agents in contact with the Tal Shiar, and if Norinda would allow him to use those agents, then it could still be possible to make contact with the Tal

Shiar and relay the Federation's offer of support in return for peace.

"Norinda, I can't tell you what this means to me, what this means for the possibility of peace." A dozen questions came to Picard then, but the most important had to do with time. "You say you know the Tal Shiar's plans. Do you know if they are following a timetable? Is there a specific date? A specific action that they've chosen to signal the beginning of the war?"

"The Hour of Opposition," Norinda said.

Picard shook his head.

"Once each Romulan year," Norinda explained, "Remus catches up with the homeworld in her orbit, and the two planets reach their closest approach. This year, in less than three days, they will be no more than a million kilometers apart. Traditionally, it is a time of celebration on both worlds, though more so on Romulus. There, schools and businesses close. Families travel to be together and share meals. Game birds are consumed to instill the spirit of the Imperial raptor which has brought the worlds together again, as they were in the beginning."

Picard nodded, understanding. "There are similar celebrations on my world." Intent on her words, he no longer noticed Norinda's Reman looks or voice. Their conversation held his interest fully.

"It is a time of peace, Picard. At least, as close as a warlike world such as Romulus can get to peace. That is when the Tal Shiar will strike."

"You must believe me, Norinda. My friends and I have come here to stop that war."

"I do believe you. That is why I saved you from the Remans working for the Tal Shiar."

"The Tal Shiar are here? On Remus?"

"They never went away. Their greatest strength is that no one believes they still exist."

"Then, is that who attacked my friends and me on our ship?"

"Mercenaries of the Tal Shiar. Yes. That is what we believe."

Picard hesitated, troubled, doubtful about her version of events. Had Norinda's cooperation come too easily? Was he in danger of being manipulated again?

"But . . . why would the Tal Shiar want Jim Kirk's son?" he asked.

Norinda began to walk again, as if she had grown impatient with his persistent questioning. "The Remans believe T'Kol T'Lan is the Shinzon. I do not know if this is true. But the possibility exists that if enough Remans believe he is, then someday, the child of Kirk could be their liberator. Of course the Tal Shiar would try to destroy him, to prevent that from happening."

Picard walked at Norinda's side, wishing she were in human form again so he could read her expressions, sense the truth behind her statements. He suddenly wondered if she had chosen this form precisely because of that reason—there was no way he could be certain which of her responses were truthful, which were lies.

"But the intruders who attacked us, they didn't try to kill Joseph." Picard remembered that part perfectly. "They wanted to take him. They didn't even kill the rest of us, when that would have been an easy matter."

"I do not know everything the Tal Shiar has planned," Norinda said. "Whatever they wanted with T'Kol T'Lan, they failed when you saved him. There is no need to wonder further."

Picard stopped again. "But we didn't save him."

Norinda stopped a few steps past Picard, looked back at him. "The Tal Shiar transmissions we intercepted, they claim the child was beamed off the ship by a Starfleet transporter."

"I saw it happen," Picard said. "I recognized the transporter signature. So did Kirk. But there are no other Starfleet vessels in orbit of Remus." He listed for her the other possibilities that could account for what they'd seen, and the objections Scott and La Forge had raised to all of them. "None of us knows who's responsible for beaming Joseph out. None of us knows where he is."

The Reman form of Norinda darkened, broke apart at the edges, shifted out of focus, coalescing so rapidly into her smaller Romulan form with its Assessor uniform that Picard heard a gentle rush of air.

"Is something wrong?" he asked.

Norinda's quick smile stirred desire in him instantly and Picard pushed the bloody cloth against his ragged ear. Before he could protest aloud, her smile had faded, as if she had reacted by instinct to male presence, forgetting their new arrangement.

"Nothing is wrong," she said calmly. "But I am troubled that there could be ships of unknown capabilities in orbit of Remus, without our knowledge."

Picard tried to understand why that would disturb her, could think of only one reason. "You're worried the Tal Shiar have cloaked vessels already in position?"

"Yes," Norinda said, but something in her tone made Picard feel there was more to her concern. The only thing Picard could link it to was their discussion of Joseph. But why would the child be of any interest to her?

Another question came to Picard. "If you know when

the Tal Shiar will strike, do you also know where? And how?"

Norinda nodded. "On the Hour of Opposition, the Tal Shiar will strike Remus, at three key targets."

"Which three?"

"Worker communes."

To Picard, Norinda appeared to be having some difficulty choosing the right words to describe the concepts she was trying to impart.

"Understand, Picard, that the vast majority of Remans are male. The sex of children is controlled by the Assessors in the breeding facilities."

Picard had his own difficulties suppressing his reaction. Again he wondered how the Federation could contemplate entering negotiations with any government capable of propagating such evil. Even though he knew that with the lives of billions at stake, compromises sometimes were inevitable. It was an unfortunate truth, but a truth nonetheless, and one the Vulcans knew well.

"Those males," Norinda said, "millions of them, are confined to miners' barracks, deep below in the rock. But there is a secondary workforce here as well—engineers, ore processors, maintenance workers, trauma specialists, cooks, protein harvesters . . . the support personnel who make it possible for so many miners to be fed and clothed and managed. Those Remans live in worker communes, and miners who survive twenty years in the rock—and there are very few who do—are rewarded by being permitted to take a support job and live closer to the surface in the communes. To the Reman mine worker, they are as close to paradise as their existence offers."

Picard had another question for Norinda.

"If the communes house the workers who support the mining operations, why destroy them? Why wouldn't the Tal Shiar strike the mines first, to shut down operations at once, and save the communes so operations could be restored after the war?"

"The communes have another purpose. You know of Reman soldiers?"

Picard frowned. He knew of them. He knew how much the Federation owed their bloodthirsty savagery in the Dominion War. Another compromise.

"And you know of the three warbirds that patrol this world's orbital reaches, also staffed by Reman crews."

Picard had been briefed on them as well.

"But have you asked yourself how are they kept in control?" Norinda asked. "Brutalized, exploited, angry slaves, given warp-capable ships with full armament. What holds them in check?"

"They're strictly for local security," Picard said, wondering what point Norinda was trying to make. "I've been told they're limited to warp factor two, so they can't possibly outrun a bird-of-prey. Their fuel supplies are kept low, so they can't reach another system. And they have no cloaking devices, so they can't hide."

Norinda nodded in confirmation. "Plus all their security codes are programmed into every ship in the Imperial Fleet, so their shields can be switched off at will."

"I understand the conditions," Picard said. "It would be suicide to use those warbirds to attack Romulan interests."

"But knowing all that you do of conditions on Remus, do you believe any Reman would hesitate to lose his or her life to strike at a Romulan?"

Picard understood then. It wasn't just the certainty of death that kept the commanders of the Reman warbirds from acting against Romulus. It was the certainty of retaliation.

"Each warbird is linked to a commune," Picard said. "Is that it?"

Norinda nodded again, her grim mood matching Picard's. "And if that warbird acts against Romulus—if any of the crew as individuals breaks regulations, strikes an Assessor, fails to keep a perfect record—then the commune assigned to that warbird is punished, in ways I will not describe."

Now Picard knew what Norinda had been concerned about. Now he was, too.

"The Tal Shiar plans to destroy the three communes linked to the warbirds," he said. "There will then be nothing to prevent their commanders from launching full-scale suicide attacks on Romulus, when the worlds are less than three light-seconds apart."

A single warbird with a miniature black hole in her hull, striking a Romulan city at warp two, wouldn't have to fire a single shot to take out tens of millions. And by attacking from so close, Romulan planetary defenses wouldn't have a chance to respond in time.

"And thus a civil war begins," Norinda said.

Picard was at once disheartened and encouraged. Disheartened, because the Tal Shiar plan was brutally simple and bound to succeed. But he was encouraged because it was a plan that had a definite starting time and a single specific action. If within the next three days he could convince the Tal Shiar not to take that action, then there was a possibility the war could be stopped before it began.

Picard had only one more question to ask of Norinda.

"You told me the *Jolan* Movement was attempting to stop the Tal Shiar's plans. How?"

"As the Hour of Opposition approaches, all the followers of the *Jolan* Movement, on both worlds, open and hidden alike, will join in an emanation of love, sending our thoughts through the fabric of the universe, to dissuade the Tal Shiar from having thoughts of war."

"I see," Picard said, giving no sign that might reveal what he thought of such a plan. "And if that plan doesn't work?"

Norinda looked genuinely puzzled. "How can it not?"

Picard had learned enough. All his questions had been answered. He had less than three days, but he still had a mission.

"Norinda, what if I could stop the civil war before the Hour of Opposition?"

"That . . . would be wonderful. Love would prevail."

"Well, I believe I can accomplish that, but what I need to do first, is to contact someone within the Tal Shiar. Can you arrange that for me, through whoever you have who's infiltrated their organization?"

Norinda grew reserved. "That would put lives at risk."

Picard found that a startling reply. "Norinda, lives *already* are at risk. Tens of millions in this system alone. Billions in the two quadrants."

Norinda appeared to be as confused as Picard felt. "Why should billions of lives in other systems be affected by what happens here?"

Picard sighed. For someone able to master a myriad of details of life on one planet, Norinda seemed curiously uninformed about interplanetary politics. And he had no time to educate her. "In this region of space, the Alpha and Beta Quadrants, each spacefaring culture is connected to the next. A war here will definitely reach out to involve other systems. Believe me. It *will* happen."

A faraway look came to Norinda then. "I didn't know," she said. "Billions?"

Picard nodded, wondering how else he could get through to her the urgency of his request.

"Billions of people, needing love." She smiled.

"Will you help me?" Picard demanded.

Norinda regarded him earnestly. "Of course I will. How can I not? We must bring peace to this world, and to Romulus, and to the Alpha and Beta Quadrants. We must bring peace to the galaxy."

"Fine," Picard said, steering firmly away from any further discussions of love. "Will you put me in contact with the Tal Shiar?"

"Certainly."

"Thank you," Picard said with honest relief. "When?"

Norinda paused to think.

"We only have three days," Picard reminded her.

"More than enough time," Norinda said. "The Tal Shiar have agents on Remus. I will arrange a meeting for later today."

"Thank you," Picard said again. He still had a chance.

From the other side of the chamber, someone called out for "the *Jolara*."

Picard and Norinda both turned to see the young Romulan, Nran, running across the greenhouse chamber, La Forge beside him.

Nran stopped by Norinda, saluted her, gasped out, "*Farr Jolan*. There's been an explosion. Sabotage."

Picard stepped back as Norinda appeared to increase her height by several centimeters.

"Where?" she demanded, and her voice was deeper than it had been a moment ago.

"Processing Segment Three. The cargo terminal." Nran nervously wiped at the curious patch of metallic gold under his left eye.

Norinda appeared to calm slightly when she heard the location. "What kind of ship?" she asked.

Nran held his fingers to the patch as if trying to remember. "A transport shuttle," he said at last. "It jettisoned its warp pod . . . because . . ." His eyes popped open in surprise. "Kirk escaped."

Norinda, Picard, and La Forge all said "What?" at the same time.

Nran squinted, keeping his fingers on the patch, and Picard concluded that it was part of some sort of subcutaneous communicator. "He and his friend . . . they stole a transport shuttle, blew up an ore hauler, then . . . then cloaked. They're gone." Nran shrugged. "And that's all."

Norinda smiled at Nran, and subtly became a younger, more voluptuous version of herself, even as her uniform grew more snug. Picard saw the yearning expression that swept over the young Romulan, knew what he must be feeling, remembered feeling that way himself.

"Thank you, Nran," Norinda whispered.

Picard knew Nran couldn't speak to save his life.

She took his hand, held it close in hers to make a fist, then held it to her heart.

Nran's face flushed bright green. His mouth opened.

"*Jolan True*," Norinda said, as soft as a kiss. Then she

released his hand and he slowly backed away, unsteadily turned, and headed off in silence.

But by the time Norinda had turned her attention back to Picard, she had regained what Picard now thought of as her normal Romulan form.

"Kirk must have found his son," she said.

Picard didn't know how she had come to that conclusion. "Was his son reported to be with him?"

"No. But why else would he leave?"

"If he was being treated like us," La Forge said, "then he was a prisoner. I'd say he escaped, but there's no way he's leaving without finding out what happened to Joseph."

Norinda looked at Picard. "Do you agree?"

"Most assuredly," Picard said. "In fact, I know exactly where Jim's going. Because it's where I'd go, too."

Norinda smiled, and waited patiently.

Picard did not disappoint her.

20

Kirk had found food packs in a cooler, and McCoy had found a medical kit with a Romulan compound that eased the discomfort in his legs. But the most restorative part of their flight to orbit was dialing back the shuttle's gravity, eventually reaching Mars normal, one-third of Earth's.

In the copilot's seat, McCoy was thinking of a few more modifications to make life simpler in the future. "I might have to give up on my internal leg implants," he mused. "Maybe face the inevitable and get a powered chair when we get back to Earth."

Kirk moved his attention back and forth from the shuttle's controls to the viewport, looking for anything out of the ordinary. *So far so good*, he thought. "That sounds encouraging."

"Encouraging?" McCoy snorted. "Me in a hover-chair?"

"You're talking about *when* we get back to Earth, Bones. That implies you expect we'll find Joseph, Scotty, Jean-Luc and his crew and get out of this."

"Well, of course we will." McCoy patted Kirk's

shoulder. "Someone's got your boy, Jim. I know as well as you do that you'd never let anyone get away with that. And I don't care if I have to cut off my legs and crawl to get him back. So we *are* going to get him back. And everyone else. Even if we are a mite shorthanded."

Kirk didn't require, but appreciated, the additional confirmation that the greatest treasures his career and adventures had brought him were Joseph and his friends—his family. Spock's loss remained raw.

McCoy seemed to sense what he was thinking. "I wish Spock was here, too."

Kirk rallied with some effort. For Joseph's sake, he had to focus on the present, not the past. "C'mon, Bones. You're supposed to say, Spock's the one who got us into this mess."

"Exactly. Which is why I wish he was here, so I could tell him **so**, to his face."

A chime sounded from the board and Kirk shifted in his chair to check the distance readings.

"Is that her?" McCoy asked. He leaned forward to peer through the viewport.

The *Calypso* floated a half-kilometer ahead of them. She had no running lights, and her navigation beacon was off, but her distinctive lines were just perceptible in the backscatter of light from the night side of Remus.

"Right where we left her," Kirk said.

"You sound surprised."

"Bones, we were told she was adrift. Generators out. No power."

"You're right," McCoy exclaimed. "Scotty said the boarding party shot her up."

"But there she is," Kirk said. "In trim. And the passive sensors show she's warm."

The captain and the doctor looked at each other.

Kirk was already planning his next move. He knew he couldn't risk using active sensors while cloaked. The Remans would be looking for their stolen shuttle, and an inexplicable sensor burst from empty space would be little different than decloaking and firing all the plasma jets at once.

"You think someone sent up an engineering crew?" McCoy asked.

"I would have thought they'd tow her to a salvage dock," Kirk answered. "Reman resources seem to be spread pretty thin. I can't imagine they'd think it was a good idea to repair a ship they didn't own."

"You think there's someone aboard her now?"

"I think we're going to find out." Kirk placed his hands on the inertial maneuvering controls, and the *Calypso* suddenly filled the viewport as he swiftly brought the shuttle to within ten meters of the ship, then began to slowly travel around her, as if conducting an inspection tour.

After a few minutes, the shuttle neared the primary cargo airlock on the deck above the engine room. Kirk was still using passive sensors, but this close he was able to use light amplifiers to bring up detailed images of the *Calypso*'s hull on a control board display. "Something's not right."

"Care to be more specific?" McCoy asked.

"Scotty said the intruders' ship grappled onto us, but there're no signs of it on the hullplates around the airlock."

"Maybe they came in through the emergency lock."

"Already checked that. We passed it a minute ago. And if they'd come in at any other entry point, we'd have depressurized."

"Which means," McCoy said, caught up in Kirk's

reasoning, "they must have transported in. The same way Joseph was transported out."

Kirk stared at the image of the cargo airlock, wrestling with the mystery. "A small ship, like this shuttle, can pass through navigational shields—provided it moves slowly enough. Fast-moving objects are hazardous, so they get deflected. Slow-moving objects are likely friendly, so they can pass through."

McCoy voiced Kirk's supposition. "You think a shuttle—a cloaked shuttle like this one—slipped through the nav shields, *then* beamed the intruders in and Joseph out?"

"If they could do that, why make us think we'd been grappled? Why send intruders aboard?" The scenario was possible, but it didn't feel right to Kirk. Joseph's life-sign readings were unique. A standard scan could pick him up anywhere on the *Calypso* in under a second and he could have been beamed away without a fight.

"There's got to be a simpler explanation."

"Two explanations, actually," McCoy said. "How did the intruders get aboard? And how did Joseph leave?"

Kirk sat back in his chair as an electrifying idea came to him. "Bones! Remember what Spock always said . . ."

"Jim, Spock was always saying everything."

"No, about mysteries! Sherlock Holmes mysteries! Vulcans love him. 'When you have eliminated all which is impossible, then whatever remains, however improbable, must be the truth.' "

"That sounds like Spock."

"So if it's *impossible* for Joseph to have left the *Calypso*, then the only improbable possibility that remains is that—"

They said the last words together: "—he's still on board!"

The transfer from the cloaked shuttle to the *Calypso* was as straightforward as Kirk had hoped. The shuttle's autopilot was easy to set for stationkeeping, and he locked its position a mere five meters from the *Calypso*'s emergency airlock. Then he and McCoy floated over in their Romulan environmental suits.

Five minutes after blowing the hatch on the shuttle, the two of them were standing in the deck four corridor of the *Calypso*, still in their Romulan suits, though with their helmets and gloves off.

The ship sounded as she always had, even to the background hum of the warp engine on standby. The deck was level and the gravity felt normal.

McCoy sniffed the air. "It even smells better," he said.

Kirk sniffed. McCoy was right. The damp, musty, livestock smell he had found so objectionable was gone. But another scent had taken its place. "What is that? Cedar?"

McCoy shrugged, the motion of his thin shoulders barely noticeable within the heavy folds of his yellow suit. "Some kind of disinfectant."

"Well, that proves my son didn't have anything to do with it." Kirk unstrapped the green-metal cane from McCoy's safety harness, handed it to him, then began peeling off the remainder of his own environmental suit.

They placed the yellow suits back in the emergency airlock, then headed for the bridge, walking quietly, avoiding the turbolift. Though Kirk was convinced Joseph was somewhere on board, he was worried that his son was not alone. It was the type of question he could have answered quickly and easily with a standard tricorder, but doing so could alert Reman surveillance satellites that someone was aboard a supposedly abandoned spacecraft.

The bridge wasn't quite as squared away as the rest of the ship. Kirk noted evidence of the disruptor fire Scotty had described. But he also saw a few places where disruptor scorches had been scrubbed or painted over. More importantly, though, all the duty stations were operational.

"Elves," McCoy finally said. "That's your answer, Jim. The ship has elves."

"Or that ghost Joseph was looking for."

"Right," McCoy said. "I'd forgotten that. He was convinced there was . . ." McCoy tapped his cane on the deck. "You don't suppose we have a stowaway?"

Kirk hadn't considered that. But someone was responsible for cleaning up the ship. "Let's check the galley, find out what's missing from stores."

The galley was in better shape than the bridge. No sticky mess of empty *tranya* glasses and chocolate pudding cups—no reassuring evidence that through it all, his child's ordinary life had continued on. If anything, the smell of disinfectant was even stronger here.

McCoy sniffed the air again and smiled. "Now I've got it. It's the disinfectant that's stocked in sickbay."

Kirk checked the maintenance readouts on the replicators. "Well, someone's been eating something . . . this replicator was used three hours ago. Milk? Apple? One chocolate-chip cookie . . ."

Kirk's heart skipped a beat.

McCoy beamed. "I know what that means, Jim.

There's a five-year-old boy on this ship, and there's someone here taking care of him."

"Someone let him eat only one cookie." Kirk desperately wanted to believe McCoy was right.

McCoy squeezed his arm. "He's here, Jim. I know it. Let's go check sickbay."

"I could perform surgery in here," McCoy said approvingly.

If the bridge was partially squared away and the galley clean, then sickbay was immaculate.

Kirk immediately scanned the cramped medical facility looking for any sign of his child. Nothing. If Joseph were on the ship, he was somewhere else.

McCoy, however, already seemed to have found something of interest in a supply locker. Kirk looked over the doctor's shoulder, saw medical supplies and standard instruments, but nothing that appeared to warrant the examination McCoy was giving them.

"Something in there?" Kirk made an effort to curb his impatience to continue the search for his son.

"Nothing's missing," McCoy said. "But it's all been . . . rearranged."

Kirk saw a flicker in McCoy's eyes, as if he had just had an idea, but then censored himself.

"Bones . . . ?" Kirk was about to tell him to say whatever was on his mind.

But McCoy narrowed his eyes, gave an almost imperceptible shake of his head.

Someone's watching us? Kirk covered and played along. "Where do you think we should look next?"

"Engineering." McCoy limped toward the door, keeping his eyes resolutely focused straight ahead.

Kirk followed, almost hoping that his reading of the situation was correct. If someone were watching them, that someone could be the person guarding his son. Not a Reman, nor a believer in Joseph as the new Shinzon. Either of those would have taken Joseph off the ship.

McCoy paused in the corridor outside sickbay, then waved his cane forward. "Let's take the turbolift."

"I thought we were trying to keep a low profile."

McCoy tapped his hip. "My leg won't handle the ladders. Besides, if whoever's on this ship hasn't heard us yet, then there's probably no one on board."

Again, McCoy followed his words with a subtle shift of his eyes, and Kirk accepted that for whatever reason, he was simply to follow the doctor's orders.

McCoy motioned him into the turbolift, then stepped in after him, staying as close to the doors as possible as they slid shut behind him. But as soon as the car began to move, McCoy spoke quickly and urgently. And what he said made sense.

"Jim, it's Janeway's EMH. He's Joseph's ghost. He's the one who rearranged my sickbay. And from what I've read about him, I think it would be the simplest thing in the world for him to create a holographic *illusion* of a transporter effect to make it *appear* that Joseph had been beamed away. He's the one taking care of Joseph!"

Kirk stared at McCoy, both angry and relieved by the doctor's speculation. What was the Doctor doing on *Calypso* in the first place? And why wouldn't he show himself now?

The turbolift car stopped.

McCoy's reasoning reached its natural conclusion.

"Is Picard keeping secrets from you?"

The lift doors opened before Kirk could tell McCoy that he'd guessed right. But from the way McCoy turned away without waiting for his answer, Kirk was almost certain McCoy already knew the truth.

The engineering compartments were nothing like those on a starship. The warp core and engine components filled almost all available space and were accessible only by catwalks and narrow ladders.

Kirk was like a man on fire, intent now on flushing out the captor of his son. But there was room for a dozen flesh-and-blood stowaways behind the power conduits and life-support regenerators. The steady rhythmic rush of the engine would preclude hearing any of their movements. And if the holographic doctor was able to duplicate the cloaking effect of a Starfleet isolation suit, then he could stand unseen only inches away.

There was only one place he and McCoy could converse privately and securely. "Let's get back to the shuttle," Kirk said loudly. "I think you're right: Whoever was here is obviously gone."

McCoy signaled his agreement, and they left the engineering compartments together. When they boarded the turbolift to return to deck four, they entered the lift more slowly than the last time so as not to cause suspicion, making room for an invisible passenger, just in case. They kept their conversation innocuous.

Ten more minutes, Kirk told himself as he and McCoy walked without hurrying toward the emergency airlock. Then they'd be in the shuttle, where he could work out the final, comprehensive strategy. *Soon, Joseph, soon,* he vowed.

And then, like so many of his plans on this tortuous voyage, that vow, too, became meaningless.

The *Calypso* rang with the sound of an airlock mating to its cargo door.

Intruders.

Again.

21

Picard stepped from Norinda's orbital transport into the *Calypso*'s cargo bay, and resisted the impulse to shout Kirk's name. He knew that to make the most of this opportunity, he had to let events unfold slowly. Somehow, he had to make certain that whatever happened, he ended up with at least ten minutes alone at the communications console on the bridge. He had to report to Janeway over a secure subspace channel, and then get word to Will Riker to have the *Titan* standing by to show support for the Tal Shiar.

Picard had had only a few minutes to discuss this in private with La Forge, and his engineer understood the need to report, and that a distraction would be in order.

La Forge stepped into the cargo bay, then rocked back and forth from one foot to the other. "The gravity alignment feels off," he said with a tone of professional concern. "We should probably run an emergency diagnostic in engineering to be sure all systems are stable." He turned to the young Romulan who had accompanied them. "Nran, I could use your help."

Nran hesitated, looked to Norinda.

She shook her head with a smile. "Stay with me."

With those three words, Nran was enthralled, and Picard knew the young man wouldn't stray more than a few steps from Norinda for the duration of this visit.

"And I'll stay with you," Norinda said to Picard.

He nodded, already thinking of how he might arrange to be isolated on the bridge. Perhaps a decompression event?

"And you will stay with us," Norinda told La Forge.

"This ship could lose power at any second," La Forge said earnestly. "And if a propulsion system goes, we could drop out of orbit quick as that." He snapped his fingers.

"If that should happen at this altitude, it won't happen quickly. We'll have more than enough time to return to my transport." Norinda pointed ahead. "Considering what happened here yesterday, it is safer for us all to remain together. The bridge is that way."

Picard thought it was most interesting that she knew the way. But then, he had also been surprised when she'd led them to the airlock chamber in which her transport was stored.

It was an Assessor's vehicle, strictly limited to orbital flight and a passenger load no greater than nine. Yet Norinda had piloted it smoothly, and as far as Picard had been able to determine from his passenger seat, had not had to request clearance of any kind. He didn't know if that was a sign of Assessor privilege, or a breakdown of Reman security. Then again, if all transgressions against the Romulan authorities were as strictly punished as Norinda had intimated, then perhaps strict oversight of Reman operations was not required.

With any luck, Picard tried to console himself, if an

arrangement could be made to cooperate with the Tal Shiar, then perhaps the Federation could begin to have some influence in Reman affairs, and someday the Remans truly would be free.

The thought was a sobering one. After all that Shinzon—his clone—had gone through in an attempt to free his Reman brothers, it had come to the original Picard to try again.

Thinking about fate and destiny, Picard followed Norinda to the bridge.

In the aft of the bridge, in the office beyond the transparent wall, behind the desk, Kirk was sitting where he had sworn he would never sit, doing what he had sworn he would never do. But he had chosen a position of control, which might be necessary depending on the intent of the new boarding party.

Whoever they were, at least the holographic doctor had decided to remain hidden, still protecting Joseph. Kirk was ready for, and expected, the worst. At any moment he would be faced with the prospect of battling a team of Romulan Assessors or Reman salvagers. Without weapons, the only advantage he had was McCoy.

Strapped in at the environmental and life-support duty station, McCoy was ready to switch off the artificial gravity, then hold on as Kirk pushed the ship into a series of spins guaranteed to have the boarding party bouncing off the walls. Wherever Joseph was hiding on this ship, Kirk hoped his son was tucked in tightly.

The turbolift began to operate.

Kirk's gaze whipped to one of the many screens that faced his desk and found the right display. The car was rising to the bridge.

He waved through the transparent wall at McCoy.

McCoy waved back, standing by.

The lift doors opened.

Four figures were crowded inside.

Two were known to him—Picard, La Forge.

Kirk's relief was momentary. The other two wore the dull gray uniforms of Romulan Assessors.

The young male he recognized as Nran and instantly dismissed him as a possible threat. The other, female, was—

The shock was overwhelming.

"*Norinda . . .*" he whispered in the silence of his sealed office.

Their encounter in the Mandylion Rift still baffled him—everything this woman was, everything she had done, no matter all the years that had since passed.

And to see her now, at a time when all of his life seemed to be measured by loss and longing, Kirk wondered if he could withstand her again.

But Norinda shared none of his apprehension. Her face was transformed by a welcoming smile—*the* terrible smile he'd feared and craved.

And with that smile, Kirk had his answer.

After what Mister Scott had reported about the state of the *Calypso,* Picard was surprised to find it in such relatively good condition. Even the air smelled fresher, as if the recirculators had been repaired. If he hadn't known that Kirk and McCoy had just escaped from their Reman captors within the past few hours, he might have thought that Kirk had been aboard for days, toiling incessantly to bring the ship up to Starfleet standards.

Then Picard had stepped onto the bridge from the

lift to see Kirk in the captain's office, and was appalled by what he witnessed next.

The moment Kirk glimpsed Norinda, Picard saw the flash of recognition quickly turn to shock, and shock to horror.

Picard knew the reason and pitied Kirk.

With each step Norinda took toward that glass wall, she *changed*.

Her reflection in the glass wall showed her Assessor's uniform shrinking round her, molding into a glossy black jumpsuit that was a second layer of skin, until . . . she became the image overlaying Kirk's stricken face: Kirk's love, his life, his greatest joy and deepest sorrow.

Teilani. Kirk's lost wife, mother to his son. Cruelly returned to him.

Picard felt almost mesmerized as he saw Kirk press his hand against the clear wall.

As on the other side, Norinda/Teilani raised her hand to—

"Stop it!" McCoy shouted, startling Picard out of his near-trance state. The doctor stood on the lower level of the bridge. "For the love of God, man, make her stop!"

McCoy was right! Picard rushed at Norinda, grabbed her by the shoulder, pulled her away from the clear wall and the tortured man behind it.

"Change back!"

"Jean-Luc, you're hurting me!" Teilani gazed up at Picard in hurt appeal, her beauty captured to the last frightening detail, from her delicate Klingon forehead ridges to the Romulan sweep of her ears. But she was younger than she had been when Picard had met her, with no trace of the virogen scar that had marked her later in life. Picard realized he was looking at Kirk's idealized memory of his beloved wife, pulled from his mind, his heart, his soul.

"Let him go!" Picard commanded.

"I can't," the apparition said. "He loves me, and I must love him." She held up her hands in supplication to Picard, and the black jumpsuit she wore, its plunging neckline reaching almost to her navel, began melting from her.

Picard forced himself to slap her, hard across her face. He winced. Siren she might be, but she still felt all too real.

She gasped, and for an instant, her face seemed to flicker into shadow. But then Teilani looked up at him again in defiance, and she snarled at him in Klingon, *"I must love him!"*

Picard seized hold of her again, determined to break whatever telepathic bond this alien creature had forged with Kirk. *Remember she's an alien shapeshifter,* he told himself. He pictured her as the Reman female who had towered over him, with the strength to throw him across the bridge. He readied himself to strike again.

"Let her go or I'll kill you!" It was Nran who shouted at him, sobbing.

Picard heard the scuffle that told him how La Forge was keeping the Romulan youth from interfering.

"Can't you see what you're doing to him, woman!" McCoy stomped up the steps to the upper level of the bridge.

But Teilani shook her head back and forth like a child having a tantrum. "No, no—*he's* doing it to me!"

Picard raised his hand, then stopped hearing the whisper of the transparent wall opening, as Kirk emerged from his sealed office.

"No, Jean-Luc," he said. "That's not necessary . . ."

Picard stepped back and Teilani turned to face the man whose memories had somehow brought her into being.

Slowly she spread her arms wide to him.

"James," she said, and her voice *was* Teilani's. "I've missed you so much."

"Your name is Norinda," Kirk said, his voice unsteady. "Not Teilani. Never Teilani."

But Picard heard the last traces of uncertainty still in his voice. And so did she.

"But I *am* Teilani for *you*." She stepped closer to him, within reach of his embrace, and Picard knew the struggle Kirk endured not to simply give in and hold her close once more.

"No," Kirk told her, "you can't be. Because I won't let you."

She touched his face, his tears.

"It's what you want," she said. "I know what you feel."

Kirk nodded. "It's what I wanted," he agreed, and took her hand from his face, pushed it gently away. "But now there's something else, someone else, I need even more."

Pain, Picard thought suddenly. It was what had freed him and La Forge from Norinda's influence. It was the one force stronger than love. And just like love, there were many forms of it. The pain of Teilani's loss had at last freed Kirk, as well.

Teilani's perfect skin became the drab gray cloth of an Assessor's uniform once more. Then Norinda, as a Romulan, looked back at Picard, eyes dark with pain of her own.

"I understand none of you," she said. "When all I offer is love, and peace, and understanding. . . ."

"We need other things as well," Picard explained. He decided he'd try to take advantage of her undisguised distress. "Why don't you take Nran back to the galley. I think some tea would help—"

Norinda slipped her arm through Nran's, and with that simple movement, her figure became fuller, her face younger, her uniform snugger. For the first time, Picard found himself wondering if she was as vulnerable to others' influence as others were to hers.

"It is you who refuse to accept the gift I offer, who need my help," she said with a touch of petulance. She looked over at Kirk in pity. "Where is this thing you want more than your own happiness? Where is your son?"

Kirk looked at Picard, as if expecting Picard to say something.

But Picard said nothing, not certain what Kirk wanted.

"Jean-Luc," Kirk said at last. "You know."

Picard shook his head. "I'm sorry, Jim. I don't."

"But he's here with—"

A new voice burst out across the bridge, sweeping Kirk's confusion aside.

"Daa-ad!"

It was Joseph.

22

Kirk whirled around to see Joseph charge at him from behind his own desk!

Kirk opened his arms to his son and lifted him up in an unbreakable bear hug. Beyond maintaining any semblance of composure, he kissed his son's head, his cheek, held him out to look at him, then pulled him close again. The heart-stopping shock of seeing Teilani again hadn't faded. The moment of recognition had been electric, resonating within him still. Her hair, her skin, her eyes so bright, so full of life, all caught in one exquisite, painfully sharp instant, had left him drained, numb.

There had been too much loss in his life. Teilani. Spock. Only holding his son in his arms once more could renew Kirk's strength to keep grief at bay.

"Where have you been? Where have you been?" Kirk said.

Joseph's answer was incredible. He had been close by ever since Kirk had entered the bridge. Very close.

"Right here, Dad!" Joseph squirmed impatiently in his arms, pointed back at Kirk's desk. "There's a crawl-space. Uncle Scotty told me. For boxes and old stuff. That's where I hid when the bad guys came." Joseph suddenly looked worried. "I wasn't supposed to talk to anyone until I knew it was safe. Not even you, Dad. That's okay, right, Dad?"

Kirk squeezed his son one more time. "Perfectly okay."

Joseph squirmed again, and Kirk reluctantly let him down and unleashed him on the other adults on the bridge.

The child quickly made the rounds, calling out, "Geordi! Uncle Jean-Luc! Uncle Bones!" Then he stopped quietly in front of Norinda, and put on his best manners. "Hello, ma'am." He stared at her ears. "Are you a Romulan?"

Kirk felt uneasy the way Norinda gazed at Joseph. "Do you like Romulans?" she asked.

Joseph nodded eagerly. "I'm Romulan. Sort of. I'm Reman, too. And Vulcan, and human, and Klingon. Uncle Bones says that makes me pure trouble!" Joseph glanced back at Kirk. "It's okay to say that, right?"

Kirk nodded, still shaky with relief. "Pure trouble is all right." He and Joseph had had talks about the concept of species being "pure." It was an outmoded concept, reeking of past injustices and bigotry. As a Vulcan-human hybrid, Spock had directly experienced such prejudice, and Joseph had been an attentive audience for Spock's stories of his own childhood.

"Well, I'm not Romulan," Norinda said. "But I like Romulans."

Joseph looked at her skeptically. "Then what are you?"

"What would you like me to be?"

Kirk went on alert, looking for any sign that Norinda

was reaching into Joseph's mind, ready to step in if she showed the slightest indication that Teilani was to reappear.

But all that happened in response to her question was that Joseph gave an elaborate shrug and said, "I dunno."

Norinda stared at Joseph for several silent seconds, then said, "I believe you." She smiled. "Would you like to see where I live on Remus?"

"Sure," Joseph said.

That was when Kirk knew it was time to bring this to an end. "There's no time, son. We have to leave soon."

"No. You don't," Norinda said.

"He's not going down to Remus." Kirk wasn't about to let Joseph out of his sight again. He stood beside his son, put his hand on his shoulder.

Norinda turned her attention from Joseph and Kirk to Picard. "Jean-Luc, you asked for a favor from me, to meet some friends of the *Jolan* Movement."

Picard seemed apprehensive. "Yes . . ." he said cautiously.

"For me to do that favor for you, I need you to do a favor for me. Convince Captain Kirk that his son should visit me on Remus." She glanced at Kirk, but there was no power to her smile, no subliminal connection. "Just for a day, Captain. Jean-Luc and I will take good care of him."

Kirk moved to forestall Picard, who clearly was trying to think of something to say to him, as if the favor Norinda mentioned could in any way be as important as his son's safety.

"I don't care what favors anyone has promised," Kirk said. "Joseph is not leaving this ship."

"Aw, Da-ad," Joseph said. "I really want to go! Really really! Can I? *Please?*"

Kirk stared at his son in surprise. Joseph loved to negotiate, but it had been more than a year since he had whined to get something he wanted. Kirk had never responded to that tactic, so Joseph had quickly learned to abandon it.

"Joseph, that's not—"

But then Joseph did another atypical thing—he interrupted, swinging on Kirk's hand like a little tree sloth. "I'll be careful! And I'll be safe! We can use secret codes, like when you told me to hide in the cabinet when the bad guys came, and then you'd tell everyone that I got beamed up by a Starfleet transporter so the bad guys would think that I was someplace else but all the time I was safe right here, right?"

Kirk's surprise gave way to a stunning realization.

"And I kept busy up here, like you told me. And I cleaned the recirculators and the walls and—Uncle Bones! Did you like the way I cleaned sickbay?"

Kirk let Joseph's hand slip from his. His child stood alone on the deck looking up at him.

"I really really want to go, Dad. You really really should let me. Okay?"

It couldn't be more obvious what was expected of him, so Kirk did what he had to. He shifted gears, looked at Norinda with stern parental concern, and said, "Just one day."

She nodded in agreement.

Kirk pointed a finger at Joseph. "And you behave yourself, young man."

"Yes, sir!" Joseph ran at Kirk again, gave him a hug, then ran over to Picard and Norinda. "Let's go!"

Picard seemed confused. "You're sure, Jim?"

Kirk shrugged as if his son hadn't been missing under dire conditions for the past two days. "If I can't trust you, Jean-Luc . . ." He waved at Joseph. "Have . . . fun."

Joseph waved back. "Thanks, Dad."

And as simply as that, Kirk said good-bye to his son, and Norinda and Picard and Nran were in the turbolift, on their way back to the cargo bay and Norinda's transport.

La Forge had stayed behind because of his insistence that the *Calypso* could fall from orbit at any second, unless he ran his diagnostics at once. But instead of hurrying down to engineering, La Forge remained on the bridge with Kirk and McCoy. "I don't think Captain Picard was expecting you'd do that," La Forge said to Kirk, with unconcealed puzzlement. "I mean, I know he'll appreciate it. It could mean the difference that'll stop a war, but . . . well, I'm surprised."

Kirk enlightened him, grinning. "Commander La Forge, I'm going to take a wild guess that you don't have children."

"No, sir, I don't."

"Well, I do," Kirk said. "And trust me, the little boy who just left here with your captain and that shapeshifter isn't my son. He's Admiral Janeway's EMH."

La Forge whistled in amazement. "You're kidding!"

Kirk stepped back to the open door of his office. "Joseph, if you're down there—everyone's gone! It's safe!"

Kirk smiled hugely as he heard a scrabbling under his desk, then the clank of a square of decking as it was shoved aside.

He beamed as a familiar little bald head popped up from behind his desk, and as he had the pleasure of being reunited with his son a second time in one day, this time it was for real.

As soon as the cargo-bay status lights indicated that Norinda's transport had undocked, La Forge was at the communications console on the *Calypso*'s bridge. He made a halfhearted request for privacy, but Kirk leaned against the console and McCoy sat in the chair beside La Forge's and neither he nor the doctor gave the engineer any indication they were ever going to move.

So, while Joseph happily went down to the galley to replicate meals for everyone, Kirk and McCoy listened as La Forge reported to Admiral Janeway, repeating everything Norinda had told Picard about the Tal Shiar's plan to ignite a civil war at the Hour of Opposition.

La Forge did not mention that he was not alone, and neither Kirk nor McCoy made their presence known. Kirk wanted the admiral to feel free of her burden of bureaucratic deception, so she would speak the whole truth.

Kirk greatly appreciated Janeway's decency as she began by expressing her genuine relief that Joseph was safe, and how she regretted ever allowing the child to be part of the mission, even though she had had no reason to suspect he would ever be in danger. And he was able to deduce from the rest of the conversation exactly what Picard's third mission had been, and how with Norinda's help in making contact with the Tal Shiar, the threat of civil war might yet be averted.

By the end of La Forge's report, Kirk found himself agreeing with Starfleet's intentions, but taking exception with their plans and tactics. *As usual*, he thought.

He especially found it galling that even in light of

the breakthrough Picard was poised to make with the Tal Shiar, Admiral Janeway refused to order the *Titan* to Romulus. Somehow, an emergency conference called at a starbase that was little more than a glorified repeating station for subspace radio signals didn't seem like reason enough to leave a single starship to cover the entire Neutral Zone. Not on what might be the eve of war.

But Kirk decided that Starfleet's biggest blunder in this matter had been not telling him the truth from the beginning. Had he known the stakes involved, he would have had no objection to accepting the assignment. He certainly would have been willing to investigate Spock's murder on Romulus as a cover for Picard's attempts to stop a civil war.

But by not trusting him, by believing that everyone they dealt with had the same compromised standards as the leaders of Starfleet, it was Command that had made the situation worse than it needed to be. At least, that was the way Kirk saw it. Starfleet, it seemed, was no different for Picard today than it had been in his time.

His report over and his subsequent discussion with the admiral at an end, La Forge cut the channel, then leaned back in his chair. "So that's everything."

"Somehow, given Starfleet's track record, I doubt it," Kirk said. "But thank you for letting us listen in. I take it that was a breach of your orders."

"Not at all. We have contingency orders and some of them cover the circumstances under which we were authorized to tell you everything. The way I interpret those orders, this was one of those circumstances."

"Good," Kirk said. "I'd hate to see the admiral make you walk the plank for insubordination."

La Forge laughed. Kirk looked at him, waiting for an explanation. "Everyone on Captain Picard's command staff has walked the plank at one time or another. He has this holodeck program that . . . well, it's historical."

Kirk held up his hands. "Say no more."

The turbolift opened and Joseph slowly came out, carrying a precarious stack of trays and food containers. Kirk rushed to help him, but not so urgently that Joseph might think he had done anything wrong.

Together they spread out the trays, then reallocated the food packs, so everyone got a version of the same meal. Kirk noticed that Joseph's tray had four chocolate-chip cookies. The Doctor's influence hadn't lasted too long.

They ate on the bridge, sitting on the steps and the upper level. And Joseph finally told them all the story of what had really happened when the "bad guys" came. How he was frightened and backed up against the wall in Picard's cabin, and then how everything had shimmered with light and he was suddenly in a park and the Doctor was there, telling him he had to play a game where he must stand as still as he could for as long as he could, without making a sound. And if he could do that, then he'd get a big reward.

Kirk was grateful for the lack of trauma in Joseph's account, knew he would have to thank the Doctor for thinking so quickly to save his child. Then he thought to ask Joseph what his reward had been.

Joseph leaned forward over his tray, and gestured emphatically with his spoon. "Dad," he said conspiratorially, "he gave me *all* the ice cream I could eat. *All*."

McCoy, La Forge, and Kirk laughed at that, so Joseph did, too. And as their laughter faded, a new sound rose on the bridge—a series of electronic chirps.

"That's a hail," La Forge said. He pushed his tray aside to return to the communications console.

"Don't answer that," Kirk said, tensing for trouble. "There's not supposed to be anyone on board this ship."

But La Forge was already at his console. "That's a Starfleet code, sir. Set for this ship and this mission. We have our own code to respond with."

Kirk relaxed, waved La Forge on. "Just stop calling me sir. It's Jim."

The next sound to come from the console was even more unexpected.

"Hello, Geordi—it's Will."

"Captain Riker . . ." La Forge answered. "Did you send that approach code?"

"Technically, Worf sent it. He's in the copilot's chair."

"But I just spoke with Admiral Janeway. You're supposed to stay on station at Latium Four."

"Another technicality, Geordi. The admiral's orders refer to the Titan, *and the* Titan *is right where she's supposed to be."*

Kirk smiled. There was hope for some in Starfleet.

Then another familiar voice joined the circuit. *"We are approaching your aft cargo-bay airlock,"* Worf brusquely announced. *"Request permission to dock."*

Kirk was anxious to give it. Now that he had Joseph back, he could finally think of Spock. And the more people he had on his side in that fight for justice, the better.

23

JOLAN SEGMENT, STARDATE 57488.1

As the craggy black rock of Remus stretched to a horizon over which a bloated green Romulus peered like a baleful eye, Picard knew how close he was to success, and how close to disaster.

With two days remaining until the Hour of Opposition, there was still time to convince the Tal Shiar they had an alternative to war. But the key to Picard being able to offer them that alternative rested with Norinda, the being who flew this transport, the being he had just betrayed.

Picard knew it wouldn't matter that the betrayal had been unwitting. On the bridge of the *Calypso*, he had been shocked that Kirk had so willingly given up his son to Norinda, to allow him to journey to Remus. But as they had made their way back to the cargo bay and the transport, Picard had reflected on what Joseph had said to his father, and before they had left the first corridor, Picard realized what Kirk must already have known.

Joseph wasn't Joseph.

The singular child strapped into the passenger seat

across from him in the bare, unfinished shell of the transport was the holographic doctor. Engaged in a flawless deception.

So far.

Because once this transport landed and Joseph was brought before the followers of the *Jolara*—which was surely what Norinda intended—as perfect as the Doctor's illusion was to all physical senses, it would have to withstand the inspection of any telepaths among the Reman population.

And there would be telepaths, some no doubt as skilled and powerful as the first Shinzon's Viceroy had been.

Even more worrisome, the Doctor might already have faced his first telepathic test and failed when Norinda had stared so closely at him on the bridge, and asked him what he would like her to be.

Clearly, she was opening herself to him, and had Joseph been a real being, whatever idealized images he had in his mind of females important to him—memories of his mother, of playmates, or even of the dabo girls who apparently had made quite an impression on the boy—should have filtered out to Norinda, whose appearance would have altered in response to those images.

But Norinda hadn't changed at all. Merely agreed that the "boy" did not know what he wanted her to be.

Picard could only hope that the shapeshifter's calm acceptance of her inability to access Joseph's thoughts indicated she had had similar negative results with other subjects. Ferengi were certainly resistant to almost all forms of telepathy. But as Deanna Troi had often said about her experiences with Data, it was one thing to attempt to probe a mind, and find resistance, and quite another to sense that there was no mind to probe.

Picard was relieved that the Doctor was not bubbling over with observations and insistent queries the way the real Joseph would be, if he were in this ship, on this adventure. The fewer the interactions between Norinda and the Doctor, the better for everyone.

What Norinda's reaction to the revelation of his betrayal would be then, Picard couldn't be sure. For a being who professed to be the bearer of peace and love, she seemed to dispense anger and impatience almost as often, and in what she had done to Jim by appearing as Teilani, cruelty as well.

To Picard, it almost seemed as if Norinda's fundamental personality were as mutable as her body. But where it was becoming easy to predict how she might change her form in order to create a powerful sensual connection with her followers, Picard had yet to detect the pattern of her changes of mood. And it was a given in warfare that the most dangerous enemy was the one whose actions and reactions could not be predicted.

"Jean-Luc," Norinda said from her pilot's chair, "look ahead: Workers' Segment Five, protectorate of the *Warbird Atranar*."

The transport banked under Norinda's guidance, revealing a collection of ribbed domes spread across a black plain. Twisted tendrils of exhaust billowed up from geothermal vents. Lights sparkled behind the domes' few transparent panels.

A million slaves at least, Picard estimated. *Poor wretches*. And because their fates were linked to a Reman warbird, the Tal Shiar had marked them for death, along with the inhabitants of two other segments.

The transport returned to its original course, and once again Romulus lay directly ahead, three-quarters full, its seas and land masses clearly visible, as were several storm fronts and the intense, glowing red pinpoints of active volcanoes. The yearly close approach of Romulus and Remus, with the resulting tidal stresses, kept both worlds tectonically active. On Romulus, the results were magnificent seasonal firefalls. Whether there were similar features on Remus, Picard did not know.

Casting his eye on Romulus, he tested his memory by identifying continents and regions, and as he did so Picard began to notice that a haze was developing around the planet. He checked the ground below and saw that the haze was a band of light hugging the horizon.

The transport was approaching the terminator, passing from eternal night to eternal day.

Of course, Picard thought. He remembered the ceiling domes in the chambers of Norinda's *Jolan* Segment. She and her followers lived on the dayside of Remus. That fact raised a question.

"Norinda," Picard asked. "Is there a difference between those Remans who live on the dayside of your world, and those who live on the nightside?"

Norinda looked at Nran, and he turned in his copilot's chair to answer Picard's question.

"Almost no Remans live on the dayside. The geologists say the sunward side has been more . . . geologically active?" He looked to Norinda for confirmation he had his facts in order.

"Continue," she said, and Nran beamed like a pupil eager for the teacher's praise.

"More eruptions because of . . ."

"Tidal stress?" Picard suggested.

The Romulan nodded. "So to mine, we'd have to dig deeper. But on the nightside, not as deep. So that's where the mines are and . . . that's where most of the miners live."

Picard mulled over Nran's information. Given the two extremes of illumination on the planet, he'd wondered if there might be a second offshoot of the Romulans with eyes that could tolerate bright light. But if most of the Remans lived underground in darkness, then it followed that most of the Remans would be intolerant of light.

"So, how is it that you came to live on the dayside?" Picard asked.

"We chose to go there," Nran said. "After Shinzon."

"You're allowed to do that?" Picard asked, truly puzzled. "Choose your own living arrangements? On Remus?"

Nran looked at Norinda again, and if she said something to him, Picard couldn't see past the back of her chair.

"Since Shinzon," Nran said, "things have been different on Remus."

"Different in the sense that things are better?"

Nran was about to answer again, but Norinda reached out to touch his arm, the contact instantly making Nran lose his train of thought.

"Just different," Norinda said. "Almost home."

She touched a control and the viewport darkened. A moment later the swollen red star of the Romulan home system blazed against the viewport, and Picard thought it likely that without its protective tint, they all might have been temporarily blinded.

A chime sounded from the controls, and Picard felt the transport dip, and even through the darkened port, he could see that on this side of Remus, the black rock shone with a glaring brilliance.

He wondered how it came to pass that Norinda and her followers had been allowed to relocate to this side.

He wondered why they would want to.

But then he put those minor questions aside, and thought again of war and betrayal, and how he might be responsible for both.

Not for the first time, he remembered when he had been an explorer, and wondered if that life would ever be his again.

The next betrayal was Norinda's.

The transport landed smoothly on a target pad, then floated on antigrav skids to an airlock carved into the side of a small mountain.

An armored door swung down, and the entire chamber, easily the size of the *Enterprise*'s own hangar deck, was repressurized in seconds.

Norinda opened the side hatch of the transport and was the first to leave. Nran followed. Picard helped Joseph out, treating the hologram exactly as he would the real child, not daring to pass a signal even by the slightest eye contact, having no way to tell what level of surveillance they might be subject to.

Then they stepped down from the transport's hatch ladder to find three Reman guards waiting for them, eyes protected by dark visors, armed with drawn disruptors.

With the deadline of Opposition so close and unchangeable, Picard abandoned civil negotiation. "What is the meaning of this?" he demanded.

Norinda seemed unperturbed. "For your protection. The Tal Shiar is everywhere, and now they know you've been trying to reach them. Some among them aren't pleased by that, Jean-Luc. They think it means you've stumbled on their plans, and so they'd prefer to kill you rather than talk."

"But I have to talk with them. I must!"

"And I do know that," Norinda said. "And I will arrange it. But I am sure you'd prefer to speak with a member of the Tal Shiar who will listen to you, instead of shooting you on sight."

Now Picard felt awkward for having jumped to a negative conclusion. Norinda had been following up on her promise, after all. Complications had arisen, but that was understandable. If it was troubling for him to think of an *entente* between the Tal Shiar and the Federation, it was reasonable to think that the Tal Shiar would be equally skeptical.

"Thank you," Picard said, deciding a little civility was called for after all. "But with so little time remaining, you can understand my urgency."

Norinda smiled, but did not use whatever power she had to make a connection, mind to mind. "I do understand. And you will have your meeting." She glanced at Joseph as she continued to address Picard. "I appreciate what you've done for me and my followers in convincing Kirk to let Joseph visit today. And I will show my appreciation in return." Then she motioned to the guards. "Be patient, Jean-Luc. Not much longer."

Norinda and Nran left through one personnel door. The three Remans directed Picard and Joseph to another. Picard was intrigued to see that the guards had to duck their heads to step through the door. This facility had not been built with Remans in mind, but for Romulans.

The corridors here were also much different from

the first ones Picard had encountered when he and La Forge had escaped with the help of Norinda and her mysterious mercenary—the apparently self-propelled suit of combat armor.

Picard still hadn't reconciled those events with Norinda's protestations of love and peace. The armored unit, or hollow robot as Picard was coming to consider it, had killed the Reman doctor—hardly the act of a follower of the *Jolara*. But if it had been a robot, little more than a tool, then perhaps Norinda hadn't understood the nature of its programming.

Or maybe Norinda is simply lying about everything, Picard thought, then sighed, dismissing his paranoia with a wry smile.

"What's so funny, Uncle Jean-Luc?"

Picard gazed down at the holographic child, remembered a phrase from his own childhood. "When you're older."

Joseph grinned maliciously. "Awww, geee, you always say that!" Then he began to skip along the corridor to join the guards and pester them with childish questions.

Picard passed door after door, none of them hidden as they had been on the nightside, many of them marked in Romulan script, which Picard regretted he did not have the skills to read properly.

He did recognize some engineering terms, though, and one door was clearly marked for orbital operations—likely the flight control room. But other doors seemed to be identified simply by numbers and a single icon, as if in code.

Then the Remans stopped before a specific door, and one of them operated a control pad on the wall beside it.

The door opened, and it was clear from their body language to Picard that the Remans wanted him and Joseph to step inside. The guards would not be following.

Picard had no choice but to trust Norinda, so he took Joseph's hand and together they stepped inside where—

—Beverly Crusher ran into his arms and held him as closely as Kirk had held Joseph.

Picard was so startled, and suddenly so fearful that this was another of Norinda's manifestations that he actually pulled away.

But when he saw Crusher's expression of hurt surprise, he immediately regretted it, knew it was her.

"Jean-Luc, what's wrong?"

Honesty was always best, no matter how strange, so Picard told her the truth. "There is an alien here who is a shapeshifter, and she once appeared to me as you."

Crusher narrowed her eyes, put her hands on her hips. "Details, Jean-Luc."

"It was for just a few seconds," he said reassuringly.

"If ye don't mind, I'll just settle for shakin' your hand, Captain Picard."

Picard turned to see Mister Scott, hale and hearty. He shook the engineer's hand with enthusiasm.

"This is a most unexpected and welcome surprise," Picard said with great relief. "The last any of us had heard, you were both in need of extensive surgical treatment."

"The Remans excel at repairing traumatic injury," Crusher said. She ran a finger along her forehead and under her right eye. "I've seen the before and after imagery on my skull fracture, broken nose, and cheekbone. But look, not a scar."

Scott tapped his jaw. "Same for me. Quick treatment. But no pretty nurses."

Picard looked around the room they were in, and was surprised by how pleasant it was. In addition to a bookcase full of Romulan scrollbooks, through which Joseph now pawed, there were plants, several group-ings of what looked to be comfortable furniture, and woven wall hangings, which Picard recognized as stunning examples of a Romulan craft style about a thousand years old. These were the furnishings he would expect in a senator's country home on Romulus, not in an Assessor facility on Remus.

"When did you arrive?" he asked.

"This morning," Crusher said.

"Aye, there were a crowd of others," Scott added. "The *Jolan* people. But if you'll pardon me interrupting, is there any word on the captain and the others?"

"Jim's fine. We just left him back on the *Calypso* with La Forge."

Scott grimaced. "Och, th' poor lad'll have his work cut out for him."

"Actually, the ship's in better shape than we thought. It's a long story, but there're no surprises up there."

Crusher was in tune with him. "But surprises down here?"

"Many," Picard said. "Each with an equally long story."

"Which you will tell us another time, no doubt," she said.

"No doubt at all." Picard looked past her and Scott to see Joseph intently reading a scrollbook. "Joseph? You're being rude not saying hello to your Uncle Scott and Doctor Crusher."

"Sorrr-eee," Joseph said, but he made no move to stop reading.

"Why is he down here?" Crusher asked.

"Aye, I thought the captain was dead set against th' lad setting foot on Remus."

Picard knew he couldn't risk saying anything, or even hinting what the real story was. "It's a favor to me. I'll explain later."

"Any idea when that might be?" Scott asked. "Have they said anything about how long they might be keeping us here?"

"I . . . would hope we'll be back on the *Calypso* within the day."

"That's good to know," Scott said.

"But why the delay?" Crusher asked.

"Norinda—she's the woman, actually, she's the shapeshifting alien who founded the *Jolan* Movement—she's arranging a meeting for me. Then we'll go."

Scott scratched the back of his head. "Norinda . . . I know that name . . . but a shapechanger?"

Before Picard could remind Scott where he had first encountered Norinda, the door swung open, and a Romulan entered carrying a small silver case.

"*Farr Jolan*," he said. "I am Zol. I am here to see the child."

As if they had discussed what to do beforehand, the three adults turned to form a wall, shoulder to shoulder, blocking Zol from Joseph.

"For what reason?" Picard asked.

Zol placed his silver case on a table and opened it, as if there were nothing Picard or the others could say or do to keep him from Joseph. "I am here at the request of the *Jolara*."

"I understand that," Picard said. "But I ask again: What do you want with him?"

Zol held up a slender, silver object and made an adjustment to it. It looked familiar to Picard, but Crusher recognized it right away.

"That's a blood extractor. Are you a physician?"

Zol took another instrument from his case, laid it out beside the first. "I am."

"Well, so am I," Crusher said. "And Joseph is my patient. And I absolutely forbid you to perform any procedures on him until you gain the consent of his father."

"Consent has been given."

"Show it to me."

Zol gestured to Joseph, who now stood behind Picard, looking past him as if he were truly frightened. "The child is here."

Picard had no intention of letting the Romulan anywhere near the holographic boy. "Joseph is here to meet his mother's relatives and for no other reason."

Zol approached the adults with a larger instrument in hand. "How are we to know his kin without having his genetic profile? You will stand aside."

"I will not."

Zol didn't argue. He simply raised the instrument he carried and the moment Picard recognized it as a disruptor, Zol fired.

The setting was low stun, and Picard fell back onto a chair, gasping for breath, without the muscle coordination to stand. Two more quick shots took care of Crusher and Scott, and no one was able to shout at Joseph to run.

Joseph was doing his best to act the part and keep the Romulan away. He screamed in terror, threw every object he could find—including Zol's own medical case—and ran back and forth with speed that Picard could see bordered almost on the impossible.

Another doctor might have given up, affected by the child's reaction. But Zol wasn't that kind of being. Distress in others did not concern him.

So he did what Picard knew he would do.

He shot Joseph.

The disruptor blast made Joseph's form shimmer, like a faulty holodeck image, and Picard saw Zol's shocked reaction.

The disguised Doctor tried to cover for his mistake, spoke into his wrist as if he wore a communicator there, and shouted, *"Beam me up!"* A moment later, he disappeared in a curtain of light, as if he had been beamed away.

But Zol appeared to be prepared for that subterfuge, and immediately pulled a tricorder from his belt, scanned the room, and fired a wide burst.

Picard saw the sparkling outline of the Doctor take shape, as if he were a sculpture made of water.

Zol fired again, this time with pinpoint accuracy, hitting the one part of the Doctor that wasn't illusory—his holoemitter, no larger than a combadge.

A flash of sparks burst from the small device, and the outline vanished as the holoemitter dropped straight to the floor.

Zol walked back to Picard, looked down on him with a sneer.

"Jolan True," he said.

And then he left.

24

Kirk enjoyed seeing Riker's and Worf's reaction to the bridge of the *Calypso*. They were both as aghast as he had been.

"This is not a Starfleet vessel," Worf had grumbled.

"Is too," Joseph had countered.

And then Worf had fixed the boy with a steely glare and growled, "Is *not*," and that had been the end of the debate.

In the briefing that followed, Kirk was determined to bring together all the information the participants in this mission had previously kept compartmentalized. So La Forge again recounted, for Riker's and Worf's benefit, everything he and Picard had learned from Norinda about the Tal Shiar's plans for war. Riker relayed Admiral Janeway's analysis of the situation as established by Starfleet Intelligence. Kirk explained what he knew of Norinda's first arrival in this galaxy.

And when they had shared all that they knew, Kirk could see that each of them, McCoy and Worf and even Joseph included, felt stronger, more secure. Stronger because, no longer in opposition with one another, they could now face the enemy together. More secure, because their stories fit together. They at last knew the truth.

But afterward, Riker still felt the need to take Kirk aside by the steps on the bridge. Kirk knew why, and asked McCoy to join them.

"Aren't you feeling used?" Riker asked.

"By Starfleet?" Kirk said. "Always."

"But Janeway sent you to search for the people who murdered Spock, even though Starfleet already had that information."

"No, they didn't," Kirk said.

McCoy supplied more explanation. "Jim means Starfleet might have known the group responsible—the Tal Shiar—but they didn't and still don't know the individuals who did it. Those are the people we have to find."

Riker shook his head, still conflicted. "But Starfleet's going to make a deal with the Tal Shiar," he said. "At least, the captain is going to attempt it." He studied Kirk closely. "If I was asked to be part of a mission to negotiate with the murderers of someone close to me, I don't think I could do it."

Kirk pitied and envied Riker's relative youth—the passion of a freshly minted starship captain. "The deal Jean-Luc wants to make with the Tal Shiar isn't to reward them, Will. It's a way to contain and diminish them. Is it the best way? I don't know. But what's important, and what Spock would want, is that Starfleet isn't turning a blind eye to what happened."

Kirk put his hand on Riker's shoulder, as if giving a benediction. "You're a starship captain, not a god. There are going to be times when you won't be able to find solutions for the problems you face; you'll only be able to choose directions that someday, maybe, if you're lucky, will take you where you want to go. I think even Jean-Luc would agree with me that most of the times, it's the journey that's important, not the destination."

Riker's quick smile was infectious. "And the rest of the time, it's the waiting, right?"

"Until you're my age," McCoy said. "Then it's *all* waiting."

As the men laughed, their discussion over, Joseph apparently deemed the moment right to hold Riker to his promise.

"Captain Riker—can you show me your yacht *now?*"

"Is that how you got here?" Kirk asked sharply. "Captain's yacht? Not a shuttle?"

Riker grinned. "The yacht can do warp nine. Rank hath its privileges."

But Kirk didn't share Riker's levity. "Weren't you challenged?"

"I filed a flight plan from Latium. I was already in Romulan space."

Riker hadn't understood the point of his question. Kirk quickly made it clearer.

"We're a civilian ship," he said, "and we had to hold position at the Neutral Zone, at gunpoint, until we were escorted here. A captain's yacht is not a diplomatic vessel—it's a nicely appointed troop carrier. I don't see how the Romulans let you into their home system without firing a shot across your bow."

Kirk had gotten Riker's attention. Riker swirled the liquid in his coffee cup, thinking. "Maybe the difference was . . . you originally had a flight plan for Romulus, and mine was for Remus."

"So all of a sudden the Romulans don't care who shows up around their sister planet?" Kirk asked.

Now even McCoy looked thoughtful, trying to make sense of the idea that the Romulans, renowned for their paranoia and sense of intrigue, apparently saw no need for either in Reman space.

"In fact, gentlemen," Kirk continued, "when you think about it, if the Tal Shiar *are* planning to take action against Remus, then they'd *have* to be watching every ship arrival and departure here. Because if their enemies have discovered their plans, this is where and when an enemy would take action to stop them."

"And here we are," McCoy said slowly, "an abandoned Federation-registry vessel allowed to remain on orbit, and a Starfleet captain's yacht docked with us . . . and no one's even been by to shine a searchlight on our hull."

"It is as if we're being deliberately ignored," Riker added.

Kirk didn't agree. "Ignored? Highly unlikely, especially among Romulans."

"Or else," Riker offered, "they already know all about us, and know we aren't a threat."

But Kirk pointed out the flaw in that reasoning, too. "There's only one way anyone could know who we are and what we're doing here, Will. Instead of Norinda's *Jolan* Movement having infiltrated the Tal Shiar, the Tal Shiar has infiltrated them."

McCoy intervened abruptly. "I hate to use this kind of language, but if *that's* true, then . . . then logic dictates everything Norinda has told us about the Tal Shiar and their plans is a lie, unknowingly, or otherwise."

"Which means," Kirk said, "we've just gone from

having all the information about what's going on here, to having none of it, in less than five minutes."

Their somber and discouraging realization was interrupted by La Forge calling out from communications. "Captain Kirk! We're getting a hail. It's Norinda."

Kirk reached out to rub his son's head, thinking with a guilty start that his young son had again perhaps heard more than he needed to. "Sorry, Joseph. Captain Riker's tour has to wait. And you have to stand way over there by Geordi and keep out of sight."

When Joseph was dutifully beyond the range of the bridge's visual imagers, Kirk called down to La Forge, "On screen."

Norinda appeared in the center viewscreen on the forward bulkhead. The banks of exotic, multihued flowers behind her strongly reminded Kirk of the greenhouse deck of her ship, where they had first met in person. If she had chosen the backdrop for that reason, she'd done so in vain. He was immune to such nostalgia now.

"Listen carefully, Kirk." Norinda's tone was cold, implacable. "We discovered your deception. Steps—"

"What deception?" Kirk interrupted as innocently as he could.

"The holographic replica of your child."

"What? That's impossible. You think I don't know my own son?"

Norinda's voice hardened. "Steps are being taken to punish Picard, and Crusher, and Scott. However—"

"Harm them and I'll—"

This time, Norinda cut him off. "However! They will be returned to you, and Picard will be free to contact the Tal Shiar, once you have sent T'Kol T'Lan down to me—to learn of his true heritage on Remus. In exchange, I offer you the *lives of Picard and your friends and the billions of others who will be drawn into the civil war. In nineteen minutes, your ship's orbit will bring you within transporter range of the Jolan Segment. Beam down T'Kol T'Lan then, or everyone dies.*" She pressed a control offscreen. "*Transmitting co-ordinates. Nineteen minutes.*"

Norinda's image winked off the screen, replaced by a forward sensor view of Remus, the terminator on the horizon, the dayside glowing brilliantly beyond.

Kirk was left staring into the expanding field of light, and slowly he became aware that everyone on the bridge was waiting for the captain to give the word; fearing that the father would be unable to do so.

But what the others didn't understand, Kirk knew, was that this was not a decision that belonged only to him.

"Joseph," Kirk said.

His son stood up beside La Forge. "Yes, sir."

Kirk chose his words carefully. "Did you understand what that woman said?"

Joseph chewed his lip for a moment, troubled. "If I don't beam down, then she's going to hurt Uncle Jean-Luc, and Uncle Scotty, and Doctor Crusher. And there's going to be a war."

"What do you think about that?"

"I don't think she should hurt anyone. And there shouldn't be a war."

Kirk used every technique Spock had ever taught him to keep his face from registering what he felt. He could not lead his child in this. "What do you think we should do?"

Joseph straightened, as he had when he had spoken to Admiral Janeway. "She's a bad guy. We should stop her, Dad."

"You mean, beam down there, as she said?"

Kirk saw Joseph's eyes register apprehension. At far too young an age, he was faced with what all children want and fear at the same time: control.

"By myself?" he asked.

"No," Kirk answered. "Never by yourself."

"Us?"

Kirk nodded. As terrifying as this felt to him, the decision had to be his son's. Kirk knew it was the only way either of them could ever live with the results of what might happen.

Joseph held firm. "We should beam down, Dad. We should stop the bad guys from hurting anyone."

Pride and fear mixed equally in Kirk as he motioned to Joseph to come to him.

"Mister La Forge," he said, "contact Norinda. Tell her Joseph and I will beam down together in a transporter swap. Tell her that Captain Picard, Mister Scott, and Doctor Crusher are to be on the pad at her location or there is no deal."

"Aye, sir," La Forge said, and he turned to his board.

With Joseph at his side, Kirk went to Worf. "Mister Worf, by any chance would you have a *bat'leth*?"

Worf squared his shoulders. "A *bat'leth* would be difficult to conceal. But I am a Klingon warrior in Romulan space. I sharpened my *mek'leth* on the journey here." He leaned forward. "And I have daggers."

Kirk approved. The *mek'leth* was the Klingon short sword. And he was familiar with it. "May we borrow them?"

Worf bared his teeth as if he were personally going into battle. "I would be honored."

Riker joined them. "You know, we do have hand phasers on the yacht."

"I doubt they'll make it past the transporter filters, but you know what else we could use?"

Riker's broad grin eclipsed his beard. "A starship? Fortunately, I know just where to find one."

Kirk looked across the bridge, saw McCoy's scowl, knew he didn't approve. But it was far too late to worry about exposing Joseph to danger. Starfleet Intelligence had failed them all in that regard.

All Kirk could do now was remain determined not to repeat the error.

And with his son at his side, he was ready to stop the bad guys.

25

JOLAN SEGMENT, STARDATE 57488.2

"Two minutes, Captain," La Forge said.

Kirk crouched down by Joseph, to look into his son's eyes as an equal. "Say it again," Kirk prompted.

Joseph sighed, and Kirk could see how nervous he was. But he knew that would pass once they were on their way.

"The bad guys won't hurt me," Joseph recited. "They think that I'm special and that I can help them. But they might tell me lies about Mommy and you. And I don't believe lies."

"I love you," Kirk told his child. "And your mother loved you."

A small smile appeared on Joseph's face as he fell into one of their bedtime rituals. "How much did she love me?"

"More than all the stars you can see. More than all the stars you can't see. More than all the stars that ever were or will be . . ."

They recited the last line together, each tapping a finger against the other's nose. "And that's how much I love you, too!"

Kirk prepared himself and Joseph. "Whatever they tell you, don't ever forget that."

"I won't," Joseph said, then added in Klingon, *"jIH lay'."*

"One minute," La Forge said. "I have three life-forms on the pad in the target chamber . . . Picard . . . Crusher . . . and Scott, confirmed. Linking carrier waves."

Kirk stood beside Joseph on the single large pad in the bay. Kirk wore the same civilian clothes and jacket he had on when the *Calypso* had been boarded by the still unidentified intruders. He had a hand phaser in one pocket, a large civilian communicator in another, and Worf's *mek'leth* slung in a back harness under his jacket. The phaser would not get past the weapons filter on Norinda's transporter, but if it were a typical Romulan installation, bladed weapons were so common that the *mek'leth* might not be noticed.

Joseph wore clean overalls, bright red, with a civilian communicator sealed in his chest pouch, and a *d'k tahg* dagger in a scabbard attached to a loop at his waist. He was under strict orders never to use it against a person, but Kirk could imagine many scenarios in which a good knife could be a useful tool.

"Carrier waves linked," La Forge said. "Fifteen seconds."

"Just remember the plan," Kirk said to Riker, Worf, and McCoy, who stood with La Forge behind the operator's station at the front of the bay. "You've got twenty-four hours to stop that war. So get Picard to the Tal Shiar first, *then* come looking for us."

Kirk could see that they all had a comment they wanted to add, probably saying how much they hated that plan. But Joseph's presence constrained them.

"Energizing . . ." La Forge said.

Kirk's hand squeezed Joseph's shoulder as the transporter bay dissolved into light all around them. A moment of nonexistence later, the light shimmered away, to show that the bay had been replaced by a vast greenhouse dome, with a grass floor, large shade trees, and even a rushing stream.

Kirk looked around from the vantage point of the raised transporter platform he and Joseph stood on. Immediately, he saw Norinda, standing by a transporter console with Virron, Sen, Nran, and a fourth Romulan unknown to him.

Kirk checked his pocket and the phaser was missing as he had expected. But he felt the welcome pressure of the *mek'leth* on his back, and the civilian communicator was with him as well.

He pulled it out, switched it on. "Kirk to *Calypso*. Are they on board?"

La Forge replied promptly. *"All present, in good health. Captain Picard requests the contact information for the . . . representative that Norinda promised him."*

Kirk stepped down from the platform and Joseph followed, staying close.

"Do you have that information?" Kirk asked.

Norinda held out her hand for the communicator.

Kirk gave it to her.

"Captain Picard," she said into the communicator, "I offered you love. I offered you peace. I offered you understanding. You rejected it all. You lied to me, and you deceived me."

Kirk stared at Norinda. She was building to something. She was speaking as if she did not even need to hear Picard's response.

Picard did not seem to sense what Kirk had.

"I told you the truth. I told you that sometimes there were other things we needed, but that we were both committed to stopping this war."

"I think you don't fear war enough," Norinda said. "I think you do not really know what war is. So now, you will have your chance to learn. And perhaps when the war is over—in the months or years or decades it will take to spread through your precious galactic quadrants—*then* you will know what it means to reject love, and so, at last, you will come to embrace it."

"Don't do this," Kirk said to her. But she wasn't listening to him any more than she was to Picard.

"Norinda," Picard's voice pleaded. *"I do know war. That's why I must stop this one. Give me the name you promised! While there's still time."*

"You should not have rejected me," Norinda said. *"Jolan True."* Then with sudden violence, she threw the communicator onto the grass and in the instant it hit, Nran fired a disruptor and destroyed it.

Kirk reached for Norinda's arm, forcing her to listen to him. "You *can't* condemn millions to death because Picard disappointed you!"

With unexpected strength, Norinda pulled her arm from his grip. "Picard chose death over love. You all do."

"Picard did what he thought best—for peace! If you're angry about the holographic duplicate of my son, look!" Kirk waved his hand at Joseph. "Here he is! I've kept my word! Show us all that you know what love is. Show us all that you can forgive!"

Norinda shook her head. "You understand nothing about love. When *all* are loved, when *all* share peace and understanding, then *all* are the same, and there is no need for forgiveness."

"But you heard Picard. We're not all the same."

"In time," Norinda said, "you will be. Totally the same."

With that, she took her attention from Kirk, held out her hand to Joseph. "T'Kol T'Lan, I am Norinda."

"I know," Joseph said in a sullen, challenging tone.

Norinda smiled.

Kirk watched with horror as her features began to subtly change, with her Romulan forehead smoothing and expanding, growing fine Klingon ridges.

"Joseph! Look away from her!" Kirk called out in warning to his son.

Norinda's face reset to its Romulan form in seconds as she turned to Kirk. "Why deny your son? You all want something. Something I can give." She pointed to the four Romulans. "They understand. They accept my gifts. But not your friends. Not you. Why?!"

To Kirk, the answer was simple. "Because your gifts aren't real," he said, moving to stand between her and his son. Shielding Joseph from what he should not see.

But Norinda merely reached out to the portable transporter console, and activated several controls and a transporter warble began to sound.

She was beaming something—or someone—in.

A column of light formed on the raised platform.

Kirk readied to defend himself and Joseph should a Reman bodyguard suddenly appear and attack. He knew it couldn't be anyone from the *Calypso*. The ship was already out of range.

"Here is a gift," Norinda said. "It is what you want. And it is real. Will you reject this, too?"

And then the light faded.

Kirk gasped.

It was Spock.

26

S.S. CALYPSO, STARDATE 57488.3

Beverly Crusher was insistent. "We have no choice, Jean-Luc! We *have* to warn them. It's the last chance we have to stop the war."

"And it could be just the thing that starts it," Picard argued.

Crusher threw her padd on the fold-down chart table in the *Titan's* yacht, still docked with the *Calypso*. He, McCoy, and Scott were seated at the table. Crusher, Riker, Worf, and La Forge were standing around it.

"If we do nothing, Jean-Luc, it's going to start anyway. So what do we have to lose?"

Picard matched her throwing of the padd by banging his fist on the table. "I will not gamble with the lives of billions of people simply because I don't know what else to do!"

"How about a measured warning?" Riker suggested, and Picard understood he was trying to find a middle ground. "I could get word to the commanders I deal with in the Romulan Fleet."

"But what could they do in less than a day?" Picard asked.

Worf snorted in derision. "They would evacuate their friends and family from likely target zones, then applaud the destruction of Remus."

"We have no time left for diplomatic initiatives," Picard said. "Even if we had tried that from the beginning, there are too many factions on Romulus, too many differing opinions on how Remus should be handled. And there'd be no way to tell if Tal Shiar operatives were manipulating the message."

"There is another possibility," Worf suggested. Picard and everyone else in the passenger cabin looked at the resolute Klingon. "The *Titan* will arrive in less than six hours. That will give us approximately ten hours to attack and disable the three Reman warbirds that the Tal Shiar hope will launch a counterattack on Romulus."

"Now that's a Klingon for you," McCoy said. "Stop a civil war by starting an interplanetary one."

Worf growled under his breath. "Our attacks on the warbirds will not be an act of war. It will be a preemptive strike to preserve peace."

Picard knew they didn't have time for McCoy and Worf to start a debate that was in reality an argument neither could win, so he intervened at once. "That still does nothing for the millions of Remans who will be killed when their communes are destroyed at the Hour of Opposition. And in the confusion that would certainly arise between a Starfleet vessel attacking Reman ships . . ." Picard locked eyes with the two verbal combatants. ". . . followed by explosions in Reman communities, there is a very good chance that interplanetary war could be triggered."

"Then why don't we find the bombs," La Forge said, "or whatever it is that the Tal Shiar are going to use to destroy the communes? No bombs. No destruction. No reason for the crews of the warbirds to take revenge."

"Unfortunately," Picard said to clarify their situation, "Norinda did not specifically say that bombs would be used. Life-support systems might be poisoned. Ships might be deliberately crashed into the surface domes. Power plants could be sabotaged. The food and water supplies. We just wouldn't know what we were searching for."

"But surely there's nothin' wrong with at least makin' the attempt?" Scott asked. "We don't have all the answers, but we do have some. We know the three communities that have been targeted, the ones linked to the warbirds *Atranar, Braul,* and *Vortral.* With the *Titan's* sensors, we'd have a very good chance o' spottin' the most likely means of mass destruction." He listed them on his fingers. "Antimatter bomb. Fusion. Fission. And if we pick th' proper orbit so we're equidistant from all three communities at th' Hour of Opposition, then we can certainly protect them from missiles, torpedoes, or crashing spacecraft."

No one objected right away, and Picard took that as a good sign.

Then La Forge added his support. "Captain, I agree with Scotty. It's a place to start."

"Very well," Picard said, looking around at his team. "Do we have any way of accessing the Romulan Central Information Net? Is there a Reman equivalent? Anything that would give us maps and specifications for the three communes so the *Titan* will be able to identify anything out of the ordinary?"

Riker seemed confident he could access the necessary information as part of a general request for trade data. He knew the people to contact on Romulus, which by now was only a few minutes distant by warp.

"Then let's get started," Picard said, and dismissed the group to begin their work.

Scott was right; the attempt had to be made.

Even if it was too little and too late.

27

Kirk stared at a ghost.

He told himself that what he saw stepping down from the transporter pad in the center of the greenhouse chamber was just another of Norinda's cruel illusions.

Spock was dead. Three thousand Romulans had witnessed his murder. Kirk had seen the visual sensor recordings. Felt the agony of loss.

"Captain," Spock said.

He stood before Kirk in a version of a Romulan assessor's uniform. He looked more gaunt than the last time Kirk had seen him, somehow frailer, as if he had succumbed to an illness or—

"Spock?" Kirk said. "Is it you?"

"Given that we are both acquainted with Norinda's skill as a shapeshifter, your hesitation in accepting the evidence of your eyes is understandable. However, logic suggests that—"

"It *is* you!" Kirk just managed to refrain from embracing Spock, but Joseph felt no such constraints.

"Uncle Spock? Are you all right?"

"As well as can be expected," Spock said as he gently extricated himself from a hearty hug around his legs.

Kirk shot a glance back at Norinda and the Romulans. They were huddled together, discussing something of greater importance than Spock's return from the dead.

Kirk looked down at his son, who now stood between him and Spock. "Joseph, this is a time to be quiet and stay close, okay?"

"Okay." Joseph looked up wide-eyed, but unafraid.

"I *need* to know," Kirk said to Spock. "How is this possible?"

Spock raised an eyebrow, as if Kirk had asked a question to which he should already know the answer. "Captain, 'when you have eliminated all which is impossible'—"

Kirk finished it. "—'then whatever remains, however improbable, must be the truth.' You didn't die."

"Not this time."

"The assassination was staged?"

"I believed a dramatic event was necessary to appeal to the emotionalism of the Romulans, in order to call attention to reunification of our people."

"*You* believed?" Kirk said. "*You* staged your own murder?"

"I was unwilling to risk anyone's life but my own. And my time in the public eye is over."

Kirk looked again at Norinda, this time saw her watching him, or, more probably, Joseph. "You can tell me more later."

He dropped his voice. "Spock, how did you get here? Why are you with her?"

Spock shrugged. "I am her prisoner, for reasons which I do not entirely fathom."

Kirk saw Norinda smile at the fourth Romulan whom he had never met.

"Spock, this is important. These people think that Joseph is the new Shinzon."

Kirk could tell Spock was startled by that fact by the quiet way he said, "Indeed."

"But right now there's a civil war about to start, between Romulus and Remus."

"Tensions have been high since the coup, but—"

"No," Kirk urgently interrupted. "The situation's being manipulated. Staged. Spock, I have to know. Was *your* staged death completely your idea? Or did you have help?"

"I had help, of course. It required considerable logistical support."

"Then tell me if any of this sounds familiar," Kirk said.

"In what way?"

"Just listen. Starfleet was convinced you were murdered by agents of the Tal Shiar."

Spock blinked, another sign of intense reaction. "That is not logical."

"I don't care what's logical. I'm telling you what Starfleet believes. They sent Bones and me here to investigate your death, to find your murderers, and then Picard came with us so he could make an offer to those same people."

"What is the nature of the offer?"

Norinda began walking toward the transporter platform and the fourth Romulan was at her side. Kirk spoke quickly in the few private moments that he and Spock had left to them.

"In addition to being responsible for your death, the Tal Shiar are also supposed to be the ones who are

going to stage a series of attacks that will lead to an outbreak of war between Romulus and Remus. But if the
Tal Shiar didn't murder you—"

This time, Spock completed the conclusion for
Kirk. "—then logic suggests they are also not responsible for whatever staged events are intended to start
the war."

"But there is one person who's tied to both events."

"Then logically, that person is the one responsible."

Kirk turned to face Norinda as she stepped up behind him.

"It's you," he said. "There is no Tal Shiar. It's the
Jolan Movement that's going to start the war."

For a moment, Kirk thought Norinda might deny his
accusation. But she didn't. "This war is how peace will
come to you."

"Insane," Kirk said.

"Illogical," Spock added.

"You're a bad guy," Joseph told her.

Kirk did not admonish him for breaking silence. His
son was right.

But Norinda didn't respond to any of those pronouncements. "I offer you love and peace and—"

"Understanding, I know," Kirk said. "We've all
heard it. And we'll all keep rejecting it because you're
not offering love at all. All you want is for us to accept
you. But you're not willing to accept *us*. You don't want
to be loved—you want to be worshipped."

Norinda seemed to grow taller, her shoulders
broader. "When the Hour of Opposition comes and the
bombs go off and the war begins, you will see your
worlds and your people consumed by hate and war
and confusion. And when you have seen worlds die because you would not accept the true reality of exis-

tence, *then* you will understand. And then, you *will* accept the Peace of the Totality."

Kirk stepped back from Norinda as her features continued to change, becoming Reman.

"When we met," Kirk said, "you told me you were running from the Totality. But you're part of it, aren't you?"

"So are you, Kirk. You just don't know it yet!"

Norinda loomed over Kirk now. Ears and face and fangs carved from gray stone, eyes disappearing behind the impenetrably dark visor that grew and formed across them, she pointed a jagged claw at Joseph. "Zol," she growled, "take the boy!"

Those three words freed Kirk.

Without thought he slapped his hand to his back beneath his jacket and in one swift arc had drawn his *mek'leth* and slashed at Zol.

The Romulan stumbled to the grass with a cry of pain, green blood spurting from the deep cut on his forearm.

Kirk kept in front of Joseph as Norinda backed away.

"Spock—there's a communicator in Joseph's pouch. Hail the *Calypso.*"

Norinda shouted to the three Romulans cowering by the transporter console. "Raise transport shields! Activate subspace jammers!"

Kirk didn't care that he was too late to stop those orders. He just wanted to stop Norinda.

So he ran at her, *mek'leth* held high, and even as she shrank before him, he spun the weapon in a gleaming arc to deliver a *k'rel tagh* stroke that angled down through her shoulder and into her chest and—

—Norinda's torso *exploded* into a spray of black

powder and all resistance to the *mek'leth* vanished, throwing Kirk completely off balance and sending him tumbling to the ground.

Kirk twisted to avoid landing on his own blade, then looked back at Norinda to see her torso re-form out of a swirling black cloud, as if he were watching a fire in reverse, with the smoke billowing back to its point of origin.

Then she was whole again, but in a patchwork confusion of different aspects. Her face rippled from Klingon to Andorian to Romulan, while her chest heaved out, becoming Tellarite, then collapsed inward, human.

But like ripples in still water, the confusion slowed and she settled into a single form—Romulan. But she fell to her knees without awareness, unconscious.

"Spock! The transporter!"

Kirk sprinted for the transporter console, hoping that Virron and Sen and Nran were all so terrified by what they had witnessed that they had neglected to follow Norinda's orders. To keep them terrified, he slashed his *mek'leth* back and forth while shouting a Klingon battle cry.

They scattered like panicked antelope bounding away from a lion.

Kirk swiftly checked the transporter controls as Spock and Joseph hurried to join him. "Everything seems functional. Did you raise the *Calypso?*"

"No response," Spock said.

Kirk turned the transporter controls over to Spock, took the communicator. It was functioning properly. "Kirk to *Calypso!*"

Still nothing.

"Captain, the transporter is operational. But I will need coordinates for our destination."

"Understood, Spock."

Why wasn't the communicator working? It didn't make sense. Unless there was something wrong on the *Calypso.*

Kirk tried again, and as if his *Enterprise* herself had suddenly entered orbit, he had his answer. The right one.

"Scott here, Captain."

28

S.S. CALYPSO, STARDATE 57488.3

Picard entered the bridge on the run, brought by Scott's urgent summons.

"It's Captain Kirk," the engineer said as he stepped back from the communications console. "He needs to talk to you right away. And he's with Mister Spock!"

Picard didn't even stop to consider the startling news. He sat down in Scott's place and hit the transmit control.

"Picard here, Jim. And did I hear correctly. Is Ambassador Spock with you?"

"He's here, Jean-Luc, and it's quite a story. But what we've found out is that there is no Tal Shiar involvement in the attacks that are planned to start the civil war. It's the Jolan Movement! They're the ones responsible."

"Norinda's people." Picard suddenly realized that Norinda had not been talking about war in the abstract. "Did you find out anything else about the attacks? We need to know how they plan to destroy the workers' communes."

"All she said was that the bombs will go off at the Hour of Opposition."

"You're sure of that? She said *bombs* will go off?"

"*Her words exactly.*"

Picard decided he might as well wish for the impossible. "I don't suppose she told you where the bombs are hidden?"

"*No,*" Kirk replied. "*But there seems to be a pattern to the type of environment she likes, and it's not one that many Remans would ever enter. Check for greenhouse domes, anyplace hot and too bright for Remans.*"

Picard agreed with Kirk's logic. "That's a good place to start. Now what is your situation with those people? Any idea when they'll permit you to come back?"

"*Right now, everything seems under control. All we need are some transport coordinates and a friendly starship.*"

Picard heard the ease in his friend's voice and was curious to know what had happened. When Kirk and his son had beamed off the *Calypso,* Picard had even wondered if he might never see Kirk again. Evidently, things had taken a turn for the better, especially with the miraculous return of Spock.

"I'd be happy to oblige," Picard transmitted. "Let me check our position." Picard looked over to find La Forge at navigation. "Geordi—how long until Kirk will be within range of the *Calypso*'s transporter?"

La Forge checked the numbers. "On this orbit, thirty-two minutes." He exhaled noisily. "I sure miss the *Enterprise.*"

Picard agreed wholeheartedly. The transporters on that starship had enough range and power to beam people from the opposite side of an Earth-sized planet. For most transporter operations, he rarely, if ever, had to take into account the ship's orbit.

Picard hit the transmit control. "We'll be by in half an hour, Jim. Can you hold out till then?"

Picard got his answer when he released the control. Joseph was screaming in fear.

Kirk whirled around and dropped the communicator the instant his child cried out.

It was impossible, but Norinda had him, one arm clutching his chest, the other squeezing his neck in the V of her elbow.

How had she moved so quickly? While he was using the communicator to talk with Picard, he'd kept watch on her unmoving, kneeling form at least fifty meters away.

Kirk shot a glance back to where she'd been only seconds ago and—

—*she was still there!* Unraveling strand by strand as a long black cord snaked from her kneeling figure to the Norinda who held his struggling child.

The kneeling Norinda was nothing more than a paper-thin shell, used to create a duplicate Norinda. Somehow the shell's interior volume had become a tendril that could reach out unseen, behind his child.

But Kirk was immune to awe or fear of alien life-forms, no matter how incomprehensible. The safety of his son was at stake. Remembering Norinda's reaction to his first *mek'leth* attack, Kirk rushed for the black cord, the weapon already in his hands.

Spock was doing his best to keep Norinda distracted, by circling around her to keep her back to Kirk.

Kirk swung the blade down to sever the cord of what he guessed was some type of nanotechnology. That was one way to explain Norinda's particular abilities.

But when the *mek'leth* sliced through the cord, the section of it leading to what was left of the kneeling Norinda shell suddenly puffed into a cloud of black dust. The side leading to the second Norinda snapped like an elastic cord and hissed through the grass and was instantly absorbed by the duplicate's body.

With Spock on one side of her and Kirk on the other, Norinda began to back toward the transporter console, as if seeking its shelter.

Joseph screamed again and kicked his legs violently against Norinda's side. Norinda's hand clamped over his mouth, and Joseph's screams faded.

"Put him down," Kirk called out, tortured by his son's cries. "He's a child. There's nothing he needs that you can give him."

Norinda did not answer. She had not spoken since she had captured Joseph. Kirk worried that meant she had no further interest in bargaining.

He was now within two meters of her, but knew he wouldn't dare take a chance at swinging his *mek'leth* so close to his son.

"Tell me what *you* want, Norinda."

But Norinda merely stepped back from him with jerky, metronome precision, her movements like that of a machine.

Spock took his chance. Kirk saw him stretch across the console from behind Norinda to slam his hand down on her shoulder and pinch whatever analogues of nerves and muscles she must have there.

But Spock's fingers plunged *into* Norinda, as if her body were no more substantial than froth on an ocean wave, and before he could pull his hand back, her flesh became solid again and trapped him.

"Let go of them both!" Kirk shouted to her. "Let go of them and you can have me!"

"I already do." Norinda's whisper was soft in Kirk's ear.

The Norinda that held his son and Spock abruptly imploded and a cloud of black sand rained down to the ground, freeing both of them as Kirk felt a new Norinda's arms wrap around him from behind. He shouted for Joseph and Spock to run, to wait for Picard to arrive.

Kirk tried to pull away, but the new Norinda merged with the fabric of his jacket and held him in place. He twisted from side to side, seeking any chance to drive the razor-edged *mek'leth* into his captor.

But suddenly he was yanked high in the air, then thrown down so violently that the *mek'leth* flew from his grasp.

Kirk lay flat on his back on the grass, gasping, eyes blinded by crimson fire, the Romulan sun blazing down through the overhead dome.

A shadow fell over him.

Norinda. A solid black silhouette against the sun.

Her hand reached down, lifted him to his feet. He looked past her, searching for Joseph . . . Spock.

"Don't look for them," Norinda said. "Look at me."

Kirk complied, hoping at least that with her focus on him, Joseph and Spock might escape her.

"I'm going to show you the true reality of existence."

Norinda tightened her grip on his hand.

"Now you'll understand," she said. "Now you'll know *forever*. . . ."

Kirk felt a jolt of electric pain singe his hand as Norinda's hand first lost focus, then softened, then broke up into tiny black cubes that broke again and again into smaller and smaller cubes.

Then his hand softened and broke into darkness.

Pain flashed through Kirk's dissolving arm.

But then Norinda gasped in surprise—as a *d'k tahg* blade punched through her chest from behind. An instant later, her grip on Kirk dissolved.

Kirk fell away from her, his arm on fire as it resolidified, to see Joseph, his Klingon *d'k tahg* in upraised hand, standing in a swirling cloud of smoke.

Kirk rushed forward and scooped his son up and out of the cloud of fine dark particles that had been Norinda. Joseph wriggled in his father's arms.

"Did ya see that, Uncle Spock?" the child asked excitedly.

"Indeed, I did," Spock said.

"Me and my dad, we got the bad guy!"

"Indeed, you did."

Kirk and Spock faced each other then, and without a word Spock looked to the side, and Kirk followed his gaze to see a dark column of smoke beginning to gather by a bank of flowers.

"Theories, Spock?" Kirk asked, still shaken by what might have been. And still might be.

"Several. But they can wait until we're safely away."

As Spock retrieved the dropped communicator to set the transporter controls for beam-out, Kirk kept a wary eye on the cloud. It was taking on a vaguely humanoid shape, and if it followed the same pattern as before, in a few minutes there could be another Norinda in the chamber. He wasn't sure they could hold their positions until the *Calypso* was back in range.

But as soon as Spock activated the communicator, Picard made contact. When he and his crew had heard Joseph's cries, the *Calypso* had changed orbits, coming in lower and faster to arrive more quickly, then climbing a higher and slower orbit to increase her time over the beam-up coordinates.

Kirk carried Joseph to the transporter platform and the child sat cross-legged in the center of it, still excited by his adventure, but exhausted.

Kirk gathered the *mek'leth* and the *d'k tahg* blade and stepped onto the pad beside his son.

Spock locked carrier waves with the *Calypso* and prepared to set a ten-second timer on the transporter console.

It was then Kirk saw that the cloud was gone.

It took only a second for the meaning of that to register.

"Spock! Run!"

Spock didn't look up. He rapidly entered the commands for the timer.

"Spock! The cloud is gone! She's coming back!"

Spock hit the activation control, then ran around the console, picking up speed as he neared the platform.

And then, for just a moment, it seemed as if Spock had stepped into a hole. His foot sank into the ground past his ankle.

"Spock?" Kirk started to take a half-step from the platform to go to Spock's aid.

But Spock waved him back. "No, Jim! Stay on the platform!"

Joseph stood up beside his father. "Uncle Spock?"

Spock dropped down another few centimeters, almost as if he were sinking in quicksand. But the grass was solid around his legs.

And then Kirk saw what was hidden in that grass.

Not a cloud of black particles, not a cord, but a mat.

And then the mat rose up and engulfed Spock in randomly crisscrossed webs of black, and where each strand touched him, his flesh dissolved into darkness, just as Kirk's arm had in Norinda's grasp. Spock did not cry out to protest the pain, but Kirk knew what he felt.

But Joseph did. And as the greenhouse chamber dissolved into light, his cries echoed in the transporter bay of the *Calypso*.

Less than two minutes later, Kirk and Worf and Picard beamed back into the chamber, and at first Kirk thought they had been transported to the wrong coordinates.

Then he recognized the transporter platform and console.

They were in the right place.

But Spock and the cloud were gone.

As was each blade of grass, each flower, each tree, each growing thriving life-form that had been in this chamber only minutes before.

All that remained was dirt and bare metal.

Kirk turned slowly in that chamber, in the heat of the Romulan sun, struggling to comprehend what had happened here, fearing Spock was finally lost forever. . . .

Because there was a war to stop and a galaxy to save.

And what was the fate of one man compared with billions?

29

At the Hour of Opposition, the three *Jolan* nuclear-isomer bombs detonated simultaneously, as they had been programmed.

But they did not detonate *where* they had been programmed.

The *Titan* had found them in the places Kirk had predicted, buried in greenhouse domes in the three miners' communes, where native Remans never ventured and the crops were tended by the followers of the *Jolara*. From there, the *Titan* had beamed those destructive weapons into deep space.

Kirk stood on the bridge of the *Titan* now, to watch those silent explosions, like three small stars burning too brightly, rushing madly to their end.

Then one star faded more quickly than the others, leaving two to shine on by themselves just a few moments longer.

Kirk turned away then, consumed by his thoughts of Spock.

But McCoy was there for him, standing with his battered Reman cane.

"We knew it couldn't last forever, Jim. That we three couldn't last."

"That doesn't make it any easier," Kirk said.

McCoy smiled at him then, and to Kirk, it was as if he looked back in time, to the first day a young Leonard McCoy had walked onto the bridge of his *Enterprise*, with that same wry smile.

"It's not supposed to be easy," McCoy said. He touched his hand to his heart. "That's what lets us know how much we had, and how much we should treasure what's left."

Kirk looked back to the screen. Only the distant stars remained, now.

Then a turbolift arrived and Kirk's heart lifted as he saw Joseph with Beverly Crusher and the Doctor.

Joseph took Kirk's hand and leaned against him, instead of giving him one of his usual hugs. He was subdued and Kirk knew why. Whatever had happened to Spock on Remus, it was as if he had died before the child's eyes, and that was something Joseph could not forget. Nor could his father.

The Doctor shook Kirk's free hand.

"Hi, Dad," the hologram said.

Kirk looked at the holoemitter on the doctor's arm. "Good as new?"

"Better."

Doctor Crusher asked if she could speak to Kirk alone, and Joseph went with the hologram to see the bridge stations. Will Riker commanded the center chair, and had none of his mentor's nervousness about having children on his bridge.

As soon as they'd gone, Crusher showed Kirk three medical instruments that resembled hyposprays, but weren't.

"I think you should take these," she said.

"What are they?" Kirk asked.

"Genetic comparison modules. When we were on Remus with the Doctor disguised as Joseph, a Romulan physician wanted to use these on what he thought was your son."

"I don't understand the significance."

"I brought them back with me because I thought they might contain the genotypes of Joseph's relatives. I thought that was why they wanted him on Remus. To trace his lineage."

"What did they contain?"

"Are you familiar with the work of Doctor Richard Galen?"

Kirk knew the name well. "Jean-Luc was one of his students. He helped complete Galen's identification of what could be the Progenitor species, the ones who may have seeded this galaxy with life."

Crusher nodded, pointed to the modules. "That's the genotype in these devices. The reconstructed hypothetical Progenitor genotype."

Kirk was perplexed. "Why would anyone want to compare Joseph's genotype to . . . that?"

Crusher had no answers. "I don't know. But I've given all my research to Doctor McCoy, and . . . well, I think you should look into it." She glanced over at Joseph where he sat at an engineering station. "He is . . . a unique child."

"That's one way of putting it." Kirk put the modules in his jacket pocket. "Thank you."

Worf and Picard arrived next. Worf carried a carefully wrapped package for Joseph that was obviously a *d'k tahg* knife. "With your approval, of course," Worf told Kirk.

"Only if you teach him how to use it properly," Kirk answered.

Worf smiled with a soft snarl and went to join Joseph at the engineering station.

Picard remained with Kirk, both men watching the knot of personnel that had gathered around Joseph.

"Quite a charming lad," Picard said.

"That's another way of putting it," Kirk replied.

Picard didn't understand the comment, but had another topic to bring up.

"I spoke with Admiral Janeway. She sends her regards, and her regrets."

"I should probably speak with her, too," Kirk said. "Give her the full report about Norinda."

"She mentioned that," Picard said. "And she also mentioned that she had a proposition for you."

Kirk forced a smile. "I like her, Jean-Luc, but she outranks me."

"You're incorrigible, Jim. Her proposition involves the *Calypso*."

"What about the *Calypso*?"

"If you want her, she's yours."

"It's a scow."

"It can be modified."

"A new bridge?"

"Anything's possible."

"What're the conditions?"

Kirk could see that Picard knew more than he was revealing. "Reasonable."

Kirk knew what a Starfleet admiral's definition of "reasonable" would be—anything but.

"The *Calypso* is a Q-ship," Kirk said. "Which means Starfleet and Admiral Janeway would expect me to carry out covert missions."

"From time to time," Picard agreed. "But the rest of the time, she's your ship, your crew. Your home." He patted Kirk's shoulder. "Think about it?"

"I will."

"And sooner, rather than later," Picard suggested.

"Something I should know about?" Kirk asked.

"Talk to the Admiral," Picard said. Then he left to speak to Riker.

For a few moments, Kirk stood alone on the bridge, surrounded by activity, but not sharing in it.

He lasted two minutes.

Then he tracked down a communicator, to contact Janeway.

What good was a captain without a ship?

What good was a ship without a mission?

Epilogue
The *Monitor* Transmission

"The signal took almost two years to reach us," Commander Soren said. She was Vulcan, chief science officer of the starbase, a specialist in communications. But unlike her audience, she already had seen the final transmission from the *U.S.S. Monitor.* And she was frightened.

From his place at the head of the long, black conference table, Admiral Meugniot objected. "From three hundred and fifty thousand light-years? Impossible." His frown of disapproval was like a slash of paint on a ceremonial mask, its shape distorted in the shadow thrown up by the reading lamps on the table, for now the only source of light in the spacious briefing room.

Soren stood beside the main viewscreen, hands held behind her back. "Subspace radio travels at a pseudo velocity of warp factor nine-point-nine-nine-nine-nine." Her voice was flat, lost in the quiet of the sound-deadened room.

"Within the galactic network," Meugniot said, not bothering to hide his scorn. "With relay stations to boost the signal, keep it bound." He made a show of impatiently scrolling through the text of the large, classified padd on the table before him. "But this signal, you claim, originated from *outside* the galaxy. One-sixth of the way to Andromeda." He shook his head. "It's a hoax, Commander. That's the only explanation. I hear the Tal Shiar are back in business on Romulus, and this is exactly the kind of false intelligence they'd develop to have us switch our defense priorities."

Soren waited for the whispered discussion among the others at the table to end. In addition to Meugniot, there were six admirals in attendance, along with four starship captains, their science officers, and three civilians—two men, one woman—who had pointedly not been introduced. Soren did not need her logic to know that meant the civilians were likely senior officers in Starfleet Intelligence. But at least their presence suggested someone at Command understood the serious nature of the *Monitor* transmission. Perhaps, Soren hoped, that person at Command was also frightened.

"There is a full engineering report included as a supplement to the main document," Soren said, her voice betraying nothing of her true feelings. "Recall that the *Monitor* was a testbed for captured Borg technology, with many novel subsystems. Furthermore, Captain Lewinski and the surviving crew had three years to refine the onboard technology. In the end, anticipating their destruction, they reconfigured their forward sensor array to emit a single, five-second subspace pulse, drawing one hundred percent of the power output of the ship's warp core."

The crew of the *Monitor* had also been afraid, Soren knew. To see the need for that transmission, to carry it out, knowing that their ship would then be adrift in intergalactic space—that was the action of a desperate crew. But a crew who had stayed true to their duty as Starfleet officers.

"I don't care how much power they had," the admiral objected. "Over that distance, there is no way a subspace signal wouldn't spread out to the point where it could not be distinguished from normal subspace static. Especially static from extragalactic sources. It's the Romulans up to their old tricks."

Soren wondered what it would feel like to take the admiral by his shoulders and shake him. To tell him he was missing the point of this gathering. The technology of the signal's transmission was not the issue. It was the signal's *content* that had led the commander of Starbase 499 to call this extraordinary meeting at Soren's request.

But, instead, the science officer calmly said, "The signal *was* relayed, sir. By at least one of the Kelvan Expeditionary Return Probes currently presumed to be en route to Andromeda."

The admiral was not one to be contradicted. "That probe is more than a century old." He appeared to have more to say, but one of the civilians interrupted.

"Commander Soren, could you show us the transmission?"

Just that one, brief request from the thin pale man in the black suit was enough to silence every other voice at the table.

"Certainly," Soren answered. "As noted in your briefing padds, this is a reconstruction based on a severely degraded transmission. Almost three months of effort has gone into restoring it to this stage, using existing engineering plans of the *Monitor* and images of the crew from their personnel files in order to create—"

"Show it," Meugniot ordered.

Soren nodded to the admiral, then turned again to the civilian, for she knew that if there were to be a defense against the threat described in this transmission, it would come from Starfleet Intelligence—the only part of Starfleet that dared consider the unthinkable.

"The majority of the signal consists of text and instrument data which is proving almost impossible to reconstruct, due to lack of redundancy. But the last one-hundredth second of the transmission included the following visual images, which represent the last moments of the *Starship Monitor*, reported lost on a routine transwarp engine trial mission, Stardate 52027.4."

She touched the playback control on her own padd. And because she had seen the transmission once, she did not need to see it again. She did not want to. Instead she watched the audience. The admirals, the captains, the science officers, the civilians. The last hope of the Federation.

The table lights dimmed, then Captain John Lewinski spoke to those people, giving his final captain's log. Their upturned faces were painted by the flicker of subspace static, and the rippling lines of distortion that could not be removed for fear of losing any scraps of information still hidden in the signal.

Soren's processing engineers had obtained recordings of Lewinski's other logs, so they could be guided in the re-creation of his voice. But it still warbled, an eerie effect, as if this really were a ghost now speaking to them across the years and the light-years since his death.

Lewinski told them about the Distortion.

It had made contact with the *Monitor* in intergalactic space, near the debris field of the first Kelvan Expeditionary Return Probe.

Lewinski's investigation of that debris revealed the probe had been deliberately destroyed, by a process that appeared to alter the fundamental constants of space-time, making it impossible for complex matter to exist.

The other revelations were even more outrageous, more unnerving.

The *Monitor* had mapped a transwarp tunnel that had been *constructed* between the Andromeda Galaxy and the Milky Way. The Distortion traveled along that tunnel at a near-instantaneous speed, approaching the theoretically impossible warp ten.

The few seconds of sensor scans the *Monitor* had been able to make revealed that the Distortion was an artifact employing dimensional engineering, one part existing in normal space while the rest of it was in warp space *at the same time*. Another impossibility.

And then the Distortion responded to Lewinski's hails by firing a dimensional weapon at his ship.

The *Monitor*'s sensors recorded its approach.

Lewinski waited until the last possible second to transmit the five-second subspace pulse that had drawn every last erg of energy from his ship's warp core.

What had happened after that, there was no way to be certain. But Soren's specialists had created a simulated engineering model of the ship. It showed how every system on the *Monitor* would have been burned out by the burst of power transmitted through its forward sensors.

The model showed the point-by-point destruction of the *Monitor*'s subsystems. It showed the warp core ejecting.

The analysts suggested that if any of the crew had

survived the shock of the ejection and sudden drop out
of warp, then they would have had, at best, three hours
of residual heat left. Provided the air was still breath-
able, uncontaminated by smoke from the fires on every
deck, some crew might have survived as long as ten
hours. But no one would have lasted longer than a day.

To Soren, though, those estimates were pointless.
The crew had survived less than five minutes.

She knew that because she had seen the analysis of
the dimensional weapon that had been fired at the
Monitor. The last few seconds of the *Monitor*'s sensor
records had not been as compressed, and had arrived
in better condition, more easily reconstructed.

Thus the last few seconds of the transmission being
shown on the viewscreen now contained crisp images
of that weapon, coming closer.

And more than impossible, that weapon was incomprehensible. Because every bit of data told the analysts
on Soren's team that they were looking *through* that
bright blue point of light, into another universe.

The flickering stopped, telling Soren that the final
frame of the transmission report was being displayed,
listing the key conclusions of her team.

She knew them well. The *Monitor* had discovered
evidence of an alien intelligence that could travel at
near-instantaneous warp ten; that had engaged in
galactic engineering; that could construct artifacts that
existed in two different dimensional realms at the same
time; that could use weapons that altered the fundamental constants of this universe; and that could open
doorways into other universes.

There was nothing in Federation science that could
grapple with such capabilities.

There was nothing in the lost histories of the first

civilizations in this galaxy that came close to suggesting that any culture had attained what the *Monitor* transmission described. The Iconian gateways, the Guardian time portal, even the Q Continuum, all had some tenuous connection to the laws of multiphysics that described the rest of the universe, and governed known science.

But there was no branch of knowledge that could make sense of what the *Monitor* had discovered.

And what so disturbed Soren was unequivocal evidence that whatever the *Monitor* had discovered, it was hostile.

And it was coming this way.

The final viewscreen image faded and the reading lights glowed brightly again.

Except for the three civilians, every person at the table was involved in conversation. Soren's sensitive ears picked up suggestions for forming task forces, for sending out more probes, for calling general meetings of the Federation Council, for holding secret meetings.

It brought her comfort to hear the explosion of ideas. Perhaps the Federation could withstand this new threat. Perhaps there was no reason to be afraid.

And then one of the civilians stood. The woman. She caught Soren's attention. "If I may?" she asked.

Soren nodded and the woman walked from the table to join her at the viewscreen. It was impossible, but in the shifting lights and shadows of the briefing room, just for those few seconds it took for the human female to reach her, she had looked just like Soren's Vulcan mother.

But in the pool of light by the viewscreen, Soren could see why she had made the mistake. The woman wasn't human after all, she was Vulcan. Then the woman smiled, and Soren hid her astonishment at that display of emotion, wondering if in fact the woman might be Romulan.

"Admiral Meugniot," the woman said, "members of the emergency board. I know that what we have just seen could be considered alarming."

Soren's face remained impassive, but she was startled by the woman's choice of words. *Could be?!*

"But as someone who has studied this phenomenon in depth—"

Soren was even more surprised by that statement.

"—I would like to explain why it's nothing to be frightened of." She looked directly at Soren then, and her smile was exactly like that of Soren's mother; the secret smile that Vulcans share only in their most private moments, with their most beloved.

"Nothing at all," the woman said. "Indeed, what is coming is something to be welcomed." She held out her arms as if to embrace everyone in the room. "Because it is the true reality of existence."

Soren stared at the woman, even as her outline seemed to blur before her. Vaguely she was aware of a distant, almost explosive shudder that passed through the floor of the briefing room. She thought there might have been alarms going off, warning lights flashing, combadges chirping.

But none of that seemed important.

This woman had something compelling to say, and Soren wanted to hear it, even as the woman turned to her and reached out to her with a hand that seemed to be made of writhing particles of black powder, stretching like dust in a whirlwind to caress Soren's face, exactly as her mother had caressed her as a child.

"No need to be afraid," the woman whispered in flawless Vulcan.

Soren took the woman's hand, ignored the screams that came from the people at the conference table, ignored the banging on the briefing room door, the even more violent explosion that seemed to tilt the room for a moment.

Soren was used to ignoring distractions. She held the woman's smokelike hand, watching with fascination as her own flesh took on the writhing character of windblown sand.

"Accept . . ." the woman whispered soothingly. "Embrace . . . Be loved . . ."

"Be loved," Soren said as she felt her body dissolve beneath her, the tendrils of black curling up, consuming her.

Commander Soren was not afraid. She was at peace.

Just as everyone else at her starbase was in that same moment.

As everyone else in the galaxy would be soon enough.

The Peace of the Totality had arrived.

James T. Kirk will return in
Star Trek®: Captain's Glory

For further information about William Shatner,
science fiction, new technologies, and upcoming
William Shatner books, log on to
www.williamshatner.com.

THEY WERE SOME OF YOUR FAVORITES WHEN
YOU FIRST READ THEM...

NOW COLLECT THE NEXT BOOKS IN SPECIAL
SIGNATURE EDITIONS!

STAR TREK®

DUTY, HONOR, REDEMPTION

VONDA MCINTYRE

HAND OF KAHLESS

JOHN M. FORD AND
MICHAEL JAN FRIEDMAN

SAND AND STARS

DIANE DUANE AND A.C. CRISPIN

STSE2.01

STAR TREK